AS LONG AS
FIELDS ARE GREEN

D1076462

AS LONG AS
FIELDS ARE GREEN

L. G. J. Layberry

SPELLMOUNT LTD

LANCASHIRE LIBRARY

Dedicated to
Alison Keane,
In the past, a helpful colleague,
In the present, an indomitable friend.
And also to
Charming Susan and lovely Sarah

EAVES LANE

02219549

First published in 1987 by
Spellmount Ltd
12 Dene Way, Speldhurst
Tunbridge Wells, Kent TN3 0NX

©L. G. J. Layberry 1987
ISBN 0-946771-16-2

British Library Cataloguing in Publication Data

Layberry, L. G. J.
  As long as fields are green. –
  (Oakleigh farm series)
  I. Title II. Series
  823'.914[F] PR6062.A96/

All rights reserved. No part of this publication may be
reproduced, stored in a retrieval system, or transmitted
in any form or by any means, electronic, mechanical,
photocopying or otherwise, without the prior
permission of Spellmount Ltd.

Printed and bound in Great Britain by
Robert Hartnoll (1985) Limited
Bodmin, Cornwall

Chapter 1

Arthur Felton's Jaguar rolled smoothly over the gritty tarmac as he directed it, without noticeable effort, along the country road. Although he had left home in a bad temper, he was in no particular hurry. Having decided to leave the haymaking to his competent staff while he performed this particular errand, he thought he might as well make the most of this bit of truancy. That was a joke, of course. He and his sister, in partnership with their father, farmed over five hundred acres of some of the best land in South Derbyshire, and farmed it well. The intensive production of the war years had provided the business with ample funds, as it had most farmers, but the Feltons had wisely invested a considerable portion of their extra capital in industry, as well as in land. Their staff consisted mainly of long-serving employees who were totally trustworthy, having learned their skills with the Ratcliffes, the family of the late Mrs Felton. Thus there was absolutely no reason why any of the partners should not absent himself (or herself) from the run-of-the-mill tasks of the farm as often as they pleased. So Arthur drove on with an easy conscience, but keenly noting everything that was going on in the fields each side of the road – for a farmer enjoys nothing better than observing his neighbours' failures or appraising their successes – while the powerful car glided along between the crowding hedges and almost filled the narrow thoroughfare.

That morning he had received a demand for income tax, boldly marked 'Second Application', in a large sum of money for the current year's tax. Remembering distinctly that he had paid this exact sum in January, he was furious at the duplication and determined to investigate personally, saying nothing to his sister Edith or his father. These days the senior Felton took little part in the paperwork. His brain was still astute and as active as ever, but he preferred to leave the details and the pen-pushing – or more properly, the typewriter-hammering – to his son or daughter. The business at Oakleigh Farm did not warrant a full-time secretary, but work could easily have been found for a part-time girl, perhaps two days weekly.

However, Edith preferred to undertake the job herself, having done it in their less expansive days before the war and prior to her own enlistment in the ATS. Her duties in the army had increased her skill with the typewriter as well as with figures, and she was therefore quite competent to deal with all the correspondence and accounts of a five-hundred-acre farm. She had a system of her own which was thoroughly efficient, but in Arthur's eyes she was a little casual in her approach and did not immediately apply herself to every item the instant it appeared, which he would have done, or so he persuaded himself. He did not give too much weight to the fact that she ran the household as well, for she had two of the farm workers' wives to help her every morning and another young wife who came along in the evening if there was extra cooking or entertaining.

Naturally, Edith arranged her multiple duties in a way to suit herself, and as Arthur dearly loved to rummage among the paperwork and claimed he had a right to do so, a certain amount of friction between brother and sister was unavoidable. They all accepted that the responsibility for the secretarial work would have to be rationalised some time but all seemed disinclined to take the first step. Arthur had opened the tax demand, and since he had made the earlier payment, decided to deal with it himself and slipped it into his pocket without mentioning it to Edith.

The weather was in one of its better moods which were not too frequent in that summer of 1950. The men could therefore be left to get on with the haymaking without fear that a sudden change of plan might be necessary. In any case, his father would be about and there were few more efficient organisers than Robert Felton. If his father were called away, there still remained the diligent and faithful foreman, Dick Marshall.

Glancing down at the winding silver of the Trent, he realised he was approaching the town and his mind came back to the reason for the journey. He would give the tax clerks a piece of his mind for their inefficiency! His irritation mounted as he turned out of Newton Road up on to the bridge, turned left into the High Street and found himself held up by shunting operations at the first level crossing. He drummed his fingers on the steering wheel with impatience.

'Who the hell drinks all that beer?' he asked himself unreasonably when several trucks, loaded to capacity with full barrels, rolled across in front of him. 'They must be a boozy lot,' he thought unkindly, still giving vent to his impatience. He was not a great drinker himself, but neither was he teetotal. Brewing was the mainstay of the town – that he knew well enough, for about half the local labour force worked in the breweries. The industry depended on farm crops, too – hops from far off Kent or

Hereford and malting barley from wherever they could get it. Not much barley grown round Burton, though – the land was too rich for it. Still, the local farmers made good use of the brewery by-products and had done so for generations – wet and dried grains, malt culms and so on. As a farmer, Arthur Felton knew perfectly well that he must spare a minute or two while they despatched their main product. After all, the townsfolk had put up with these inconvenient crossings for a hundred years.

An impatient bleep from behind startled him out of his reverie and he realised the gates were wide open, exposing him at the head of the queue. Hastily he moved off, jerking the car slightly, then to his annoyance he found he had to wait a few seconds at the next rail crossing while a fussy little shunting engine completed its manoeuvre. Setting off again, he turned right at the top of the street and pulled up outside a building which displayed a modest board beside the front door – Collector of Taxes, Burton Collection.

He had never had occasion to visit this office before. In fact, he was barely aware of its location or even existence. The Oakleigh tax payments were invariably sent, not without grumbling, by post, as were the monthly PAYE deductions.

Marching firmly up the stairs he reached a passage with several doors. One at the far end boasted a notice above it, reaching out like a signpost and reading: 'Payments and enquiries; Please enter.' Responding to the invitation, he found himself in a small room with a counter on each side of him. That on the right was protected by a glass barrier behind which three or four clerks were busy at their desks, heads down, elbows poised. As the left-hand counter showed only a blank wall, Felton stepped up to the glass barrier. The nearest clerk, a youth in his late teens, got up at once.

'Can I help you, sir?'

'I hope so. I want to complain about this.' He waved the demand note.

The young man seized it and glanced down quickly.

'You're not making a payment, sir?'

'I most certainly am not! I paid this last January!'

'We only take payments this side, sir,' he pointed to a notice which read: *Payments only this side.* 'Please ring the bell on the other counter.'

The farmer snorted irritably and turning round, thumped the little hand bell vigorously several times. Almost immediately a young man with glasses appeared through a sliding door.

'Yes, sir?'

'I've called to complain about this . . .' Felton began, brandishing the demand note again.

The clerk took it from him, read it instantly and withdrew through the sliding door, through which the farmer caught a glimpse of many desks, numerous clerks of both sexes and varying ages, most of whom were enjoying their afternoon cup of tea. The visitor gave a loud exclamation of disgust and thumped the counter with his fist.

'Bloody Revenue!' he growled, not quite under his breath. 'This is where all our money goes!'

He began to pace up and down angrily. Then a girl appeared through the door which she closed behind her. He was about to explode when he noticed how attractive she was. Medium height, glossy dark hair, wide blue eyes covered by long lashes, clear ivory skin, diminutive nose, firm lips and chin and dressed most becomingly in a cream blouse and dark grey skirt. On her forearms she carried a huge volume, with his own demand note on the opened page. Somehow she looked vaguely familiar.

'What's the trouble, sir?' she asked with a pleasant smile.

'That bill you've got there.' He reached over and took it from the book. 'We paid that sum in January and I want to know why we're being charged again. It must be a duplication, 'cos the amount is exactly the same, and here is the receipt.'

'Yes, of course. That sum was paid on January 20th. You have the receipt and I have it noted here. But that was only the first instalment. See –' she pointed to the second box on the receipt which plainly showed I.T. D.1. 'That means it was the first instalment of Schedule D tax, due and payable in January. Now we're asking you for the second instalment due this month.' She pointed with her pen to the words on the demand note.

'Do you mean we always have to pay the same amount twice?'

'It does not always work out exactly the same. The Inspectors – who raise the assessment – may have received further information which could cause part of the sum to be discharged, and the demand for D.2 would then be amended downwards. Or they may have discovered that the original assessment was too low, in which case there would be a new assessment and an extra demand sent to you with a three-digit addition to the reference number.'

She seems to be warming up to her work, Arthur thought, reeling out the information like a damned gramophone record. Pretty girl though, as long as she was talking like an expert and forgetting her earlier self-consciousness.

'Indeed?' he said acidly, unable to think of any other response.

'Why do you bother yourself about this?'

Arthur Felton was staggered. 'Damn her impertinence,' he thought while his mind groped for words.

She went on, 'I have a note here on my duplicate that your affairs are handled by this firm of accountants.'

'You seem to know everything,' Arthur said ungraciously. Then, bending a little he explained, 'Yes, we did use that firm but the senior partner who had handled our business died, and we decided we would do it ourselves rather than entrust it to his successor.'

'Then you should have seen your notice of assessment, Major Felton.'

Arthur raised his eyebrows. Major Felton? He glanced down at the demand note in his hand. It was addressed to R. Felton and Son Ltd.

'And how on earth do you know I've been a major?'

She smiled winningly, and Arthur thought how utterly charming she looked.

'Why, everyone at Hartnall knows you, Major. We know about your DSO and your MC, too. The whole village is proud of you!'

The man looked at her with furrowed brow. Then his expression cleared.

'Now I know who you are! You're one of Gene Keen's daughters from Hilltop Farm. Why didn't you say so at first, you little madam?'

She smiled again and coloured slightly but was pleased by the intimacy of his last remark.

'We're all anonymous here, Major Felton, and we don't normally give our names to taxpayers.'

'Taxpayers eh? That's all we are to you, I suppose. But what's this about a notice of assessment?'

'It is a form the Inspector of Taxes sends to you, generally in October, so you have plenty of time to challenge it if you think it's incorrect. There are two boxes which show the total of the first instalment due January 1st and the second instalment due July 1st.'

'I don't remember seeing it,' he said weakly and cursed himself for not spending time on a proper briefing. This knowledgeable chit of a girl was making him feel rather like a schoolboy, and he a veteran of the Fourteenth Army, a farmer of substance and reputation, and a qualified man to boot, for he had passed his RICS final before the war!

'Perhaps Edith opened it when you were not there and filed it away,' the girl suggested brightly.

'Huh! Is there anything you don't know about my family and business, young lady?'

She smiled knowingly.

'You know what village life is, Major Felton.'

She was becoming impertinent again, he thought, but he decided not to pull her up for he felt himself at a disadvantage.

'What I want to know, young lady, is what a farmer's daughter is doing in a tax office. Surely you could find something better to do, and more pleasant, on your father's farm?'

The dark eyes, hitherto friendly, became hostile.

'As it happens, I don't care for farm work, although I've done plenty of it, but I enjoy Revenue work and I'm interested in it!'

'I see! A farmer's daughter, finding pleasure in squeezing tax out of other poor devils of farmers who may not have the ready money to pay. Aren't you ashamed of yourself?'

The girl's eyes flashed dangerously and she seemed about to explode but, remembering that she was a civil servant dealing with a member of the public, she restrained her anger.

'All taxpayers are not like you, Mr Felton. You pay your taxes regularly and in good time. Well, reasonably so . . .'

'Thank you very much!' Arthur was becoming angry now.

'. . .but about five per cent of taxpayers don't pay readily and will try all sorts of dodges to avoid doing so. It would not be fair to the genuine, honest ninety-five per cent if we let these habitual defaulters get away with it.'

She raised her voice slightly and Felton suddenly realised their whole conversation could have been overheard by the cashiers behind him.

'I suppose there's something in what you say,' he admitted grudgingly, 'and somebody has to do it, no doubt.'

The girl went on, changing the subject, 'I suppose you'll pay the demand now you're here, Major. I can't take the cheque myself . . .'

'Why not?'

'It's against the rules. Payment must be made on the other side, and I am sure the cashiers would be glad to take your cheque.'

'I've no doubt they would.' the farmer said grimly, 'But I'm afraid I can't oblige them!'

'Why not?' said the girl in her turn, but with a solicitous tone to her voice.

'Because I just don't happen to have a farm cheque-book with me. I came here expecting to get an apology, not another receipt. I haven't even got my own cheque book with me, either, and if I had I wouldn't pay the firm's income tax with it.'

The sliding doors opened and a tall, heavy middle-aged woman came through. She had black wavy hair above pleasant features and would have been attractive if her expression had not been so severe and dominative.

'Is everything all right Alison? You seem to be making quite a meal of this interview. Can I help?'

Arthur pulled himself up to his full height of six feet and his face took on his military profile.

'Thank you, madam, there is no need for you to interfere. Miss King was merely expounding to me the ethics of tax collection and I am much obliged to her. However, I will detain her no longer, if it displeases you. Good afternoon!'

He inclined his head slightly, turned round and marched out of the room.

The pivotal officer recovered her composure but there were pink flushes on her cheeks as she said, 'What was all that about? Is he a friend of yours?'

'As a matter of fact, he's a near neighbour. But his family are far too grand to be friends with us. I've seen him about sometimes but have never spoken to him before. When I was a little girl, I can remember seeing him working on the farm before he joined the army.'

The older woman was still smarting under the snub.

'I'll throw the book at him if he falls into arrears!'

'He won't do that! They've got tons of money!'

Arthur Felton drove home swiftly. He surprised himself by concentrating his entire thoughts on the girl in the tax office. She was pretty he told himself again, but a little too knowing for a girl of her age – certainly about tax matters. Funny he hadn't seen her before, since her home was less than two miles from Oakleigh. Of course, he had been away in the army seven years, which would cover most of her girlhood. Still, he'd now been home four years and should have come across her. No doubt she'd been in the Revenue most of that time, and naturally would not be around home during the day. How did she get to Burton, he asked himself? Walked to Repton and caught the Blue Bus, perhaps?

He had vague childhood memories of Gene King coming to Hilltop Farm as a young married man in the early nineteen-twenties. Later, when he himself was old enough to get about the farm, he had noticed that there always seemed to be children around the steading. Obviously, they would be older than the tax girl. Alison, her superior had called her. A delightful name and utterly suitable.

His memory still stirring, Arthur could just recall fragments of the conversations at home when the Kings had moved in. Hilltop Farm had been purchased in 1921 by his father and grandfather who had sold it again after subtracting some of the land to enlarge Oakleigh Farm. King would not have been involved in those transactions for he had not arrived from the West Country until two or three years later. Possibly because of his distant origin, he was too reserved to mix well with his neighbours.

Arthur's thoughts took command of his driving, for as he cruised along the Repton road, he found himself turning into the narrow lane which led past Hilltop. Resignedly, he told himself he could have a look at some of the Oakleigh boundary fields before returning to the haymakers.

The brilliant sun's power was almost scorching – a rare event in that summer, Arthur reminded himself. All the farms he had passed were busy with late haymaking and the scent of it filled the air. Fragrant as it was, he took it all for granted while pondering that haymaking was not what it used to be. None was pitched loose on to waggons and mophreys any more, nor swept to the elevator for quick stacking. The pick-up baler had eliminated all that manual toil but it had also brought to an end the pleasant comradeship of the haymaking gang of five or six men. Their banter, their argument, their sarcasm, their spirit of competition as they moved every forkful, had gone for ever. Replacing it was the monotonous 'thump, thump' of the baler easily overheard above the even beat of the tractor, whose driver made his repeated circuits of the field with his neck twisted sideways. Things were definitely not the same!

With a start, Arthur realised he was thinking exactly like his father, whom he constantly upbraided for being old-fashioned!

He automatically slackened his speed as he approached Hilltop Farm, where the buildings were beside the road, the front of the neat house facing it, while the back looked out over the cowyard – a traditional design for the district. A herd of about twenty milking cows grazed the field adjoining the yard. There were a few ancient-looking multi-coloured shorthorns, but more than half were Friesians. Arthur knew that King had been using a Friesian bull for some years, progressively changing his herd, by breeding, over to the black and whites.

Beyond the farm was the Kings' hayfield, and the sweet, penetrating aroma drifted through Felton's open window as he

12

drew level. The crop was obviously quite fit, for it was neatly rowed up into thick, fluffy lanes. Phillip King stood in the open gateway looking thoughtful and displeased. Wondering at this, Arthur stopped his car. A perfect haymaking day and a splendid crop in good condition! Why should the owner look miserable?

It was not usual for a farmer to drive past another of his kind without some comment, so Arthur called out cheerily, 'Hello, Mr King! You've got a grand crop of hay! Looks nicely fit from here, too. Will you get it all baled to-day?'

Gene King walked across the road to the Jaguar. He was a slightly-built man in his mid-fifties; his dark hair showed streaks of grey, and his clean-shaven face and neat features matched the tidiness of his working clothes.

'Good afternoon, Mr Felton. Don't see you round this lane very often. You haven't come round to see me, I take it? It would be odd, after all these years!'

'Well, no. Just driving home this way for a change.

'Couldn't help admiring your cows and your hay crop. Remarkably bright and clean for this year.'

'Aye, it is, but I'm afraid it'll spoil before I get it in. The weather won't hold like this for long.'

'But it's ready now, isn't it? Why don't you get cracking?'

'I was expecting the baler along this afternoon – just about now, in fact, but the Missis has just been along with a message from the contractor to say he's broken his baler and it'll be out of action for twenty-four hours at least – maybe longer.'

'That's bad luck,' Arthur said with feeling.

'Dang these modern methods, I say.' The other man nearly exploded in his exasperation. 'If we handled it loose and stacked it, we'd ha' been right at it just after dinner. But as you well know, we're not geared up for that sort o' haymaking any more. There aren't enough men on the farms these days. The more mechanised we get, the longer the delay when anything breaks down. You can't keep two of everything, not even a contractor. This hay's perfect now, but what will it be like the day after tomorrow?'

Arthur drummed his fingers on the steering wheel as he said diffidently, 'Would you like me to send our baler along?'

King's eyes opened wide with surprise.

'Well . . . I . . . I . . . er, why should you do that? You big farmers don't usually team up with us little chaps!'

'Thanks!' Arthur grinned. 'Well, here's an occasion when I may be able to help you. Naturally, we're baling this afternoon, but he'll finish the field about four or five o'clock and we've no more ready. Now, shall I send him round or not?'

'Well Mr Felton, of course I'll be grateful if we can get this up before its spoiled. But it's mighty strange that we've been neighbours for more than twenty years and nothing like this has ever happened before.'

'Never been opportune, perhaps. I just happened along at the right time, that's all.'

'It's very good of you, Mr Felton.' The farmer seemed worried as another thought struck him. 'But what about the cost? You might charge a lot more than I can afford.'

'What does your contractor charge?'

'Sixpence a bale.'

'Then I'll charge sixpence a bale. Satisfied?'

King looked confused. 'I wasn't trying to be awkward, you know, but . . .'

'That's all right. I'd better get along and see how Dick's progressing.' He touched the clutch and the car moved smoothly away.

In a couple of minutes he was in his own hayfield. The Oakleigh foreman, Dick Marshall, was bowling along at a rattling pace, the baler working as rhythmically as a sewing machine, throwing out the neatly tied bales with unfailing precision. Machines generally worked well when Dick was in charge, Arthur thought. There were a few rows in the middle of the field, then the bulky outside row, left until last to allow the dampness of hedge moisture to dry out. Four other men were setting up the bales in sloping stooks, for in this damp summer the hay had rarely been dry enough for the bales to be carried in immediately. Arthur walked across to the baler and Dick dutifully stopped his tractor to hear what the young gaffer had to say.

'You've got on well, Dick.'

'Aye, but the conditions are just right to-day, Gaffer. This stuff's as lively as we've 'ad it this summer and it's a pleasure to bale it. The machine thinks so as well, I reckon. Everything that moves is clean and shinin' and that's 'ow it oughter be.'

'How right you are, Dick! Now, when you've finished here, I'd like you to go and bale a field for Mr King at Hilltop Farm. He's got a field just ready – grand stuff – and his contractor's had a breakdown.'

'Oh, cripes, Gaffer, Ah were goin' out to-night. Ah knew Ah'd finish early on this lot and arranged it wi' Mavis. Ah've no tea wi' me, either!'

'Very well, I'll do it,' Arthur said resignedly. 'Leave the baler by the road gate, folded for travel, clean it off a bit and see there's plenty o' string. I'll go home and change into working kit.'

Dick Marshall stuck out his lower lip.

'Ah can do it, Ah suppose. It weren't very important wheer we were goin'. But gaffer, next time you want me to work late when it's not obvious, let me know afore dinner-time, will you? An' p'raps you'd call at home an' tell Mavis our plans are changed, and ask 'er to send me some tea.'

He slipped into gear and moved off, the whirring and thumping of the machine preventing his boss from replying, even if he had wished to.

'That's the second time I've been ticked off this afternoon.' he muttered, 'Once by a tax girl and now by our own foreman. Some of 'em take a deal o' pleasing.'

Chapter 2

Somewhat chastened, Arthur returned to Oakleigh where he found his father and sister enjoying a cup of tea in the kitchen. He joined them expectantly and Edith did not disappoint him. Normally the Feltons followed the old-fashioned practice of sitting down to high tea as soon as the farm staff finished work – currently at five o'clock or five-thirty. This left the evening free to supervise overtime, if any, or to achieve some activity in the period, which could not have been attempted had they eaten a seven o'clock supper. However, a cup of tea was a different matter and the teapot was likely to be in use on the kitchen table at any time of the waking day.

'Just sent Dick off to bale a ten-acre field for Gene King,' Arthur remarked casually.

'Bit of a back-door job, wasn't it?' his father enquired, equally casually. Robert Felton was rarely enthusiastic about anything these days. Although as active, healthy and alert as ever, his feelings seldom erupted. His formerly dark hair was now quite grey, the only dark colouring being under his eyes. His wife had been dead for nearly five years but he still mourned her in a silent but totally controlled manner. His son and daughter were well aware of this and made no attempt to deprive him of the solace his thoughts gave him, for they had also loved their mother dearly.

His father went on, 'I should have thought King was too independent a chap to ask us – or anybody – for help! He certainly hasn't been in touch here.'

'He didn't ask. I offered,' Arthur said briefly.

His father opened his eyes a little wider.

'What the devil d'ye want to do that for? Better to let these smaller chaps manage their own affairs. We don't want to patronise 'em and we don't need the work nor the money. In any case, there are the contractors to consider – I'm sure King uses one – and we don't want to take the bread out of their mouths. They provide a valuable service, but they might not give King such good attention another time if they get to know – as they will – that we've been doing work for him.'

'He's got a grand field of hay there – about half his total crop I reckon – perfectly fit and his contractor's had a major breakdown. I was passing and stopped for a chat and he told me of it so I offered to send Dick, since we've nothing of our own to bale this evening. The price is the same the contractor would have charged – sixpence a bale. Make a note of that, Sis. You'll get the number from Dick.'

'Not so free with your orders, Knight-errant!'

'I hope you're not going to make a practice of this, Arthur,' pursued his father. 'Touting for orders in a 3-litre Jaguar seems a bit undignified to me.'

Arthur sighed. He was not prepared to argue over such a triviality. Just another irritating pin-prick in an unsatisfactory afternoon. He changed the subject, or thought he had.

'King's got a useful herd of cows round there. Using a Friesian bull has paid good dividends, I should say.'

Robert Felton looked strangely at his son.

'What's the matter with you? King came to Hilltop Farm when you were about eight years old and now you're thirty-five and you've only just realised that he's a tidy-minded farmer who knows his job.'

Arthur sighed again and tried another angle.

'Ede, I've been into the tax office this afternoon, about that demand that came in this morning. I was sure it had been paid last January so I went in to check up on them. Apparently I should have looked at the notice of assessment.'

'Well, I don't know! What are you talking about, Arthur? And what demand? I didn't see it!'

'No, because I put it straight into my pocket to deal with it myself.'

'Then I damn well wish you wouldn't. You know nothing at all about the tax system. If you want the assessment notice you'll find it in the big grey folder on the second shelf. It's marked "Income Tax" which should help you to identify it!'

'Don't be sarky!'

'As a matter of fact, that demand which you seem to have got so het up about was paid yesterday. They should have got the cheque this morning.'

'You sent off a big cheque without consulting me?'

'We only need two signatures and Dad was here, while you were not. And it wasn't all that big – just under a thousand pounds.'

'It's a lot to pay out for no return, all the same.' He thought for a moment. 'But this means that they had the cheque in their office when I was there shooting off my mouth about wrongful claims. They must have been stringing me along, thinking me a fool!'

'Well, you were a fool Arthur, sticking your nose into things you know nothing about. Why don't you leave the book-work to me, or take it all on yourself?'

'Here, hold on,' their father said in some alarm, which they were not sure was simulated, 'you stick with the office work, Edith. At least you've proved your worth at it. We know exactly where we are and where everything is kept, but Arthur'd be an unknown quantity. I wish you two would stop arguing. Pour us all out another cup of tea, lass.'

'It's a new departure for someone from Oakleigh to visit the tax office,' Edith said as she complied.

'It was a new experience, anyway,' Arthur admitted, 'but I was surprised to find that our affairs are dealt with by a Hartnall girl.'

'Really?'

'Yes – er – I spoke to a young girl who turned out to be the daughter of that chap King we were talking about just now.'

'Oh, now I see! Were you in there a long time? What did you think of her?'

'She's a dark girl, pretty as honeysuckle and as full of knowledge as a dictionary, reeling off civil service jargon at nineteen to the dozen.'

'They're trained to do that. Dad, now we know why Dick's baling King's hay!'

'Don't be so damned silly, Edie!' Arthur said angrily, reddening in spite of himself.

'Don't call me Edie! You know I don't like it! Anyway, Alison King's too young – you're nearly old enough to be her father!'

'What, at thirty-five? Don't be daft.'

'I tell you the girl's only about nineteen! I can remember when she was born. It was just before I left the village school at eleven. There were two other King children at the school then – Frank, who was about three years younger than I, and Katherine, who hadn't started school long. She was full of the new baby and was always chattering about it.'

'What, a kid of five confiding in a girl of eleven?'

'Yes of course. Mum insisted that I should take an interest in the infants as they started school. Said we owed it to the village, or something. Yes, Alison would be nineteen. But she's got a young man. I've seen her out with him.'

'You seem to know a lot about the King family all of a sudden.'

'You seem to have been smitten all of a sudden!'

'Don't be so damned silly! I only mentioned the girl because she's a neighbour. I don't suppose I'll see her again. By gum, I will, though! I'll give her a piece of my mind for stringing me along while she had our cheque up her sleeve, the cheeky so-and-so! That's typical of you, though. As soon as I mention a girl you start ringing the wedding bells.'

'Well, it's about time you were married, and that's a fact.' interrupted his father, seizing this golden opportunity to air his standing grievance. He was fifty-five and had no grandchildren to carry on the Oakleigh tradition. 'But I thought you might go further afield than our eastern boundary. Still, you could do a lot worse, I daresay.'

'He could do a lot better, too,' Edith pointed out, disregarding her brother's mounting anger. 'Linda Ratcliffe's waiting eagerly in the wings.'

'That's enough of that, Edith,' her father reprimanded her, showing a trace of anger himself. 'That marriage *would* be impossible! Not that I've anything against Linda herself. She's pretty, capable and well-mannered . . .'

'Of course, what you would expect from the old squire's family.'

'. . .but her father's beyond the pale. There couldn't be a union between his family and ours! There's been bad blood between him and me for forty years!'

'Some of that must have been your fault, Daddy,' Edith said persistently. 'Major Ratcliffe's always been quite charming to me.'

'Oh yes, he's full of charm! But he was a lot more than charming to certain women of my generation, as perhaps you know – or, well, you may not. I don't want it all brought up again.'

'But that's all so long ago . . .' Edith argued, but Arthur got up from his chair abruptly.

'I'm going to have a word with Alf before he turns the cows out. I'll come in again when you have the tea on the table, Edith. In the meantime, perhaps you and Dad will finally decide whether I'm to marry Alison or Linda, or some other girl within fifty miles. Let me know, 'cos I'm going to cricket practice after tea.' As he strode out his back registered his disapproval of their attitude.

'Doesn't do to pull his leg too hard, apparently,' Robert Felton said when his son was out of earshot. 'I wish he would tie up with somebody, Edith. If only your mother was still alive! She'd soon have picked a girl for him!'

'Dear old Mum! We shall never get used to being without her, Daddy. She would have tried her hand at matchmaking, you can bet on that. How I'd looked forward to introducing Peter to her. Now he's gone too and there's nobody!'

'He died doing his duty, Edith,' her father said uncomfortably, for he was unaware that she still mourned her fiancé, Colonel Peter Green, who had lost his life in Palestine two years previously.

'His duty!' Edith repeated bitterly. 'Went through the whole of the war without a scratch and then blown to pieces while trying to keep the peace in a sordid squabble between Jews and Arabs!' She ended with a choked sob.

Robert Felton got up and put his hand on Edith's shoulder as he walked past her.

'I'm sorry, lass. I wouldn't have brought the subject up if I'd known it would upset you. All of us in this family have our own private griefs, and with me they go back a long way. But the sun still rises every morning, love, and one day it'll rise especially for you.'

* * *

Alison King sat down purposefully to her desk the next morning. The payments for the July instalment were coming in quite fast and she was given a thick batch of receipt carbons. Each one of these had to be checked and she posted the figures with great care, for she was interested in her work and hated to make mistakes. Moreover, she knew well enough that an error in posting could cause extensive searching and endless delay when the accounts were balanced in the autumn.

She read each receipt carefully before she transferred it, face down, to the pile on her right, stopping in surprise, when the next voucher was in the name of R. Felton & Son Ltd, and the amount £992, 17s 6d. Glancing across at her working sheet she found that the amount was correct and it tallied with that which she had discussed with Major Felton the previous afternoon. It was all very strange, for the taxpayer had definitely stated he did not propose to pay at that time. Could he have returned home for the correct cheque and delivered it by hand to the cashiers? In that case he would have been given the receipt and the carbon copy would show a large 'C' to indicate that the payment had been taken over the counter. Here there was no such endorsement.

The Control Officer, Miss Hall, walked by a few feet away and Alison called to her.

'You remember that chap we had the barney with yesterday afternoon?'

'That autocratic-looking young farmer who tried to flatten me?'

20

'Well, yes.' Alison smiled. 'He made all that fuss about the demand being wrong and then gets the cheque here instantly. We must have made an impression!'

'You mean you did. I saw him looking you up and down, rather hungrily, in fact. But he couldn't have got it here before the cashiers banked up, unless he had an aeroplane.'

The girl glanced at the receipt number.

'But look here! This receipt was quite early in Johnny's first book. That means it was written well before lunch!'

'Then it came with yesterday morning's post. What sort of a chap is your Major Felton if he writes a cheque, posts it, than chases it here to say he's not going to pay it because it's wrongly charged? He must be a nut-case.'

'He's certainly not that,' Alison said sharply, somehow feeling she ought to defend her important neighbour. 'He's about the sharpest chap in Hartnall.'

'Not very sharp if he acts like that! I suppose he did sign the cheque himself. I'd like to see it, but it must be sealed up in the bank wallet by now.'

'He may not have done, Miss Hall. There are three in the family and I think they're all directors. Perhaps two signatures are sufficient.'

'No doubt his two co-directors signed this particular cheque and despatched it. Your Major'll be mad when he finds out and serve him right, too. He'll be less rude next time.'

'It must be his fault, certainly. I've always understood that his sister's most efficient at office organisation.'

'Pity she can't be more efficient at seeing that her brother keeps his nose out of it,' Miss Hall said unkindly as she moved on.

*　*　*

The weather remained fine for the rest of the week and Arthur Felton withdrew from the village cricket team for the Saturday match and allowed the vice-captain one of his rare opportunities to take charge. There was a good deal of hay lying about at Oakleigh and Arthur decided that it would be discouraging to his staff if he allowed cricket to take precedence. Of course his father was there to organise, but for maximum effort the men liked to see the 'young gaffer' there as well.

One machine was tedding the hay and another rowing it in and the baler was working apace with a relief driver for meal times, and two teams of other workers were hauling off the bales with tractor-trailers. Arthur took over the baler while Dick ate his dinner, then drove home for his own late lunch. Everything was going smoothly and if the men worked really late they could complete the season's baling that evening, with or without his help. Arthur decided to take the opportunity of calling at Hilltop to see King's daughter and make her explain about the fiasco at the tax office. As it was Saturday she would have left the office at one o'clock and would undoubtedly be at home this hot afternoon.

He drove the Jaguar into the field which Dick had baled on Thursday evening. Some of the bales had been collected and a trailer pulled by a Ferguson was being re-loaded. In the distance, out of sight over the hedges, Arthur could hear the 'thump, thump' of a baler at work. Obviously Gene King had another hayfield.

The visitor walked quickly over to the vehicle. King was loading the bales and another man was pitching them up to him with some difficulty. Not yet tempered for the job, Arthur thought automatically. He looked across at Alison who was driving the tractor. She looked the picture of elegance in her Land Army trousers and a cream shirt, casually unbuttoned. Arthur looked pointedly at the exposed top of her bra, and the girl coloured slightly and fastened one more button. He smiled at Alison but addressed himself to the man on the load.

'Afternoon, Mr King. You've got a rare lot of bales here. Pretty well tied too, aren't they? Not many loose ones.'

'There aren't any,' the man replied. 'There wouldn't be would there? Dick Marshall's the best farm chap for miles round, I reckon.'

'He's had a lot of practice, you know.'

'This is my brother Pat, Mr Felton. He comes up every year to help with the bale-carrying. But he's a bit soft yet. Hasn't toughened up at it.'

'I came to have a word with your daughter, when she's free.'

'Oh – ah – well – we've about finished loading and us two can take it in while you see Alison. Nothing wrong, I hope?'

'No, no, not at all. Just a little matter to square up.'

Mr King finished his load off quickly with a single row of bales along the centre. His brother pushed his fork hard into the side of the load and leaned on the end while the loader placed his left hand on the shaft of the fork, steadying himself, then easily and slowly slid down the side of the load to the ground, bending his knees to their full extent to take the strain of landing on the hard ground.

'Right! Alison, I'll take that tractor over while you talk to Mr Felton. Come on Pat, we'll just about get this unloaded before milking.'

The little tractor stuttered away with its swaying load, Arthur and Alison watching its progress as a matter of course. The man smiled down at the girl, thinking how desirable she looked. Surprisingly, she spoke first.

'Now Major, perhaps you'll tell me what it is you have to say which is important enough to interrupt our haymaking. And how did you know I would be here?'

'Where else could you be on such a fine afternoon?'

'I might have been playing tennis!'

'And I might have been at cricket, and should have. But I thought you didn't like farm work.'

'I don't – much, but I'm always willing to help. Do you only do the jobs you like?'

'As far as I can,' he admitted with a grin, 'but, being one of the bosses I often have to do things I don't like – such as ticking people off.'

'You'd better not start ticking me off!'

'I ought to, young lady. You really had me on a string on Thursday afternoon, didn't you? Made me feel a right fool, letting me rampage on even though you already held our cheque!'

'Hold on a minute, Major! You were making a fool of yourself, barging into the office without troubling to investigate first.'

'But you let me continue!'

'Yes, but only because I didn't know payment had been made.'

'You must have known, Alison. Our letters are always posted to catch the evening collection and they never fail to reach Burton or Derby the next morning.'

'I tell you I didn't know! You don't understand our system. Payments go direct to cashiers who write the receipt, despatch it and then bank the money at the end of the day. The carbon copies of the receipts are passed through to Control to be checked and posted the following morning.'

'Posted? Where do you post them to? I thought you'd keep such vital records in your office.'

'Posting means entering the figure in our duplicates.'

'Oh, I see – more jargon. Control – posting – duplicates – what a way for a farmer's girl to talk.'

'I'm not a farmer's girl – at least, not often. I'm an Assistant Collector.'

'And a very pretty one, if I may say so. But I accept your

apology and am prepared to forget the whole thing!'

'Accept my apology!' the girl spluttered, reddening in her anger. 'You've got a nerve, Arthur Felton . . .' she stopped suddenly and looked down. 'Sorry, I shouldn't have said that – at least, not so rudely. Revenue Officers are supposed to be patient with taxpayers at all times, no matter how stupid or unreasonable they are.'

Arthur threw back his head and laughed noisily.

'That's a nasty dig, I must say. However, I forgive you, even those red cheeks and flashing eyes. You look prettier than ever in a temper. Now, when are you coming to see us at Oakleigh? You have never been there, have you?'

While chatting they had been drifting in the wake of the tractor and were now within earshot of Mr King, his brother and the cowman who had turned out to help them unload the hay into the steel barn. Seizing her cue, the farmer's wife appeared from the direction of the house carrying a tray loaded with glasses and a very large jug. She proffered a drink to each of the bale-handlers, then called across to the field.

'Will you have a glass of ale with us, Mr Felton?'

'Well . . . I – er . . .'

'You might as well,' Alison chipped in. 'I'm going to have one.'

'Well, thank you, Mrs King.'

So Arthur remained a few minutes drinking harvest beer and chatting with the people of Hilltop Farm, feeling rather like a trout among minnows. Casually he scrutinised Mrs King. Her dark hair, barely touched with grey, looked attractive in its fashionable roll. Her skin was obviously well cared-for and her slight figure looked trim and active. A neat family altogether, Arthur told himself.

Since he did not wish to become involved in a family discussion which might savour of too much intimacy too quickly, he drained his glass and prepared to depart.

'Do drop in and see us,' he said as if it were a general invitation, but looked directly at Alison who smiled and dropped her eyes. He walked with long strides in the direction of his Jaguar.

The cowman also left to get in the cows, and Mrs King emptied the jug into the remaining glasses.

'Isn't Arthur Felton like his mother?' she remarked nostalgically. 'That's the first time I've been within a hundred yards of him, and we've been here for twenty-seven years. I can remember seeing him riding about in the carts when we first came.'

'Well, I think you're going to see a lot more of him in the future,' her brother-in-law remarked shrewdly. 'Seems to me he's got his eyes on young Alison.'

His niece laughed heartily, but not without satisfaction. 'That's a good 'un,' she said. 'In the first place he's nearly old enough to be my father and, secondly, everybody knows that Linda Ratcliffe's after him and bound to get him in the end.'

'Don't be too sure of anything,' her father commented. 'The Feltons are a stubborn, determined lot and are more likely to hold out for their own way than to give in to somebody else's.'

'I'm engaged to Adrian,' Alison reminded him.

'That won't make much difference to a Felton.'

'Perhaps not, but it does to me! Did you know Arthur's mother well, Mum?'

'Before the war, when you kids were small, she used to drive round these lanes in her trap – and ride as well, of course, and she would drop in and see us three or four times a year maybe. But during the war I suppose she hadn't the time to get around much – not in this direction, anyway. It's a pity she was taken so young. She was really a fine woman.'

'She certainly had the finest funeral, Mum. I remember seeing her, of course, but I don't think I ever spoke to her, unless it was at school. She came in, once or more, every term and we all admired her.'

Arthur was in a thoughtful mood as he drove away from the Kings'. There had been absolutely no need for the visit, but he had enjoyed it. What a pleasant family the Kings were – especially Alison. He was attracted not only by her looks but also for her refreshing self-assurance. He was not an amorous man and certainly no philanderer. Since he had been discharged from the army in 1946, women had meant very little to him, for his whole life had been absorbed by the farm. He accepted that when the farm came to him, it would need a mistress and to fulfil this requirement he would have to choose a wife. Alison? Perhaps, but there was no need to hurry.

His route took him round the back lanes, for he had decided to take a look at the feeding cattle in Hartnall park where he had rented some of the grazing. Some of them should soon be fit for grading and slaughter. He drove in between the two entrance lodges, mourning the absence of the magnificent wrought iron gates, removed in the wartime seizure of ornamental ironwork for smelting. The tiny cottages were in a sad state of disrepair. There were broken windows, collapsing guttering, tiles missing and the gardens a wilderness of overgrown shrubs, riotous flowers and towering weeds. More than three years had passed since the army had derequisitioned the property and in that time the vandals had been active. Why did young people have to smash things up to express themselves? It wasn't so in his day. They must have a screw loose thought Arthur.

The park was about seventy acres altogether, but divided into three sections, one on each side of the curving drive and a third area to the rear of the mansion. Many of the splendid ornamental trees had disappeared, leaving only decaying stumps. Some, close up to the house, had been cleared to provide for playing fields, for the property had been used as a girls' boarding school from the mid-twenties to the outbreak of war when it had been instantly requisitioned by the military. Although long gone, many ugly traces of their occupancy remained – two Nissen huts beneath a group of shrouding walnut trees, cement foundations here and there where other buildings had stood, and deep marks from army transport being parked on the old playing fields, plus the inevitable litter.

The Hall itself, a late-Stuart edifice, peeped forlornly from its crowding greenery and seemed to have sunk lower since Arthur's childhood. The blank windows – some broken, one or two boarded up – told their own anguished tale of neglect. Arthur parked his car on the spacious but weed-covered gravel in front of the magnificent portico which was a Georgian addition, and walked through the untidy bushes to the back premises, where dandelions and mayweed grew vigorously in the stone-paved yards. Stables, coach-houses, garages and living-quarters remained intact, mute evidence of the splendour that was. The huge gilded clock in its own handsome tower showed the time, as it had done for years, at twenty-seven minutes to five. Arthur thought he heard the tea-cups rattle. Among such desolation of neglect and silence the clock could have been an upright sleeping beauty of masonry. As always, Arthur felt he had stumbled on a lost village of a dead civilisation.

He walked down past the walled kitchen-garden, now tended, somewhat half-heartedly, by an absentee market-gardener tenant, and entered the back park. There was still plenty of grass, and the cattle, all Angus crosses, had thrived well and he decided that at least a dozen could be sent to the grading centre at Derby market on the following Tuesday. They could be sorted out and loaded in the stable yard with the aid of a few hurdles, and he made a mental note to bring them from Oakleigh on a trailer together with four or five men first thing on Tuesday. There couldn't be too many hands on the job when sorting cattle.

He finished his appraisal, drove thoughtfully up the drive and turned left towards Oakleigh. When past the lodges and the high hedges surrounding them, he had a full view of the park through its open fence. A few yards back from the road a huge 'For Sale' notice had been erected on stout poles with shoring timbers back and front as if it was meant to be a permanency. It might be that, thought Arthur, for it had been there for three years already, but as he glanced up to read the glowing description for the thousandth time, he was staggered to see the word 'Sold' in bold, exultant red letters, pasted diagonally across the fading board.

Chapter 3

'That's something to be chalked up,' thought Arthur as he drove back to his hayfields. A new owner at Hartnall Hall could make a tremendous difference to the village if he (or she) were the right sort and intended to live there. More probably it had been bought for institutional use – a lunatic asylum, or perhaps a hospital. A factory possibly, but he thought special planning permission would be needed for that and any application would first be made to the parish council of which he (and his father) were members. Such a project had certainly not been mentioned at the last meeting. However, there was no point in idle speculation. The purchaser would reveal himself in due course.

Arriving at the hayfield, he found Dick had just finished and was adjusting the width of the machine to travel to the next and final field of the season. He jumped down from the tractor seat to peer in at the string-box. Arthur joined him.

'When you've been two or three times round Flowery Mead, Dick, I'll take over while you have your tea.'

'You might as well come round there now, Gaffer, and move the fust round o' bales for me afore Ah 'ook on the sledge. Or Ah'll shift 'em while you drive.'

'I'll do that for you. By the way, you did a splendid job of baling at Hilltop Farm. Mr King seemed right pleased.'

'Ar, 'e were pleased all right, Gaffer. Give me ten bob!'

'That was generous of him.'

'It were that. Different to the last job Ah did for somebody else!'

'What was that?' asked Arthur, guessing that Dick had a tale to tell and would feel deprived if not allowed to repeat it.

'A couple o' wiks sin', owd Mrs Foster o' Lower Sucklings asked me to trim off 'er back paddock one Sat'day afternoon, wi' 'er own tackle, o' course – owd standard Fordson an' trailer mowin' machine. Said 'er'd gie me a drink. Took me 'alf the afternoon to get th' tractor runnin' an' the owd machine in workin' order, so it were nigh on six o'clock when Ah finished the job.'

'Did she give you a drink?'

'Oh ar, 'er give me a drink aw reight – glass o' lemonade an' two fags!'

His employer grinned.

'I've heard a better one than that, Dick. Mrs Foster has a little wire-haired terrier she's very fond of, as I expect you know. A week or two ago, he disappeared for a day and a night and she was right worried. Anyway, young Tommy Gretton found him up in Marlpit wood, with his foot in a rabbit wire. Mrs Foster was so pleased to get him back she rewarded Tommy wi' two sticks o' rhubarb. When the lad mentioned it was his birthday, she gave him a third stick o' rhubarb!'

'Ah can't believe that, Gaffer.'

'Well, that's the story, Dick. If you do anything else for Mrs Foster, you should ask for payment in advance.'

'Is 'er as poor as all that, Gaffer?'

'No, I think she's fairly well off. Owns the little farm, you know and her son has one o' the biggest garages in Derby. Well, we'd better move on and bale this last field. I'll follow you along.'

Dick was a great character, thought Arthur and wondered idly what Oakleigh would be like without him. He had worked there for as long as Arthur could remember – thirty-two years in fact, coming there as a lad of fourteen with his father in 1918. There had been vast changes in farming and he had absorbed them all. Now his nineteen-year-old son, Arnold, worked at Oakleigh, keeping up the family tradition.

With the haymaking out of the way Arthur was in a happier state of mind as he led his staff down to Hartnall Hall on the following Tuesday morning. The bullocks were unwilling to leave the saturating dew at first, but on the drive the rough surface of the hard gravel must have tickled their feet for they set off in a wild stampede, heads lowered and tails outstretched. Only some valiant sprinting by Billy and Arnold, the two youngest hands present, prevented them from invading the public highway. Wild-eyed but winded, they returned at a sedate trot and were skilfully steered into the capacious stable-yard, where various alleys had earlier been sealed off by hurdles.

The yard was so big and the cattle so restless that Arthur was unable to judge their condition by handling, as he had hoped, but had to depend on visual appraisal. The sliding doors of one of the roomy garages was pushed back and the chosen animals were directed into it to be contained there by Arnold and Billy. Arthur and his two senior men walked in among the main herd, cutting out the meatiest bullocks. The cattle were excited and full of lush grass and soon the yard was covered in splashing dung. The men did not escape quite all of it, either. Arthur was glad he had brought wellingtons and the old raincoat he kept for such occasions.

The twelfth and final beast for the market consignment had been drawn out when the farm men were surprised by the silent appearance of a Bentley on the drive outside the yard. A big man levered himself out of the driving seat.

'What the 'ell's going on 'ere?' he demanded loudly.

Arthur looked round enquiringly for he was not used to being addressed in such emphatic terms. His workmen stood around in silence.

'We're sorting out cattle for market,' he remarked mildly. 'But what is it to you, may I ask?'

'I'm the owner of this property and I don't expect to see somebody else's cattle in my yard, mucking the place up. What a bloody mess! Who are you and who gave you permission to come in here?'

'I rent the grazing in the park,' Arthur explained patiently. 'I know the agent pretty well, I pay a good rent and I'm certain he would not object to our using this derelict yard to sort out the cattle.'

'P'raps he wouldn't, but I bloody well would and do. You're in 'ere without direct permission. Get these cows out of 'ere and you'll get this bloody filth cleaned up or I'll know the reason why!'

'There's no need to get heated,' Arthur said, warming up slightly himself. 'I haven't been informed of any change of ownership, but we're about to take the cattle out, anyway.' There was the sound of heavy traffic approaching down the drive. 'Two lorries are coming in to pick up these beasts. Perhaps you'll move your Bentley before it gets damaged, either by the lorries or by the cattle in the loading.'

'Right! I'll shift the car but, apart from that, I'm not leaving this yard until I've got satisfaction from you, young feller.'

Arthur motioned to three of his men to return the unwanted cattle to the back park, leaving Billy to hold the market animals in the garage. When they returned, the lorries backed into the yard one at a time and after initial hesitation the unwilling bullocks were herded up the ramp with much scrabbling, shouting and thumping, followed by the usual swaying of the loaded vehicles.

Arthur, after being fully engaged supervising the whole tricky business, turned round to find the aggressive Bentley-owner beside him, watching the proceedings with apparent disfavour. He was a short, thickly built man in his early forties. Most of his blond hair had disappeared, leaving a large bald patch in the middle of his teutonic-looking head. His eyes were grey, shrewd and cold, and his chin jutted out militantly.

'I'm Arthur Felton,' the farmer said, as cordially as he could persuade himself to feel. 'My father and I, and my sister, run Oakleigh Farm on the other side of the village. May I ask your name?'

'You may! You'll hear plenty about it soon enough! I'm George Clark and I own G. C. Plastics in Derby. I've bought this property and I intend to live in the Hall. We're moving in practically at once.'

'Welcome to Hartnall, Mr Clark,' Arthur said, holding out his hand.

The other ignored it.

'I'm a self-made man and, I may say, a ruthless man. When I speak, people jump to it. I don't want local farmers loitering round this place now I've bought it. Get your cattle away from here, pronto!'

'For your information, Mr Clark, I've bought the grazing here until October 1st and paid for it. These cattle will stay here until then and there's nothing you can do about it! I may say you won't be popular in this village if you act this way.'

'I don't set out to be popular, farmer. I just want people to know I'm boss o' me own place! We'll see about this grazing. But get this muck cleared up or you'll find yourself in court. I'm goin' to wait 'ere and see it done!'

'We'd better be gettin' back to Oakleigh,' Dick Marshall said loudly, using the liberty his long years of service had given him. 'Accordin' to this chap, if 'e talks long, we'll soon 'a to start jumpin' around like fire-crackers! Ah'll tek keer that one o' my jumps lands right on 'is bloody feet!'

Arthur was pale with anger and ignored the broad grins of his men. 'Frank, come back from Oakleigh with brush and shovel and get this yard cleaned up – properly, I mean. Oh, better bring a hosepipe as well and wash it down. The water is still on at the stand-pipe.'

'Let me do it, Gaffer,' Dick pleaded, not caring if the retreating George Clark heard him. 'Ah'd turn the hose full on that bugger afore Ah left 'ere.'

'You've given me an idea, Dick,' Frank said thoughtfully.

'That's enough of that talk,' Arthur said sharply. 'If this man's going to live here, there'll be plenty of ill-feeling about without deliberately creating it.' He took off his wellingtons and his dung-splashed raincoat and tossed them into the boot of the Jaguar which had been left in the shrubberies well out of the way of the moving cattle. The car was nearly new and Arthur kept it very smart. He derived some satisfaction from accelerating powerfully past the unpleasant Mr Clark who stared at the car in some surprise.

Knowing the grading centre would have a great many cattle to deal with, Arthur decided to go home for a coffee and to change into market clothes before driving to Derby. As he dawdled along the farm drive he found himself following a girl cyclist whose back seemed familiar. As she moved her head slowly he realised, to his great surprise, that it was Alison King. He recalled that he had invited her to visit Oakleigh but had not expected her to do so before ten in the morning on her bicycle. She did not ride into the yard and approach the house through the cooling shed like some callers, but dismounted at the wicket gate which led to the front of the house and the office at the far end. Knowing that Edith would be at her desk at this hour, Arthur drove into the yard and walked down to the milking parlour to have a word with Alf the cowman.

Taking her briefcase from the carrier on the front of her bicycle, Alison walked along the gravel path between the garden and the house and knocked at the office door, which was opened at once by Edith.

'Good morning, Miss Felton. I'm from the Collector of Taxes –'

'Do come in. It's Alison King, isn't it? What can we do for you? It's not just a neighbourly call, I take it?'

'No, it's official, Miss Felton . . .'

'Call me Edith. I'm going to call you Alison.'

The girl looked at the older woman with admiration for it was generally known that Edith Felton had been the belle of the village as a teenager, as had her mother, Meg Ratcliffe, before her. Alison could hardly remember Edith before the war, but she recalled seeing her several times in her ATS uniform and had sometimes seen her at a distance since the war had ended.

Edith was tall with a full figure. Her light brown, almost chestnut hair glistened attractively in its high roll, and the bright blue eyes were disconcertingly penetrating. Her complexion was smooth and unblemished, her features, firm, even and comely. Alison wondered why this queenly young woman had never married.

'All right, Edith, then. I've called for your P35 and deduction cards which we don't seem to have received.'

'But that's ridiculous! I sent them off in April. This is mid-July. Have you only just discovered you haven't got them?'

'There are an awful lot still outstanding, I can assure you.

We've just started a major effort to get them in.'

'Well, ours went off between the 6th and the 19th April, I can assure you. Those are the dates required by you, and I keep to them. It's just as easy to be in time as to be late.'

Alison glanced round the comfortable office, which could more accurately be called a study. The wall above the desk was covered with divided shelves and pigeon-holes and in each section were groups of hardback files with a bold white label gummed on the back of each. Clearly the very essence of efficiency. She had heard that Edith had been a captain in the Pay Corps, and she was clearly putting her military experience into operation.

'Did you post them yourself?' Alison enquired.

'I certainly did! No one else in this house thinks of posting letters.'

'If you say you have posted them, I accept they have been sent, so the fault must be at our end. We receive a great many schemes in April, sometimes more than a hundred a day, so it's possible one could have been misdirected, although it's not usual.'

The office's inner door opened, and Arthur walked in from the kitchen.

'Good morning, Alison. Glad to see you were able to visit us at last. How are you getting on with my efficient little sister?'

'Don't be ridiculous, Arthur,' Edith said sharply.

'This isn't a social call, Major. I'm here for the annual PAYE returns.'

'The devil you are! Hasn't my competent partner sent them off? For shame, Edith!'

'I accept that they have been sent off, Major Felton, but we don't seem to have them in the office. It is essential for us to have the P35, the P9s which are the deduction cards and any P45s which you may have received during the fiscal year. Part Three, that is. Since they are missing, I am afraid I shall have to reconstitute the scheme so that it can be processed.'

'My God!' Arthur pretended to groan. 'Edith, how have you been getting on with little Miss Jargon here?'

'Don't be rude, Arthur. I won't have you insult visitors in my office.'

'Your office? Anyway, this young lady is not a visitor, she's a tax officer. And we are not hosts, we're taxpayers.'

'Now you're really being rude and I won't have it! Go and make a cup of tea while Alison and I sort this out. I suppose you're capable of that?'

To the utter astonishment of Edith and himself, Arthur obeyed.

When he returned to the office ten minutes later bearing a loaded tea-tray, his father accompanied him.

'Hello, young lady,' Robert Felton said genially. 'You're Gene King's youngest girl, aren't you? Pleased to welcome you here.'

Edith dispensed the tea and they partook of it together. Alison felt she had seldom met a more pleasant man than Arthur's father. There seemed to be an aura of kindness and consideration around him, as shown by his next remark.

'I hope you can supply Alison with the information she wants, Edith.'

'Yes, of course I can. We were just arranging it when you came in,' his daughter replied, somewhat testily. 'Tell me again what you propose, Alison. I always keep a copy of the P35 for my own records.'

'If I could borrow that, and your wages book, so that I can make out a pro-forma P35 and dummy cards, I would be grateful. May I take them back to the office with me?'

'No, I don't think I can agree to that, Alison . . .'

'Why not?' interrupted Arthur.

'. . .They might be lost as the originals were,' Edith went on, ignoring the interruption. 'You can work here and use what documents you need to make copies.'

'And if it's a long job, you can stay to lunch,' put in Robert Felton. 'We'll be glad to have you.'

'That's very kind of you, Mr Felton, but I hope to be away before lunch-time. I have a lot of calls in my case!'

'Is this part of your regular duties?' queried Arthur aggrievedly. 'Biking round the countryside, calling on people, some of whom may not be helpful or even polite?'

'No, but some of our officers – the cashiers – do. Someone is out everyday. Personal application, when written reminders have failed, is part of the system. I've been loaned to the Pay-As-You-Earn section for a few days, because I know this part of our area so well.'

'You would call here on the day I have to go to Derby,' grumbled Arthur in mock annoyance. 'I could have shown you round the place when you'd done your figuring.'

'I couldn't possibly have agreed, Major Felton. My time belongs to the Inland Revenue – in office hours, anyway.'

'Good for you Alison. That's put you properly in your place, Arthur,' chuckled his father.

'Well then, I'm off to market. You two girls can get on with your copying conference. Don't lose your way among the jargon.

34

Coming with me, Dad?'

'No thanks, Arthur. I get weary, hanging about that market for half the afternoon. It's bad enough when it's my turn on the grading panel.'

Later that day, over the evening meal, when the market returns for the ten bullocks had been examined, digested and approved, Arthur described his encounter with the man who claimed to be the new owner of Hartnall Hall.'

'It's a great shame,' Edith said with feeling, 'to think the house has been empty for so long and then to fall into the hands of such a disagreeable character. I wonder where such an ignorant man got the money from? A war profiteer, perhaps.'

'The purchase money wouldn't be so difficult to raise, Edith,' her father pointed out. 'The place is so run down and it's been on offer for so long the owners wouldn't expect much for it. We could have bought it ourselves easily enough, but what would we want it for? Living in a mansion's not our life style.'

'I wouldn't want us to leave the dear old farmhouse —' Edith began when she was interrupted, rather rudely, by her brother.

'We could have bought it all right, Dad, but would we have been able to foot the bill for the extensive repairs? That's going to cost a fortune.'

'Let's hope this newly-rich Mr Clark has the money to do it properly and that his character mellows a little. I wonder what the Ratcliffes will think of it. Perhaps you'll find out if you see them on Saturday, Arthur,' Edith said mischievously.

'You know perfectly well I'll see at least one of them on Saturday, Sis. Linda never misses a home match.'

'Yes, you'll have to make do with Linda in place of Alison at cricket.'

'How can you say that? Alison might well be there, for all you know.'

'She won't! She's a tennis enthusiast and has a tournament on Saturday at Burton.'

Arthur grunted and did not pursue the matter.

Linda Ratcliffe was at the cricket ground as usual, very much in evidence with Mrs Dickens and Mrs Marriott, in the centre compartment of the splendid three-roomed pavilion which had been a gift to the cricket club from her grandfather forty years previously. The three women were laying out the tea things on a small trestle table. Linda fondly imagined she supervised the cricket teas, but in fact the other two did most of the work at the ground, leaving Linda to make eyes at the captain of the home team.

She tripped over to meet Arthur Felton as he got out of his car. The young farmer, himself already resplendent in his immaculate cream flannels, looked at her with masculine appreciation. She was tall and graceful, her pale blue linen dress looking just right with her blonde silky hair. Her eyes were large with a mischievous twinkle, her nose small, fine and delightfully tilted, and though her lips drooped slightly as if in a constant sulky pout, she was nevertheless a remarkably pretty girl. Blond and beautiful, the young men called her.

'Good afternoon, Major Felton.'

'Good afternoon to you, Miss Ratcliffe.'

'I would like to talk to you, but do you have to be so formal?'

'It wouldn't be fitting for an ordinary working farmer to address the Squire's daughter in a familiar way, would it?'

'Rubbish! I'm not the squire's daughter. This village hasn't had a squire for thirty years, and you are not an ordinary farmer!'

This was old ground. Arthur was only plaguing her and they both knew it, but he was anxious that too much intimacy should not develop between them.

'It's about Charles. I'd like you to give him more chance with the bat. He fancies himself as an opener, and so do I.'

'Charles is only eighteen. There'll be plenty of time for him to improve later on. And why didn't he ask me himself? I don't think much of any lad who gets his sister to plead for him.'

'He didn't! I'm doing this off my own bat.'

'Remarkably appropriate metaphor!'

'He needs encouragement. Daddy's not well this summer or he would coach Charles.'

Arthur was silent for a moment or two, remembering how assiduously Linda's father had coached him in the far-off, happy Thirties. Night after night, Major Ratcliffe had turned up at the net for practice with the team, but had concentrated on teaching and advising the young Felton, although his relations with Arthur's father and grandfather were anything but cordial.

'All right, Linda, I'll send him in first in my place.'

'That's not what I wanted for him at all. I'd like you to take him in with you to open the innings!'

'Very well, if you're so intense about it, but I don't know what Fred Sands will say.'

'He won't say anything to you.'

'You've got an answer to everything.'

He walked away from her to join his team, feeling it necessary to discourage any further close conversation. Give Linda an inch and she would take a yard; tongues were wagging enough already and the change in the batting order would give the gossips another titbit. Winning the toss, he decided to bat and opened the innings with Charles Ratcliffe as his number two, much to the annoyance of his normal opening partner.

Arthur had a keen eye, could move quickly and was a fine forcing bat. He could have been successful in a higher class of cricket had he been willing to give more time to it. Although fully conscious of his understudy at the other end, he played his normal game and scored rapidly, mainly by powerful drives in front of the wicket, and soon had the opposing fieldsmen on the boundary. His partner defended well and scored a run or two occasionally. The captain reached his fifty with the total at sixty-five and immediately retired from the crease, Charles Ratcliffe having scored a round dozen. When Arthur entered the pavilion he was greeted with a chorus of remonstrance from his team mates.

'I want you all to get some batting,' he said briefly and after taking off his pads walked over to join Linda who, with her two female companions, was sitting on one of the forms beside the pavilion. As he sat down, the two older women discreetly moved away, much to his annoyance.

'I think you're an utter fool, skipper,' Linda said furiously. 'You were going so well you'd have got your century easily, and we haven't had one at Hartnall this year!'

Arthur stretched out his long legs, relaxing comfortably in spite of the girl's tirade.

'Why did you do it?' she went on. 'I know! It was to spite me because I asked you to give Charles a better chance! Well, I was right, wasn't I? He's still there, with nearly twenty to his name.'

'Don't nag, Linda,' Arthur said wearily, using her Christian name naturally, a habit which was becoming more frequent than he liked. 'You do go on, don't you? There'll be plenty of other chances to get a ton . . .'

'Don't be so sure. You're thirty six!'

'Thirty-five,' he corrected her, 'and only just that. I'm young enough for another twenty years of village cricket, but I'm too old to argue with a girl of seventeen!'

'You know perfectly well I'm twenty-two!'

'Then don't act as though you're seventeen. Having your airs with me! Young Charles is all right. I didn't know he wanted to go in first. I thought he was happy enough where he was. As to my retiring not out, how do you know it wasn't so that I could sit and talk to a lovely, if cross, young lady?'

'If I thought that, I could forgive you anything, Arthur. Why can't you pay such compliments more often? I sometimes think you don't care.'

'We've always been good friends, haven't we?' protested the farmer. 'I appreciate the interest you take in the cricket team.'

'Oh, cricket!' Linda said irritably, 'I'd do a lot more than take an interest in cricket for your sake, Arthur. I'd do anything, for you – just any mortal thing. Anything you want, Arthur, and I mean that,' and she slid an inch or two along the wooden seat so their thighs touched.

Arthur Felton gave her a startled glance. During his seven years in the army he had certainly not lived a celibate life, but he had no intention of philandering in his own village. His mother had brought him up to set an example to others. Linda's big eyes were wide open, shining and twinkling in direct invitation.

'Linda,' he said sternly, 'if you mean what I think you mean, I'll turn you up and smack your bottom!'

The girl clapped her hands.

'Oo! That would be lovely! When?'

'You're incorrigible,' the man replied, getting up and walking into the pavilion.

Chapter 4

After a few minutes of cursory discussion with his team about the game, Arthur remembered with some irritation that there was another subject he had meant to discuss with Linda Ratcliffe, so he made his way back to her. She was still sitting at one end of the form with her hands on her lap almost as if she were waiting for him to return, but in the meantime watching the cricket with rapt attention. She'd be an attractive little devil, Arthur thought, if she were not so bold and cheeky. As he sat down beside her he wondered how far she would go if she were pressed.

She looked across at him archly.

'Finished your business in the pavilion? Laid your plans for annihilating the opposition?'

'I've just remembered I wanted to talk to you about Hartnall Hall. You know it's been sold and the new owner's going to live there?'

'Yes, the agent kept Daddy informed for sentimental reasons, although it's none of our business, really. Have you met the new owner?'

'Yes, I have, and it wasn't very edifying. He's a rough diamond with objectionable manners and total conceit. He won't be an asset to the village. Has your father met him?'

'Not yet, and I'm sure he won't want to if he's as aggressive as you say.'

'The man's an uneducated boor and if he's got money enough to buy the Hall, he must have accumulated it by wartime profiteering, I should think.'

'Oh no! Daddy's had him investigated. He's genuine enough – went right through the war and finished as a sergeant-major in a front-line regiment. Used his gratuity to start a business in plastics and it's grown hand over fist. Comes from a rough family, but there's nothing shady about him.'

'Has he any family?'

'He has an inconspicuous wife, a crippled son and a school-age daughter. To begin with, they're going to live in the servants' quarters while they repair the rest of the house. Now you know as much as I do, Major Felton.'

'I shall get to know a lot more in due course, I daresay. But it will soon be teatime. Only two more of our men to go in. Hadn't you better join the other two in getting it ready?'

'Thank you for dismissing me so perfunctorily!' Linda snapped. 'You've extracted all my information, so now I can go and make the tea!'

'Shall I go and make it, then?'

'Stupid,' and Linda tossed her head prettily and marched to the pavilion. At the interval between the innings she was much in evidence handing round cups of tea, plates of sandwiches and rock-cakes with so much grace and charm that all the cricketers thought the Hartnall skipper must be crazy not to grasp the jewel which was so clearly offered. As he watched her superb carriage and aplomb, Arthur could not help thinking the same from time to time. But Alison's image would keep cropping up in his mind. Her quiet loveliness combined with her brisk efficiency crowded the vivacious Linda out of his thoughts.

At the end of the game, which Hartnall won easily, Arthur resisted the clamour of his team-mates to celebrate at The Waggoners. He was not a keen drinking man and he had been in the company of his team for five hours. No need to make an evening of it as well, for as usual he had one or two farming matters to deal with. Picking up his cricket bag he strode over to his car and to his surprise and annoyance saw Linda waiting there for him, with a basket in each hand.

'May I beg a lift home, Major?'

Arthur frowned at this obvious ploy.

'Can't you go home with Charles?' he asked ungallantly. 'I saw his Prefect here.'

Linda flushed.

'Charles has just gone off to the pub with the others, his car loaded to capacity. It isn't much to ask, is it, after I've organised the tea for both teams?'

'Of course not,' Arthur said, belatedly remembering his manners. 'I've things to do, but it will only take a minute,' and he politely opened the door for her. 'What's wrong with your own car?'

'It's being serviced. The farm foreman – you know, Banton, does it for me and he could only manage it this afternoon. I need if for my job on Monday. It's so boring and inconvenient to go by bus.'

Arthur knew she was only leading him on but he refused to be drawn. He had heard that she was secretary to a Derby firm and was not sufficiently interested to know more. He would drive her to Home Farm and pull away as quickly as possible.

The farmhouse into which Mortimer Ratcliffe had moved when Hartnall Hall, together with the larger portion of the estate, had been auctioned in 1921, had been smartened and enlarged so that it now resembled a small manor house. Arthur crunched to a halt on the U-shaped gravel forecourt by the front door. If he had hoped to drive away immediately, he was disappointed, for Major Ratcliffe and his wife were appraising their flower beds.

Linda jumped out at once, saying, 'You must come in for a drink, Major.'

Arthur cursed under his breath; he could hardly drive off under the noses of the girl's parents.

Major Ratcliffe, still tall and lean, but with a certain hollowness about the cheeks, walked across the lawn with an engaging smile.

'Had a good afternoon, Linda? Glad to see you, Felton! Successful match, I hope?'

His daughter answered him.

'Really splendid Daddy, but it could have been better. Charles opened the innings and carried his bat for thirty-two. The skipper made a beautiful fifty in quick time and then, for some inexplicable reason, retired!'

'I'm sure he knew what he was doing,' her father said reprovingly. 'It's not for the team or the onlookers to query the captain's decision.'

Arthur grinned broadly and slily pinched Linda's arm so that she coloured faintly.

'Come inside Felton,' said Major Ratcliffe cordially; then remembering the circumstances added, 'oh, of course, you haven't met my wife,' and he made the introduction.

Arthur bowed slightly as he took the proffered hand. He had seen Mrs Ratcliffe hundreds of times, and she must have seen him, but such was the schism between their families they had never spoken to each other. Arthur knew from hearsay that she was French, and that to the village she was a mystery woman. He mentally christened her the Grey Lady, for her hair was almost white and she wore a fashionable dove-coloured summer dress. Her eyes regarded him kindly, she was graceful in her movements and gracious in her manner. With a shock Arthur recalled that although the Mortimer Ratcliffes had lived here since 1921, which was as far back as his memory went, he had never called in at Home Farm before.

He was not relishing the first visit either as he followed his host into the lounge, for it seemed as if he and Linda were to be more closely linked, a state of affairs which he would have preferred to avoid. He accepted a sherry and hoped that the conversation could be limited to cricket.

'Shall we see you in the team again this season, sir?' he asked solicitously.

''Fraid not, Felton . . .'

'Next year, then?'

'Almost certainly not, I would say. I'm nearly sixty, young fellow! My joints are getting stiff and my digestion's not what it was. I must content myself with watching you, Felton, and thinking of those old times before the war.'

'They were pleasant days, sir, and I don't forget I owe all my cricketing skill to you. I'll always be grateful, for I've had a lot of fun out of the game.'

There was a nostalgic silence for a few minutes until Mrs Ratcliffe interposed gently, 'You will stay to dinner, Mr Felton?'

Arthur nearly fell over himself in his hurry to refuse.

'Oh – er – I'm sorry, Mrs Ratcliffe. Will you excuse me? I have an appointment this evening – a business appointment,' he added, realising how unlikely it sounded.

'Ah! Farming matters will always intrude, even on cricket Saturdays,' said Major Ratcliffe sententiously, although he did not believe the young man.

Arthur put down his glass and said farewell to his host and hostess.

'You must come in again, Felton,' the Major said heartily.

'Yes, please do!' Mrs Ratcliffe echoed her husband willingly for she had taken an instant liking to the young man, so much more agreeable than any of the other local farmers known to her.

Linda accompanied him to the door.

'I don't think you have an appointment at all. Just an excuse to get away,' she grumbled.

'Don't try to read my mind. I find it too disconcerting, Linda. Thank you for a splendid afternoon. At least, it's been very enjoyable for me, but it can't have been for you, because I seem to have made you angry several times.'

'I'm getting used to that,' Linda said sulkily.

'You won't take no for an answer, will you?' Before she had time to reply the Jaguar rasped away over the gravel.

'Confound the girl,' Arthur muttered to himself as he cruised along the lanes to Oakleigh. 'Why can't she lay off?' He was getting hungry and he hoped Edith had kept a meal for him. Dinner at the Home Farm would have been quite acceptable and he could have done justice to it, but he had felt uneasy in that house and disturbed at what Linda might have been reading into his presence. Damn Linda! She would keep creeping into his thoughts and his life when he wanted to think of Alison whom he found an altogether more attractive personality. He intended to get better acquainted with her and would need to devise a suitable plan of campaign.

At the Home Farm, Linda and her father were discussing their visitor, Mrs Ratcliffe having left the lounge to supervise the preparation of the evening meal.

'You're not becoming fond of Felton, are you, Linda? I'm pretty sure his father wouldn't welcome such a match.'

'Why ever not?'

'There's been enmity between us ever since he first came to Hartnall about forty years ago. He was a conceited, ignorant lout, but as sharp as a bayonet point. Ran away from his home in a London suburb where his father kept a grubby little paper-shop . . .'

'I've heard that his brother has a chain of such shops now,' Linda interrupted.

'Very likely. They're an enterprising family. As I was saying before you broke in, the lad was taken on by Arnold Ratcliffe who was our tenant then, and in a few years Felton had married the daughter of the house, and soon owned the lot! Now he's the biggest and most competent farmer round here, including us by jove! I must hand it to him for his nerve and his application.'

'But how did he come to fall out with you, Daddy? One hears rumours, but it's hard to get at the truth. How did an obscure farm boy tangle with the son of the squire?'

'It's a long story and won't bear re-telling, but it concerned first Ratcliffe's daughter and then, to some extent, Felton's sister.'

'You must have done something pretty horrid for them to hold a grudge all these years!'

Her father did not deign to answer that. He went on, 'I've got to hand it to the chap though. He's got some guts as well as brains. Did remarkably good work in the war – my war – and ended up with a commission. Then in the recent war he was a great help as my company commander in the Home Guard.'

'Yes, I remember that, but if you dislike him so much, how could you work with him and he with you?'

'That was a matter of duty, girl. Personal feelings have to be put aside in wartime, and it took me some while to make Felton see that. Stubborn as hell, but diligent, responsible and utterly competent.'

'He might not make a bad father-in-law!'

'I was very fond of young Felton. Fine fellow, keen as mustard. He reminded me of his mother when she was a girl. I was quite fond of her and she was the loveliest thing for miles round – and so was Edith in her day, and still is. Meg and Betty Felton were the prettiest and most competent horsewomen in the Hunt. The menfolk of that family did not go in much for hunting, although Robert hunted a bit for a year or two.'

The Major sighed and fidgeted in his chair.

'I love Arthur, Daddy, and I intend to have him, whether he likes it or not!'

'You generally get your own way, Linda. But mind, his family will be against you. I'd love to give you away in Hartnall church, and I daresay I can stand his father's glowering, but if Arthur's Aunt Betty turns up it might be embarrassing for her and for me.'

'You'll probably have plenty of time to make your peace. It might take me quite a while to land my fish!'

'It certainly might, my dear. Rumour has it that Felton is looking in another direction – to Hilltop Farm, in fact.'

'You mean Alison King? That little thing?'

'She's a pretty wench, nevertheless, and a hard worker, and has an office job in Burton, just as you have in Derby. It beats me why farmers' daughters take up work in town and pretend they like it!'

'I'll have to think about Alison. Where did you hear this?'

'It's only gossip among the men. Perhaps it's meaningless, but the Oakleigh foreman, Marshall, hinted it to Banton over a glass of beer in The Waggoner's.'

'It's just as well to know the opposition, Daddy, and not to underrate it!'

*　*　*

Arthur's curiosity about the new owner of Hartnall Hall mounted and he made a point of inspecting the cattle in the park himself, every morning. On the next Monday, on returning to his Land-Rover, he found a large van, bearing the legend 'G. C. Plastics' parked beside it. There seemed to be several men working in the house and another was starting to tidy up the shrubbery. Arthur would have liked to look inside the house and have a word with the men, but before he could do so, Clark drove up in his Bentley and Arthur felt that his curiosity would not be welcomed. He raised his hand in acknowledgement as Clark got out of his car, but the other man did not respond, staring straight ahead as if Arthur did not exist. The farmer shrugged his shoulders, climbed into his vehicle, turned it round and drove off noisily.

Returning up the drive, his mind became absorbed in farming problems. There was a lot of grass in the eastern half of the front park, and the reduced number of cattle would scarcely cope with the heavy growth. He could put the ewes in to flush them for breeding, but the grass was long for sheep and possibly the Clarks kept dogs – town dogs, unused to sheep. Perhaps a late cut could be taken for silage. The job could be worked in, just before and during harvest, making it into a stack at Claypits. A dressing of nitrogen would be a help – boost the growth and uplift the protein content of the silage. There was just time and he knew there was a ton or so in the barn, left over from the spring applications. He would send Frank in that afternoon. Better mention it to Dad first though. He liked to be consulted on all policy decisions. The ewes could come in when the silage was off, if no dogs had appeared at the Hall by then. He would have a word about it with the shepherd. It might be better to put the unsold lambs in the park and fatten them off with trough food. They ought to be off the farm by the end of October.

The plastics van continued to arrive every morning, bringing three or four workmen. Heaps of empty paint tins, broken plaster, wallpaper, splintered laths and other rubbish grew larger every day. In the middle of the week a large furniture van arrived and the back of Hartnall Hall soon began to take on a 'lived-in' look. Still the workmen came every day and Arthur wondered if Clark was repairing his new house 'on the side' and setting the cost of the labour among his firm's outgoings, thus earning tax concessions. If that were so, it couldn't be right, he told himself, and he was not inclined to allow this loud-mouthed manufacturer to get away with such flagrant dishonesty.

Arthur hadn't seen Alison for a week and felt he would like to see her again, if only to discuss the apparently devious ways of Mr Clark. He understood she was still spending a few days cycling round the district on 'outdoor work' as she called it. That probably meant that she also cycled to the office on those days, so there was no point in picking her up after work. Loading a bicycle in the boot of a Jaguar in busy Station Street would attract attention and might cause mischievous comment. On the other hand, if she were coming home by bus she would have quite a walk from her office to the Wetmore Road bus park.

There was really no earthly need for him to hide his feelings, so he decided to take the bull by the horns and call at Hilltop Farm. Eugene King was not in the house when Arthur arrived and his wife was a little flustered at being caught unawares by so eminent a visitor. He explained his errand briefly, saying he had a matter to discuss with Alison and driving her home in the car seemed the handiest way to do it.

'I'm sure she'll be glad of the lift, Mr Felton,' Kathleen King said, knowing full well that this was not so. 'She takes her bike on Mondays and Wednesdays only. You'll save her walking down to the bus and walking home from Repton off it. She doesn't leave work till six, though.'

Quite satisfied, Arthur departed and Mrs King immediately telephoned her daughter to warn her that a tall rich man with an expensive car might be waiting to pick her up.

'Arthur Felton, I suppose,' Alison said crossly. 'What on earth does he want? Anyway, I'll make the best of it, Mum. It will make some of the girls in the office look envious, and the boys too!'

The farmer was outside the Collector's office at ten to six and in a few minutes the Revenue staff emerged in twos and threes. Alison was in the third group. She walked straight across the pavement, calmly opened the door and settled down beside Arthur, waving to her staring colleagues as he drove off.

'Saucy little wretch,' Arthur said to himself. But aloud, 'You're a pretty cool, young lady. Were you expecting me?'

'Mummy phoned me you were coming, so when I'd got used to the idea, I thought I might as well make the most of it. One doesn't get picked up in a new Jaguar every day!'

'I suppose I could have brought the Land-Rover. Would have been less conspicuous,' Arthur said, speaking his thoughts aloud.

'Thank you! I prefer the Jag. Much more stylish! Anyway, what is the reason for this unexpected honour, Major?'

'Does one need a reason for picking up a pretty girl and giving her a lift home? I've been trying to see you for a day or two, but you're so damned elusive.'

'I'm a working girl, you know – leave home at nine in the morning and don't get back until after half-past six. Doesn't leave much time, does it, apart from the week-ends! We're not all rich farmers!' she added unkindly and then wished she hadn't said it.

Arthur disregarded the jibe. He was so keen on his own half of the conversation that he was practically ignoring hers.

'I'd like to see more of you, Alison. I'm getting right fond of you!'

The car glided to a halt where the road widened outside the inn at Newton.

'What are we stopping for? I'm anxious to get home for my tea.'

'We'll have a meal here if you like.'

'No, thank you, it's not necessary when we're only a few minutes from home where Mum's expecting me. Why can't we talk there?'

'Because I want to talk to you in private! You're not nervous are you? Here in the centre of the village in broad daylight with all this homeward-bound traffic?'

'Don't be silly,' Alison said shortly although she did have a vague feeling of apprehension. She knew nothing about this man really, except where he lived and that his family was the most respected in the village. 'I'm not nervous,' she continued to reassure herself, 'not yet, anyway,' and wished she hadn't said that either.

'I hope you never will be,' Arthur said seriously. 'Nothing will ever happen that you don't want to happen. But why not come over to Oakleigh and spend an evening with my father and Edith? Dad would be so pleased. He's got a television set now and he loves it – quite makes his evenings! You'd like it too!'

'Don't kid yourself that you're going to fall in love with me, Major. I'm certainly not going to fall in love with you!'

'You don't know that! You may do!'

'I'm already engaged and have been for two years.'

'Engagements can be broken!'

'I like that! I'm not going to break my engagement! Adrian and I are going to get married as soon as he's saved up the deposit for a house. He won't let me help, so I'm going to buy the furniture.'

She's getting conversational at last, thought Arthur, and that's some improvement. The girl went on, 'You see Major, we both have the same tastes – tennis, speedway racing and football. We never miss seeing Derby County at home. The only sport you're interested in is cricket.'

'How can you possibly know that?'

'Everybody knows it! The same as everybody knows that Linda Ratcliffe is madly in love with you!'

'Rubbish! She's only a child.'

'She's three years older than I am.'

'But you seem so much more mature,' Arthur said which was unfair to Linda.

'I don't see why. She's a working girl the same as I am and probably earns more money. She's secretary to one of the big firms in Derby.'

'I hope she's not secretary to one firm that I could name!'

'What on earth are you . . . oh, you mean the chap who's bought the Hall. I heard that he's a bit of a tartar and has had one clash with you already.'

'However did you hear that?'

'It's all over the village. Our cowman's a right gossip, you know – goes to the pub quite often and gets all the news – straight from the oven!'

'He's certainly not a very pleasant character and, I think, not very honest.'

'How can you say that?'

'Well, it's something in your line, really. He's bought the Hall to live in with his family, but he has a vanload of men from his factory in there every day, working in the house and the grounds. That can't be right – using his firm's labour to improve his private dwelling. Shouldn't you report him or something?'

'I report him? What's it to do with me?'

'Well, you're a tax officer. Isn't that your business?'

'Major Felton, we are tax collectors, but it is not our duty to snoop around and ferret out information on our own initiative. That would be very underhanded – sort of nosy-parkering!'

'But I thought that was what you did!'

'If the Inspector of Taxes wants some specific information about a certain taxpayer or about the occupant of a certain property, of course we try to get it for him, but not always by direct means. We make discreet enquiries at the house next door, or from the milkman or postman.'

'Well, I think that's disgracefully underhanded. You let all these people know that you're chasing this unfortunate party for income tax?'

'It's not like that at all!' Alison coloured with mounting anger. 'We are not allowed to divulge our business or our identity to any-one but the taxpayer. It's against the Official Secrets Act. We adopt a kind of subterfuge and pretend that we're an old acquaintance making a surprise visit.'

'Not a very respectable way of earning a living.'

'Nonsense! It's the unrespectable people who make it necessary.'

'So this chap Clark's going to get away with it?'

'Major Felton, you've no right to make that assumption!' Alison was becoming impatient with her questioner, who thought how desirable she looked with her flashing eyes sparkling in her pale face, now highlighted by a pink patch on each cheek as pretty as a June rose.

'All right then. Explain how I'm acting unreasonably in suspecting this chap.'

'In the first place, you don't know the circumstances. This man may be making an adjustment in his books, debiting the cost of the labour to the private account and crediting the business account.'

'That's not very likely!'

'You don't know. But what you should know is that a lot of that sort of thing goes on in farming and a blind eye is turned to it. Who does the garden at Oakleigh? It is beautifully kept, but not by your father or Edith. Jimmy Dunn has a few hours every week in there, doesn't he? Is that adjusted in the accounts?'

'Well . . . I . . .'

'Even on our little place the cowman puts an evening in our garden at least once a week – overtime, of course, but it comes out of the farm. The Inspector of Taxes probably knows about these cases, but so long as the practice is not abused, he lets it pass.'

'Oh, well, I'd better pipe down, I suppose.'

'You certainly had. There's another possible explanation that should have occurred to you. Mr Clark may have bought the Hall as an investment out of his firm's funds. In that case he would be entitled to repair it with the firm's labour. That's not as unethical as it sounds, since he could transfer a payment for rental from his private account to his business account.'

'It all sounds rather questionable.'

'Does it? What about this Jaguar? You don't run it out of your pocket money, do you?'

'But I use if for the farm as well, so the farm pays part of the running expenses.'

'What, when you've also got a Land-Rover and a pick-up for farm use? And what about Edith's Consul and your father's Humber?'

'My God, there's no stopping you, is there, when you get your teeth into anything. Like a terrier with a rat, and I seem to be the rat this time. Are all tax collectors as tough and fierce as you?'

'Will you run me home now, please. I'm getting hungry.'

As the car moved away she half-turned and said, 'I'm sorry I blew my top, Arthur.'

The man cocked his head quizzically. It was the first time she had used his Christian name and had obviously done so inadvertently. Perhaps he had progressed further than he knew.

Chapter 5

When haymaking ended the onset of harvesting was still a fortnight ahead, and the catch-crop of silage was not quite ready either. Oakleigh Farm was enjoying a quiet period and several of the staff agreed to take their annual week's holiday, leaving only a skeleton crew to carry out necessary stock duties. Arthur took his own annual holiday in May, when sowing had been completed and inter-row cultivation not yet begun, but in this second half of July the whole Felton family took things easier than usual. The farm, big as it was, ran like a well-oiled machine at all times, or as Felton senior put it, 'like an old-fashioned threshing outfit on a bright March day!'

Optimistically, Arthur cruised around the district in the Land-Rover on Monday and Wednesday, hoping to glimpse Alison on her round of calls. In fact, she had taken a week of her own annual leave, but had not thought it necessary to reveal this to him. Neither would it have been tactful, for she had gone to Blackpool with her fiancé.

On Tuesday Arthur drove to Chesterfield to see the final day's play between the county and the West Indies touring team, but the play was frequently interrupted by rain and he drove home in an unsatisfied state of mind. On the Friday he was better rewarded when he visited the Trent Bridge ground at Nottingham for the second day's play in the third Test Match of the series. The weather was splendid and through the whole afternoon the crease was occupied by Worrell and Weekes in a glorious partnership. Arthur drove home in a replete mood, in body as well as in mind, for he stopped at a fashionable roadhouse for an evening meal.

'Linda rang up twice,' Edith told him when he arrived home. 'She's going to ring again later.'

'What on earth for?' Arthur said suspiciously. 'We're not playing at home tomorrow!'

'Where will you be playing?'

'We're going right over to Ashby, and the following week we go to Allestree. Both teams are right out of our normal area really, but this last year or two we've been making such good scores that several high-class sides have invited us to play them.'

'Dad's been watching the Test Match on television. He enjoyed it as much as I suppose you must have done!'

Their father came into the lounge to hear the last remark.

'Never thought much about cricket until they invented television,' he agreed. 'Now I'm getting quite a fan, especially of the West Indies.'

The telephone rang and Arthur went to the instrument in the hall, leaving the sitting-room door open.

'Major Felton?' asked the familiar, cultivated voice.

'Yes, Miss Ratcliffe.'

'Need we be so formal, sir?'

'You started it!'

'I've rung twice before, expecting you to be home.'

'A farmer doesn't spend every minute indoors, as you should know.'

'But I thought this was a slack period for you!'

'Slack, but exciting. I've been to the Test Match to-day.'

'Oh Arthur! I'd love to have been with you! Why didn't you say you were going? I'd have begged the day off.'

'Made up my mind on the spur of the moment. That's one of the differences between being a farmer and a secretary!'

'Snob!'

'What did you ring me for, Linda? Not to compare our respective professions?'

'Arthur, will you give me a lift to Ashby to-morrow?'

'What on earth do you want to go there for?'

'For the match, silly.'

'But you never go to away matches!'

'Well, I'm going to from now on.'

'Oh lor!'

'Thank you very much for that involuntary exclamation! Will you pick me up?'

'Why can't you go in your little Morris?'

'It needs two new tyres. I've got them, and Bromley's going to put them on to-morrow.'

'I see. Last week he was servicing it; next week he'll be spraying the body, no doubt!'

'Don't be mean, Arthur!'

'Why can't Charles take you? He's in the team.'

'He's taking a girl-friend and doesn't want me around!'

'Well, I don't know, Linda. I may be in a hurry . . .'

'I'll come to your house on my bicycle and wait until you're ready.'

'I don't want to . . .'

Arthur paused. He was weakening and running out of excuses.

51

Linda was one hell of a nice girl if she were not so determined. He was surprised to receive a dig in the ribs and found his father standing beside him. Instinctively, Arthur put his hand over the mouthpiece.

'What is it, Dad?'

'I've been listening to you, lad. Don't string the girl along in that uncivil way. All those excuses! Act the gentleman and take her with you!'

By now Arthur did not need much persuasion, but he said, 'I thought you didn't want to get us mixed up with the Ratcliffes!'

'Giving a girl a ride in a car isn't marrying her!'

'It might be, with Linda,' his son said grimly as he removed his hand. 'Are you there, Linda?'

'Yes, of course. What was that pregnant silence? Hatching out another feeble excuse, I suppose?'

'No! My father's beside me and insists that I escort you to the match, if only as a mascot.'

'Oh, how sweet! May I have a word with him?'

With a flourish, Arthur handed the phone to his father.

'Yes, Miss Ratcliffe?'

'Mr Felton, you're an old dear! Next time I'm at Oakleigh, I'll call in and give you such a big kiss.'

Robert Felton put the telephone down hastily and made a gesture of despair.

'There's no holding these youngsters!'

'Now you know what I'm up against,' his son said, grinning.

After an early lunch the following day, Arthur dutifully collected his passenger from her home. Linda's parents were not around, which he thought strange. The girl chatted brightly on the journey, but Arthur answered mainly in mono-syllables, determined not to give her any encouragement.

The cricket ground – when they found it – was of a much higher standard than was usually provided by the Hartnall team's opponents. The wicket was firm and true and the outfield smooth and fast. The home team won the toss and batted first, scoring well over two hundred runs. However, at the tea interval Arthur confided to his team that he was not dissatisfied as that total was quite within their own reach.

'You can do it easily, Arthur,' Linda called from her seat in front of the pavilion as the captain and her brother walked out to open the innings.

Arthur did not intend to produce fireworks in this match for he was anxious to prove that their invitation had been justified. He scored at a fair rate without taking risks for he knew quite well that as long as he was at the crease the other batsmen would have confidence to play their natural game of free hitting. When the fourth wicket fell, Hartnall were within twenty runs of their opponents' score, and Arthur was still there with eighty, so the game seemed in the bag, although by then the sky was darkening rapidly.

As Arthur shaped to take the first ball of the next over, the rain began to fall in big drops. His reaction was to dismiss from his presence the first two balls, both hitting the sight-screen with a convincing thud. The third ball of the over streaked along the ground towards the square-leg boundary. The batsmen hoped to run four, but could only manage three, which left Hedley Brown, the builder, to face the bowling. He had only just come in and felt that if another wicket fell at that point, the increasing rain would send them all into the pavilion before another batsman could emerge. So he played the remaining three balls carefully, leaving it to his captain to make the necessary runs at the other end.

Arthur took guard, then stood with upraised bat while the bowler went back to his mark. One six would give him his century and win the match for Hartnall. But as the bowler started his run there was a rumble of thunder and the rain hammered down in torrents, straight, hard and heavy. The bowler changed course and headed for the pavilion and all the other players sprinted in a headlong dash, but they were all wet through before they reached its shelter.

Most of the onlookers tried to crowd in too, and Arthur was astonished to receive sympathy from none other than Linda's father.

'I'd no idea you were coming, sir,' he said as he shook the water from his hair.

'I'd no intention of missing this match, Felton. You've done well boy, and I'm proud of you!'

Arthur at once sought Linda, determined to punish her for deceiving him about the outward journey. He found her under a corner of the awning, looking very crestfallen.

'What on earth's the matter with you?' he asked in exasperation.

'Oh Arthur! I did so want you to get your century and win the match for us!'

'Don't be so silly, girl! It's only a game and it's been well fought out. I'll get changed – there can't be any more play after this deluge – and we'll set off for home, although I really ought to pack you off with your father.'

'Sorry about the little white lies Arthur, but I do enjoy your company and the end did justify the means!'

Arthur pursed his lips and tried to frown, but found he could not. He was beginning to regard the girl as a rather naughty younger sister.

'We'll go through Burton and stop at the Midland for a meal,' he said casually. To Linda it did not sound at all casual and she decided that things were going nicely. As she sat opposite him at dinner, her cup of happiness was full, especially when he mentioned that he thought of going to Trent Bridge again on the Monday.

'Oh Arthur, may I come? Please?'

'You're a working girl, remember? What about your job?'

'Oh, I won't sneak off. I'll 'phone my boss as soon as he gets to the office.'

'What time's that? I want to get there before start of play!'

'Of course! But how long does it take to drive to Trent Bridge? Not more than half-an-hour, surely? I can be ready before ten o'clock.'

'All right, you can come, but you might have to stand all day. I haven't tickets!'

'I don't mind if I'm with you!'

'Oh Linda, do grow up!'

Arthur tried to be impatient, but he felt himself becoming far less antagonistic towards the girl. She was lively, pretty, gracious, intelligent, loving, but somewhat importunate. 'If you come with me on Monday, you'll behave yourself? Now you know exactly what I mean,' and he held up an admonitory finger.

Linda blushed and looked down demurely.

'Sometimes I think you're not quite natural.'

'Just keep on thinking that, Linda.'

First thing on Monday morning Arthur and his father set most of their staff cutting and hauling grass from the park to build a silage camp at Claypits. Frank was to use his tractor on the cutlift, a machine which mowed the grass and elevated it to a trailer hitched on behind. Dick's job was to drive away the full trailers and return each time with an empty vehicle. Arnold Marshall had to level the grass in the trailer; and at Claypits, Len, the other tractor-driver, and Jimmy Dunn built the grass into a mound with the use of a buckrake.

When the continuous process was well under way, Arthur disappeared into the house to prepare for his day at cricket. He

54

collected a delighted Linda, as he had promised, and was touched to find that she had brought with her a basket containing a packed lunch for both of them. Arthur's mouth watered comfortingly for he knew Linda had an appetising way of her own in the preparation of food.

'Why are you going this way round?' she asked him when he turned right in the village instead of going straight through.

'I want to go round by the Hall to see how the chaps are getting on with the silage-cutting. You don't mind?'

'No indeed! I'd like to see them,' Linda said briskly, but what she really meant was she would like them to see her in the gaffer's car, for she thought it would add a little strength to the link she was forging.

Arthur drove the Jaguar straight through the gateway on to the cut grass and stopped, surveying the scene. Dick had just returned with an empty trailer and was waiting for the cutlift to come round to effect the change. Taking advantage of his status as foreman, Dick climbed down from his tractor and sauntered over to the young gaffer's car. He smiled his acknowledgement of the young lady's presence and gave the faintest of touches to the crumpled peak of his cap.

'Everything all right, Dick?'

'Aye, it is, Gaffer. Runnin' as neat as may be. Ah just have time to tip the load and git back 'gin they're loaded up agin. Ah've bin in twice. Take all week to clear it, I reckon.'

'You're not far out, Dick. A week of good weather. We won't carry on if it rains too much. I don't want to mark the turf for the new owner.'

He pressed the starter, drove the Jaguar round in a full circle and put up his hand in farewell as he approached the gate. Linda did the same, quite unnecessarily, thought Arthur. She was certainly an opportunist. Dick stood staring after them as Frank drew up with his train.

'Young Arthur's playin' a double game Ah reckon, Frank,' Dick said with a knowing grin. ''E's got the two prettiest gels in Hartnall in tow now. One week it's Alison King and the t'other Linda Ratcliffe. By gum, Linda looks smashin' to-day. As pretty as paint and as sweet as a nut.'

'Good thing there's plenty o' room i' the back o' th' Jag,' said the nineteen-year-old Arnold Marshall as he climbed down from his load.

'Ah wasn't talkin' to thee, lad,' his father said sharply. 'Keep them thoughts to yoursen or they may get you into trouble.'

The exchange of trailers was quickly effected and the men stood a few seconds as they lit cigarettes.

'Ah'm a bit worried about this gearbox, Frank,' Dick confided as he climbed into his seat. 'Getting very shaky. Ah'll take the top off and see what's wrong when we've done this job.'

'Th' owd thing's gettin' on a bit, in't 'er?' Frank replied. 'But 'er's faster than the others for this road work.'

'We'll get one more load afore dinner, onyway,' Dick shouted as his tractor roared away.

He drove out of the park in low gear, negotiating the narrow iron gateway carefully, and essayed to change into top gear as soon as he had straightened up on the gravel drive. The wearing cogs did not separate properly and he frowned as he pumped the clutch and joggled the gear lever. Finally the cogs meshed and Dick opened the throttle and released the clutch. The engine roared and the outfit moved backwards at an alarming speed. Surprised and dismayed, Dick threw the clutch and endeavoured to change gear, but found the lever immovable; the selectors would not function and the cogs were jammed in reverse gear. He stopped the engine and took his foot off the clutch. Seeing that Frank and Arnold had stopped to appraise his predicament, Dick waved to his son.

'Arnold, get on your bike and fetch the owd gaffer. Tell 'im to bring the big box o' tools.'

Dick considered the situation. The drive was narrow and the avenue of lime trees stood so close to the edge that the tiny grass verge did not allow sufficient extra room for two vehicles to pass. His tractor and fully-loaded trailer were therefore completely blocking the fairway. The new owner was a man of uncertain temper and would not wish to be denied access to his property, even temporarily. To remove the top of the gearbox and make the necessary adjustments, repairs or replacements would take at least an hour or two. If a new part was required, a day or two might elapse before it could be obtained and fitted. To free the gearbox and tow the vehicle away with another tractor would also be wasteful of time. Taking all these things into account, Dick thought his best plan would be to reverse along the full length of the drive to the big stable yard behind the house where there was ample room for the tractor to stand for repairs and have its trailer unhitched. The distance was several hundred yards and he would have a crick in his neck when he had reached the yard, but that was unavoidable and all in the day's work.

He climbed aboard, declutched, pressed the starter and moved off backwards. He had an over-full load and grass trailed over the sides so that he could see nothing other than by rearing up in his seat, suspending his ribs over the wing and looking past the trailer. But this position was too uncomfortable to be maintained for long, so he gave it up and trusted to luck. If a vehicle came up from behind, the driver would surely see him.

At first, progress was too slow and Dick, thinking that he had better get to the other end as quickly as possible, advanced the throttle. He kept his tractor adroitly in the centre of the drive, his head twisted to ensure that his course was parallel to the grass verge. The fast-running engine was noisy and drowned all other sounds, but he vaguely fancied he heard the notes of a motor-horn repeated several times, then a scarcely perceptible jar as the trailer stalled for a split second. He assumed that one of the wheels had run over a bigger-than-usual stone and took no further notice. Slackening speed, he steered his load into the stable yard and switched off his engine. As he turned to face forward he was astounded to see Mr Clark's Bentley parked in the space at the rear of the house, looking as though it had been involved in a head-on collision for the front of the bonnet was badly crumpled and both headlamps shattered. The owner was striding towards him with a face which looked as though he contemplated murder of the most brutal kind.

'What the 'ell d'you think you're doin', you dangerous bloody maniac? Charging down my drive at full speed in reverse gear? Didn't you 'ear me hootin'? By God I'll have you prosecuted for dangerous driving!'

Dick was mildly surprised and showed it.

'Were you be'ind me, then? Did you run int' th' trailer? Why the 'ell didn't you set back? Your car's faster'n th' tractor, surely?'

'Is this village peopled by lunatics, or what? Sendin' blokes out wi' tractors who've no idea of drivin' or the rules o' the road! When I 'oot I expect farm traffic to get out o' the way, but you kept comin' regardless. By the time I realised 'ow reckless and ignorant you were, it were too late! I couldn't get into reverse in time. You've just about wrecked my Bentley, you clod-hoppin' numbskull. Never driven on the road before, I suppose?'

'Just 'old 'ard,' Dick said grimly. His hand shot out and gripped Mr Clark's shirt front with an enormous fist. 'Ah don't allow anybody to talk to me like that! More of it and I'll set you to rights. Ah'm sorry about your Bentley, but it were your own fault. Ah were stuck i' reverse gear and if you ain't got sense enough to see what were 'appening and get out o' th' road, it serves you bloody well right!'

'You impudent yokel! 'Ow dare you argue with me? I don't allow any workman to talk to me like that! Take your hands off me and apologise!'

'Apologise?' Dick echoed and shook the man easily with one hand, although both men were about the same size. 'You may be the big man at your factory, but on this farm, Ah'm the big man except for the two gaffers, and 'ave bin these many years, an' Ah don't want ony flabby, egg-'eaded factory man to talk to me like that! An' for your information, we're on private property wheer we've a perfect right to be. So get that between your false teeth and chew it over.'

George Clark was outraged. He ought to teach this farm labourer a sharp lesson. As an ex-commando, he had all the deadly tricks of the murder trade up his sleeve and was certain he could effectively punish this upstart. He was aware that the farm man was slightly heavier and as solid as concrete; the hand that gripped him had muscles which felt as strong as steel wire. The chap was quick and active, too, for he had seen him sorting out the cattle a few days previously. Clark had no doubt that he would emerge the victor in any struggle, but since his army days he had undoubtedly become soft, and perhaps both of them would be severely hurt. Besides, how did he know that this overbearing heavyweight had not also been trained in unarmed combat? Moreover, although he pretended to be indifferent he did not in fact want to start his life in the village with a bloody struggle against a well-known native. He swallowed his pride and decided that discretion was the least painful way out.

'There's no need to get excited,' he said coldly. 'Take your hand from my jacket! That's no way to go on.'

Dick released the man but stood there, warily awaiting the next move, not quite sure what his own should be. Clark continued, 'I hope your boss is insured. All this is going to cost a hell of a lot of money, in more ways than one. It looks as if I'm going to miss an important appointment.'

'You can bet we're insured, and here comes the boss now, to prove it.'

Robert Felton drove into the yard in his big Humber which he preferred to the Land-Rover. He took in the situation at a glance.

'What the devil's going on here?' he asked them and both men started to speak at once, vehemently.

'Hold on a minute, Dick. Let Mr . . . Clark, I suppose it is . . . give his version first.'

Mr Clark did so with much invective and condemnation of the tractor-driver who, in his view, had acted dangerously in charging blindly down the road in reverse gear, irrespective of other users.

'It wasn't quite like that, Mr Clark,' the old farmer said without waiting for Dick's explanation. 'The gearbox was jammed in reverse, and if he'd stopped where he was the drive would then have been blocked, possibly for hours, which wouldn't have pleased you. By running down here he avoided that. Now at least we can work on repairs without inconveniencing anybody. What you might have done, Dick, was to send Frank on ahead to pilot you.'

'Ah didn't think o' that, Gaffer.'

'No, and I don't suppose anybody else would have done. Naturally you wouldn't have been expecting to back into a car with someone at the wheel of it and on a private drive at that.'

'If it had happened on a public road it'd have been a criminal offence,' expostulated Clark. 'Who are you, by the way?'

'I'm Robert Felton, and I farm this land in partnership. Our insurance company will indemnify you for all proven damage, Mr Clark.'

'So you're Robert Felton,' the man said curiously. 'I've heard of you. At least you're less unpleasant than that big-headed son of yours!'

Felton could not help grinning at the tactlessness of this remark and even the simmering Dick relaxed sufficiently to smile.

'I suppose the tractor can stay here a day or two if necessary?' the farmer asked politely, determined not to exacerbate matters by taking it for granted.

'Yes, but I don't think I want that load o' grass sitting there. It'll stink like hell by tomorrow.'

'You won't have to. The chap is just coming to take it away.'

Further conversation was interrupted by the arrival of Len Shaw with another tractor.

'What about the damage?' demanded Mr Clark, becoming pugnacious again.

'The NFU will attend to it and will apportion the blame in consultation with your insurers.'

'Apportion the blame? Be buggered! Your man was entirely to blame!'

'That remains to be seen, Mr Clark. Admittedly he was reversing blindly down this private road, but you were facing the hazard and did not have to wait there for the collision! But there is no point in our arguing. My foreman will make a statement and no doubt you will yourself. My other two men in the field are witnesses, of course. Anything else?'

Mr Clark was very red in the face but forebore to argue with this quiet-speaking but masterful farmer. He was as dominating as his son, but in a different way.

'Yes, there is,' he shouted. 'What about consequential loss? And I've an appointment in Derby in just over 'alf-an-hour and no means of gettin' there. What about that?'

'As one of my staff is responsible for your delay, however inadvertently, I will run you there.'

'Well, that's co-operation, I must say, and I'll be glad to take advantage of it. Now, who the hell's this gel on a bike?'

Mr Felton was surprised to see that it was Alison King. She dismounted neatly, smiled at the farmer, and approached the industrialist.

'Are you the new owner of Hartnall Hall, sir?' she asked pleasantly.

'Yes, I am. What is it to you, and who are you?'

'May I have a word in private?' Alison said evenly, looking pointedly in Mr Felton's direction.

'What about, and who the 'ell sent you? Some poverty-stricken charity who thinks I'm a soft touch? This gentleman has just offered to run me into Derby and we're in a hurry.'

'I'm from the Inland Revenue, office of the Collector of Taxes,' Alison replied quietly but distinctly. 'To maintain secrecy and to avoid possible embarrassment to taxpayers, we do not normally divulge our identity in front of third parties. Your attitude leaves me no alternative. Since you are now living in our area, we'd like to have your tax reference applicable to your former address.'

'So what? Do you think I carry it around with me, on a slate hung round my neck?'

'Nothing so absurd, Mr Clark. You are Mr Clark, aren't you? Your manners have been described to me by other people of the village.'

Robert Felton chuckled inwardly.

'Oh, you're a local girl are you? I thought so by the way you were eyeing my friend here like a fellow-conspirator. If he knows you there was no need to be so secretive, was there? Sheer bloody bureaucracy! Of course I have a tax reference and my tax office has a copy of it, so you can get it from there.'

'How can we do that, when we don't know which office it is?' persisted the girl.

'It's the Derby office.'

'The Inspector of Taxes has four offices in Derby.'

'Then apply to 'em all, one at a time. It's all you've got to do! It's ridiculous bothering me when you can get help from one of your own departments!'

'This is the simplest way, Mr Clark. If you can't tell me now I will leave you a 41C . . .'

'No, I don't bloody well see. I'm in a hurry to get about my business, and I should advise you to do the same. Can we get on Mr Felton? We've wasted enough time.'

'The girl's only doing her duty, Mr Clark. Surely you can accept the document she is offering you, and fill it in at your leisure?'

'Well, for God's sake! Give it 'ere then.' He snatched the slip and its return envelope and thrust it into his jacket pocket, looking at the unfortunate Alison quite balefully. 'Now p'raps we can get off. I don't know, though. Whose is this bloody car comin' down the drive 'ell for leather? This place is gettin' more like a race meetin' every minute!'

Chapter 6

The newcomer was Edith Felton. Parking her car beside the damaged Bentley, she emerged leggily from the driving seat, smiled at Alison, nodded to Mr Clark, who looked dazzled at her appearance and the glimpse of her upper leg, but addressed her father.

'Daddy, two truckloads of lambs have arrived at Willington from Aberdeen. They've been on rail a long time and shouldn't be left there too long, so I thought I'd better find you.'

'Damn! I didn't expect them until next week! And it's nearly dinnertime, too! Call at Bert Rawlins' house and tell him that I'll take him and the two lads in the Land-Rover after dinner to fetch the sheep. I don't know, though. I won't be back. I've to take Mr Clark to Derby . . .'

'That's all right,' Edith said quickly. 'You arrange about the sheep, and I'll take Mr Clark to wherever it is. You don't mind riding with a woman driver, do you, Mr Clark?'

'Not one as looks like you,' the man said boldly, forestalling Robert Felton's weak introduction.

'Er – Mr Clark, this is my daughter Edith, who is also my partner.'

Clark was less gracious than he meant to be. 'If you're going to be my driver, Miss Felton, p'raps we can get off before any more delays crop up!'

Edith coloured slightly but motioned him into the front passenger seat, got in very quickly herself, then drove off with a flourish and an explosion of gravel.

'You Feltons believe in gettin' on wi' things,' remarked Clark as the car swayed out of the drive on to the public road. He feasted his eyes on the magnificent young woman, thinking she was the handsomest piece he had ever set eyes on. 'I'm a bit that way inclined meself. No point in 'angin' about. Time's money to a busy man. There's no need to drive mad-'eaded, though. I'd like to get there by car and not by stretcher.'

As Edith did not reply, he continued, 'Still, I've noticed that women drivers are faster than men, on the 'ole.'

'You sound as though you're bigoted, Mr Clark,' Edith said at last.

'Me education don't extend to the meanin' o' that, but I think I know what you're getting at. What I should a' said was, "Some women are faster than some men".'

'Nobody could disagree with that statement,' Edith replied, turning her head and smiling at her passenger, who felt himself strongly moved by her loveliness.

'You Feltons are a rare family, I must say. You sittin' there like the Queen o' Sheba, your father's summat like Julius Caesar, while that brother o' yourn acts and looks like the Duke o' Wellington.'

'You appear to have a dramatic taste for the classics as well as a deep knowledge of history,' Edith said, showing her surprise.

'It's just that I've a good memory. I forget nowt, not even from me schooldays, and that's why I've been a success. And I notice things, too. For instance, you're not wearing a weddin' ring and yet you're the finest-looking woman I've ever sin.'

'You're trespassing on private ground, Mr Clark.'

'Well, maybe, but it's a bloody waste that a woman like you shouldn't be married. Now, if you'll drop me off 'ere I'll walk the few yards down the alley to my place. Thank you for drivin' me in, and I 'ope to see you again.'

'If we're living in the same village, we're bound to meet,' Edith said as she prepared to drive away, and added to herself 'unfortunately!' for she had taken a dislike to the man's blunt ways.

Later that evening, in the cool comfort of their sitting-room the members of the Felton family discussed the day's happenings from their different standpoints.

'I had a pleasant chat with that girl Alison King,' Robert Felton said as he relaxed in front of the sleeping television. 'She's not a shy girl, but she's not forward, either. Told me a few things about her job – how very necessary it was to be discreet to avoid complaints from members of the public. Imagine pleasant youngsters like that sent out to meet and discuss with ill-mannered louts like that chap Clark. You'd think they'd send out strong-arm men to deal with such characters.'

'They can't be certain what people are like until they get there,' Edith remarked. 'It's merely a name and address to begin with. I daresay they do send out a capable man when the party they have to call on is known to be tough.'

'I don't like Alison doing that work at all,' complained Arthur. 'I tell her it's not suitable for a girl, but she won't take any notice of me.'

'Why should she, Arthur?' asked his sister. 'You may be

smitten with her, but she doesn't return your feelings, being deeply in love with her fiancé.'

'How can you say that?'

'I've spoken to her once or twice at the tennis club.'

'I didn't know you'd taken up tennis again!'

'I've been a member all my life, as you should know. Linda's there too, sometimes. I like both girls, but I don't see why you persevere with Alison when you've got Linda ready made, keen on you and close to hand!'

'Linda's all right – a nice girl to take to cricket and all that – quite an enthusiast. But she's persuasive, very gushing, and takes too much for granted. And I don't like the way she looks at me sometimes. It's not modest!'

'Oh, Arthur! Grow up!' expostulated Edith, 'and don't flatter yourself. That's sheer conceit! I'm sure Linda doesn't mean that!'

'I don't like my girls to offer themselves too freely,' Arthur said doggedly. '*I'll* decide when I want to make advances, thank you.'

'Do you mind if we get the talk back to farming?' their father interrupted mildly. 'Those lambs arrived Arthur, and I've put them on the seeds in Top Long Furrow.'

'Here already? The auctioneers must have chosen them from an earlier sale. Are they any good?'

'They're a grand lot, but the price might be correspondingly steep. But as we turned 'em into the field, I asked myself, "are they really necessary?" If we're going to lose the Hall grazing, an extra hundred ewes to lamb might be an embarrassment.'

'We must keep Bert fully occupied, Dad. Wages are always rising and three hundred ewes is not quite a full-time job for a skilled shepherd. We'll have to adjust a bit – use more fertiliser, sell some of the cattle a little earlier, maybe. But I'm still hoping to get the park for another year.'

'If there's a possibility of that, I think I'd better see Clark about it,' Robert Felton said drily. 'He certainly doesn't cotton to you.'

'Better still if I go,' Edith interposed. 'He seems to have taken quite a fancy to me!'

'Is it reciprocated, Ede?'

'No, it damned well isn't, as you ought to know. I think he's a most objectionable character, and he's most horrid when he's trying to be pleasant. I wouldn't like to drive him on a long journey!'

'Then we'll certainly send you along to negotiate the deal,' Arthur said, grinning. 'Might as well make business use of her charms, eh, Dad?'

'All right, I will go!' Edith said flatly. 'It's about time I had more say in the running of this business.'

During the evening meal at Hilltop Farm, Alison had described her encounter with Mr Clark. She was shaken by the man's rudeness, and while she felt she had not allowed herself to be browbeaten, the incident had left a nasty taste.

'I shan't want to go out on calls if I meet many like him,' she told her parents. 'Tomorrow I'll ask Miss Hall if I can stay in Control.'

'I shouldn't let one rough customer put you off, girl,' Gene King said. 'If you like the outdoor work, stick to it. Isn't there a procedure whereby you can list this man as unpleasant and should be called on only by male officers?'

'We do have such an arrangement – but I don't think anybody bothers to consult the file before going out on calls.'

'If the information is there and the people don't make use of it, it's their own fault. Anyway, I don't think I like you being subjected to such bad manners, and I don't think Arthur Felton would, either.'

'What on earth is it to do with him?' Alison asked spiritedly.

'Have you seen young Felton lately, Alison?' her mother said quickly, forestalling what she imagined would be an acrimonious reply from her husband.

'Not since the week before last, when he picked me up at the office, which was a hell of a cheek, really. I'm not all that struck on him. He pesters too much.'

'I'm damned if I can understand you youngsters.' Her father came sharply into the conversation again. 'There's this young Felton – probably the biggest and wealthiest farmer for miles around. Practically every girl within twenty miles has her eye on him, I reckon, and he's not interested. He appears to be struck on you and *you're* not interested. Is it his family? What have you got against them?'

'Nothing at all. They're good people, and the more you get to know them, the nicer they are. Edith really is a charming woman. She'd make anyone feel at home anywhere in any circumstances. I've played tennis several times with her lately. Old Mr Felton's a delightful man too, always kind and polite. He chatted to me very pleasantly for a few minutes this morning. I think it was to make up for Mr Clark's rudeness. If it hadn't been for him, Mr Clark would never have accepted my 41C. We all know what an angel Mrs Felton was. I've certainly nothing against any of them as a family.'

'It would be nice to marry into a rich family like that, Alison,' her mother ventured.

'Money isn't everything, Mum. I wouldn't care to live in that big house, anyway. I want a nice new six-roomed semi-d. And I couldn't get fond enough of Arthur to marry him . . .'

'You wouldn't need to keep on with that tax job,' interrupted her mother.

'I like the Revenue work, as it happens. And you're forgetting Adrian. I love him – we wouldn't have got engaged otherwise – and when we're married I shall keep on working for a few years, so we can buy anything we want. I may even be promoted, which would be a great help.'

'Suppose a few kids came along?' her father said sceptically.

'We don't intend to start a family for five years at least . . .'

'You young people are so sure these days,' her mother sighed. 'In my time babies tended to come along whether you wanted them or not, and at times different to your own choosing.'

'That was the old-fashioned way, Mum. Things are arranged differently now. We shall have babies in due course, and Adrian will be the father of them.'

'I'd rather begun to think of Arthur Felton as a son-in-law,' Gene King persisted. 'That would 'a bin right handy.'

'He's not exactly Prince Charming, you know, Dad,' Alison reminded him.

'I don't know about a prince, but he was charming enough when he called to see me,' Mrs King remarked somewhat wistfully, then added loyally, 'but Adrian's a fine lad, and I'm right fond of him.'

* * *

Unaware that he was being discussed in such intimate terms, Arthur was at that time driving Linda home from the Test Match. They stopped for a pleasant meal, but apart from that, there were no opportunities for emotional or erotic diversions, much to Linda's disappointment. 'The time will come,' she told herself as she drank a glass of sherry with her escort and her parents.

Arthur went home in a contented frame of mind. He had enjoyed the day's cricket, although regrettably England looked like losing. Linda had been a charming companion and had been neither maudlin, precocious nor importunate on the way home, thus almost dispelling his earlier misgivings. At her home he had enjoyed a drink and a pleasant chat on cricket with her father, and as always Mrs Ratcliffe had been the embodiment of charm. So he returned to Oakleigh, wondering with amusement how Linda would persuade him to take her to the match at Allestree on the coming Saturday. Should he invite her? He thought not, and put the idea firmly out of his mind.

The silage-making from Hartnall park was completed by the end of the week, as forecast by both Arthur and his foreman Dick Marshall. No more mishaps occurred, other than occasionally meeting the glowering Mr Clark who was using one of his trade vans until the Bentley should be repaired. Arthur visited the silage field at least once every morning, and while he was at the park, invariably looked over the remaining beef cattle which still occupied the rear portion. He always left his car or the Land-Rover near the front of the house, in full view, so that his people would instantly know his whereabouts, for Arthur was prone to remain long among the beef cattle, appraising with joy their growth and fitness.

On the Saturday morning, the sun came out quite hot after considerable overnight rain and after seeing out the last load of grass, Arthur drove down to the Hall to inspect the cattle. There would be just time to do this before lunch, which he would have to take early in order to leave at about 1.45 for his match at Allestree. He still had not decided about taking Linda and, strangely, she had made no move.

He walked out into the back park, his eyes, not unusual for a farmer, set on the ground, 'looking for a lost sixpence' his mother used to say. The grass was getting stalky now and needed running over with the mower to tidy it up. He would try to spare a man next week if harvest was not too demanding. The cattle would relish the trimmings for a day or two.

Under the hot sun the cattle had retired to shade early and Arthur failed to locate them at first. Could they have got out, he wondered. But that was hardly likely for the whole area was surrounded by dug-in iron rail fencing. Focusing his eyes for distant viewing he finally spotted them as a shadowy mass in a grove of low-branched Atlas cedars in the top-centre of the pasture and strode quickly in that direction. As he did so he heard faint shouting from the left-hand lower corner of the park. Idly he supposed it was village boys at play. Being private property, the hall grounds were forbidden to them, but Arthur was no curmudgeon. However, he would circle round there on his way back to see that no damage or mischief had been inflicted.

He walked in among the bullocks, stirring them up and pushing them out into the open to make his appraisal. But they were reluctant to expose themselves to the burning sun and while he was driving out a second group, the first bunch calmly returned to their shade. There were over thirty of them, close-packed. Arthur threaded his way between, passing his hands over the ribs of an extra-sluggish beast. They were putting on flesh at a good rate, but there was plenty of keep and he need not market any more until the end of August. By that date their progress would have slowed down and the price would begin to fall because of heavier marketing. Normally he counted them religiously every time he visited them, but they were now too closely huddled for that, and he made a mental note to inspect them early in the morning or very late in the evening while the hot weather lasted, so he would see them on the grass instead of under the trees.

As Arthur walked back towards the entrance gate he remembered the shouting and changed his course to the distant corner. As he did so he heard repeated shouts again and as he got nearer, he distinguished the cry 'help'. Quickening his pace, he dropped over a terraced bank and saw an arm waving, followed by more imploring shouts. The farmer raised his hand in acknowledgement, and the waving and shouting ceased at once. At the same time a heavy black cloud started to creep up under the sun and Arthur calculated automatically that there would be a squall of rain in less than a quarter-of-an-hour.

He lengthened his strides and soon came within scanning distance of his objective. A wheelchair, facing downhill, was tilted perilously to the right and its occupant was twisting his head over his shoulder and presenting an anxious white face towards his rescuer. Arthur took in the situation at a glance. The fence at this point was set in the centre of a shallow gully, and one of the flat iron rails had become detached from its socket. The chair must have been travelling fairly fast and the offside wheel had forced itself through the larger gap made by the loose rail, and the rail itself had sprung back to trap the rim of the wheel. The chair was immovable for its occupant could not reach low enough to remove the rail and if he had been able to do so, he could still not have bounced the wheel over the bottom rail on to the free turf.

The invalid was a young man of about twenty, Arthur estimated. He had a frank open face with delicate lines and his unruly crop of fair curly hair gave him a look of gay variability.

'Thank God you've come, sir. I've been shouting for more than an hour.'

'How did your chair get in this position?'

68

'I came out to look round – explore the estate, as it were, and did not know the ground sloped so much – quite deceptively from a chair.'

'Did no one know you were here? Who opened and shut the gate for you?'

'I did it myself. I can do most things, you know,' the young man said, flushing.

'I'm sure you can. You're a member of the Clark family, I take it?'

'Yes, I'm the son, Colin.'

'And I'm Arthur Felton, and my family rent this grazing. All I can say, Colin, is that it's a bit risky taking a wheelchair out on your own over a grass park which is totally unfamiliar. You should have had someone with you until you know the ground.'

'I'm sorry,' the young man said coldly. 'I did not wish to trouble you. Can you get me out?'

'Of course I can get you out, and it's no trouble. I was thinking of you. I shouldn't have thought you could paddle the chair back up this long slope, even in the best conditions. Now hold tight to the other side, I may have to lift the wheel!'

He stooped, seizing the flat iron rail with one hand, bent it inwards slightly, then carried the wheel backwards and lifted it over the lower rail. Turning the whole chair sideways of the slope, he bent down again and deftly straightened the loose iron and forced it back into the slotted upright.

'You haven't hurt yourself?' he asked the youth.

'No, indeed. Thank you for enquiring. I was merely getting worried at the passing of time. My family are used to my going out on my own and staying away all day.'

'Well, I'll give you a push back up the slope. You chose the steepest part of the field. Did you let the chair get out of hand?'

'Not really. I like going fast, but I didn't know that gully was there until I was into it.'

'The rain's getting close. I'm afraid we'll get a soaking before we reach the buildings,' Arthur said as he slowly and strenuously propelled the little vehicle over the grass which, being tufted through undergrazing, tended to impede the flimsy wheels, although Colin was assisting by hand propulsion.

'Here's a girl on a bicycle,' the latter said, looking ahead to the distant gate. 'Perhaps she'll help,' and he gave a perfunctory wave.

The girl leant her machine against the fence and, coming in through the gate which she carefully fastened behind her, walked quickly towards them.

Arthur stared hard while the girl walked about fifty yards, then he exclaimed in surprise, 'Well, I'm damned! It's Alison!'

'A friend of yours, sir?' asked the invalid.

'Well, sort of, but not friendly enough to seek me out down here, I would have thought.'

When Alison arrived at the spot she showed her surprise at the strange tableau. She was wearing a smart blue two-piece over a paler blue blouse and her heavy black brogues were ideal for country wear, Arthur thought approvingly. Her pale complexion seemed to glow through the sultry dimness.

'What a superb-looking girl,' Arthur said to himself as Alison asked, 'What's all this?'

'How do you come to be down here, all dressed up on a Saturday morning?' Arthur parried.

'I called at the Hall to see Mr Clark. He wasn't in and as I recognised your Land-Rover I knew you were down here and I thought he might be with you.'

'Well, he isn't and I haven't seen him, at least, not *that* Mr Clark. But I suppose I should introduce you young people. Alison, this is Colin Clark, son of your elusive client. Colin – meet Alison King, the prettiest girl in the village, a local farmer's daughter and a most charming and efficient officer of the Inland Revenue.'

The girl blushed very prettily.

'If you believe *that*,' she said emphatically, 'you'll believe anything. But why are you standing here? Don't you know it's going to pour with rain any minute?'

'I just stopped for a breather. I need some help on this slope.'

'What, and you a cricketer?' Alison said, but took up a position behind the chair and she and Arthur pushed side by side, ascending the hill at a brisk pace. Colin Clark glanced from one to the other, realising wistfully that there was an understanding between them.

Although they hurried they could not beat the storm. As they weaved between the scattered oaks and limes, giving each tree a wide berth, there was an awesome flash of lightning, followed instantly by a rolling explosion of thunder. Then heavy drops of rain, striking the frame of the chair so hard as to create splashes. Alison ran forward and opened the gate while Arthur passed through at a lumbering trot. Once on the gravel they ran at full speed in an attempt to escape more thunder and lightning and heavier rain.

'Into the first potting-shed,' shouted Arthur above the storm-noise. This time it was he who ran forward and shoved open the dragging door and they halted in the musty, earthy atmosphere of a rarely-used room which still showed traces of its occupation by the army. Arthur and Alison stamped the raindrops from their clothes and Colin wiped his face and hair with a very large handkerchief.

Arthur was inclined to claim Alison's attention for himself but the girl felt strangely drawn to the invalid. Sympathetically she probed the cause of his handicap.

'You must have had a very severe accident, Colin.'

'Not the sort of accident you're thinking of, Alison. No. I'm a victim of the polio epidemic of '47, and really, I'm lucky to be alive. You don't have to be sympathetic, you know. I can do most things, although I'm not quite up to driving my car yet. I'm lucky, too, in that my father has plenty of money, so I don't go short of anything. You've met my father, of course?'

Alison and Arthur exchanged glances which Colin intercepted.

'Oh, I know he's a rough diamond – a hard man in business and all that. Perhaps that's why he's been successful. But he's been wonderful to me and I think the world of him.'

'That's how you should think of him, naturally,' Alison said firmly, while Arthur remarked that it would be a sad state of affairs if a young man did not think well of his own father. He stopped suddenly when he recalled that he'd had an unpleasant row with his father in 1939 and had joined the army in a fit of resentment. Colin went on to explain proudly, 'Dad's fitting up an office for me in his business and I shall attend every day from the autumn. I feel I've been dependent on him long enough and want to resume my place in the firm.'

His two companions were duly impressed.

As the rain slackened, so the conversation dwindled. Arthur wanted to get home for an early lunch before leaving for the match at Allestree, for he was certain that the storm, although heavy, was localised, and there was no reason to suppose the cricket would be affected.

'Damp as you are, you won't want to ride your bike home, Alison,' Arthur suggested. 'We'll chuck it in the back of the Land-Rover and I'll drive you to Hilltop.'

'I certainly shan't refuse that,' Alison said firmly. 'Shall we push you to the house first, Colin?'

'No thank you, that is not necessary,' Colin replied coldly. 'If I cannot propel this thing over level paths, I'd be a poor specimen, wouldn't I?'

Alison blushed for her lack of tact, but Arthur said easily 'We don't know much about you yet, young fellow. I'm sure we shall meet often in the future and I look forward to it.'

'And so shall I,' Colin replied, feeling contrite for his sharp rejoinder. 'You are the first two Hartnall people I've met. If others are as pleasant as you, I'm going to enjoy living here. Goodbye, Alison! Goodbye, Mr Felton!'

'Call me Arthur. Alison does – sometimes.'

Chapter 7

'Care to come with me to cricket this afternoon?' Arthur asked his passenger as they scurried through the back lanes, swerving first one way and then the other. 'We're playing Allestree and it's the first time we've been invited there.'

'Oh, I don't think so, Arthur. There are other things you know.'

'What are you doing this afternoon? Anything at all?'

'We haven't decided. Adrian's coming for me.'

Arthur muttered something which sounded suspiciously like 'Blast Adrian.'

'That's quite enough of that,' Alison said reprovingly. 'We are engaged, and I'm not likely to stand him up to go out with you.'

'I don't seem to be making much headway, do I?'

'Why do you bother? You've got Linda who's making an exhibition of herself the way she's running after you. Apart from that, she's quite nice.'

'Is she by jove?' Arthur said grimly. 'Thank you for that last qualification. I'll tell Linda when I see her – if I see her again.'

'Oh no! Please, Arthur, don't do that! I was only joking. I sometimes see Linda at the tennis club and I wouldn't like her to fall out with me – especially over you! There's no need. She can have you as far as I'm concerned.'

'Thank you very much for your tact! Any other nice things you can think of?'

'I'm sorry, Arthur. Of course I'm grateful for your attention and flattered, naturally. But we're poles apart – you must see that! Nothing in common at all!'

'I think we've a lot in common. We're both working farmer stock – my family's farming on a bigger scale – that's all. Linda's county class, and in any case, I don't want her. I prefer you!'

'Don't tell Linda that! She wouldn't believe you. Nor would anybody else. Thanks for the lift – see you again some time.'

As the Land-Rover had turned in to the yard at Hilltop Farm, Gene King, looking quite bedraggled was putting away his Ferguson tractor. When he saw Arthur come in with Alison beside him he brightened up and walked over to the vehicle, greeting Arthur through the driver's side window.

'Put paid to your harvesting to-day, Mr Felton?' he said

enquiringly, waving his arm vaguely over the dripping landscape.

'For an hour or two, perhaps,' Arthur said hopefully. 'But it was only a local storm and if the sun comes out hot, we'll still get the combine working for a couple of hours or so late in the afternoon. What have you been up to, to get so wet?'

'Puttin' a bit o' nitrogen on the top meadow. It's pretty bare, but these thunderstorms'll start the grass off again, and it's a good idea to help it on a bit. Can't have too much grass on a dairy farm.'

'Or any stock farm,' Arthur commented. 'In this sort of season I daresay you're glad you haven't any harvesting to do, Mr King?'

'Call me Gene. Everybody else does. I suppose I can call you Arthur?'

'I should think so, as you've seen me around since I was eight or nine years old! Why ever not?'

'There's been some water down the Trent sin' them days! You were talking about the corn harvest. As you say, I'm glad to be without it in a wet summer. It's hardly worth bothering with on a little place, although in a good season a few acres o' wheat'll bring in a useful bit o' cash – in a lump sum, you know, extra to the milk cheque. With your hundreds of acres there's a tidy bit o' money involved. But I were thinking, Arthur, wi' all that corn to get in, there must be times when you can do wi' a bit o' extra help. There's me and my cowman here an' all we're doing these days is a bit o' hedge brushin' and we'd be glad to give a hand in an emergency. You've only to let us know.'

'That's right kind of you. We've got a fairly adequate staff and we set the work out carefully to tally with the men available, and I daresay we'll get through. Still, it's a nice thought, Gene – if we've a lot of bales standing out, an extra team might make all the difference between missing the rain and catching it. I'll bear it in mind.'

Alison had slipped out the other side when her father appeared, but stood there uncertainly for a few seconds. As the conversation extended, she melted away, unnoticed by the two farmers. When her father perceived she had gone, his face showed his displeasure.

'Why did the girl slip away like that?' he mused aloud, 'Not very polite after you'd brought her home in the rain!'

'Alison'll do exactly as she likes. I've found that out,' Arthur said shortly. 'But I've never found her lacking in politeness.'

Their pleasant little chat had evolved into something approaching acrimony, King annoyed because Alison had disappeared, and Arthur irritated because the man had mentioned it. Straightfaced, he raised his hand in farewell as he reversed his vehicle and drove out of the yard.

After a light salad lunch provided by Edith with her usual efficiency, he changed, packed his cricket bag and set off in the Jaguar. The thunderstorm, heavy and violent as it had been, had removed the humidity and the sun shone bright and hot from an unclouded sky. Over lunch, following comments from his father and sister, he had privately decided to offer Linda a lift to the cricket match. By arriving unannounced he hoped he would catch her unprepared and unable to accompany him, but he would be absolved of the charge of ignoring her. Sure of his ground, he drove easily into Home Farm and was astonished when Linda appeared at the front door obviously dressed for the journey.

'Thanks for coming, Arthur,' she said, smiling sweetly as she took her seat beside him.

Arthur scowled his displeasure.

'I haven't invited you yet,' he replied rather rudely, but Linda refused to be disconcerted.

'You were going to, weren't you? I just knew you'd come round.'

'You knew more than I did,' he said irritably. 'I only made up my mind on the way here.'

'Ah, but I made up my mind to go with you early this morning.'

They were out of the village and well on their way to Derby. He could hardly throw her out, although he felt he would like to do just that.

'The devil you did!'

'Oh yes! I intended to go with you and as you didn't ring last night, which a well-mannered cricket captain would have done, I rang Edith this morning and had a chat with her.'

'The devil you did!'

'That's twice you've said that! Yes, and she said it would be all right and she'd send you along.' Linda giggled.

'Damn and blast you women! I won't listen to a word from any of you in future. I'll be as churlish as I like and serve you bloody well right!' He was really angry.

'Oh Arthur, you are so sweet about it,' Linda said, gently squeezing his left arm, but inwardly shaking with laughter.

'You've made me so angry, I shan't be able to bat worth a damn,' Arthur grumbled, shrugging off her affectionate grip. 'I'm just seething. If you worked for me I'd give you the sack on the spot and if you were my wife or sister I'd give you a damn good hiding!'

But Linda would not be repressed and tittered frequently for the rest of the journey.

The cricket ground was small but well kept and the pitch quite firm, for the thunderstorm had missed the area. On winning the toss, Arthur had no hesitation in taking first innings. Still feeling ruffled, he marched out to bat with young Charles Ratcliffe without saying a word, which the boy thought strange.

The home team possessed a very fast bowler who opened the attack. Arthur played forward, but at that moment was distracted by two cyclists – a man and a woman – who entered the ground by the gate beside the pavilion. The girl looked vaguely familiar, thought Arthur as he lost sight of the ball which landed with a painful thud on the little toe of his left foot. He circled two or three times, limping in sudden fierce anguish and cursing under his breath. 'Damn Linda, damn those inconsiderate cyclists and double damn this mad-headed, breakneck bowler.'

After a minute or two he took guard again, still lifting and flexing his left foot, for it hurt abominably. The bowler felt sympathy for the pain he had inflicted, but it was mingled with pleasure at having unsettled a dangerous opponent. He decided to press home his advantage and delivered another fast ball, dropping it very short. It reared dangerously close to Arthur's ear. With utter fury but superb efficiency, the batsman hooked it high and far so that it crashed through the trees well outside the long leg boundary, to the accompaniment of vigorous handclaps, not only from the Hartnall team in the pavilion but, generously, from the fielding side.

That stroke set the tone of Arthur's innings. He punished the bowlers mercilessly, penetrating the field with absolute precision and daunting velocity. When the fieldsmen retired to the boundary he took singles as he pleased. This, of course, slowed down the scoring for it brought Charles Ratcliffe to face the bowling. Feeling that his skipper could not last long in this reckless mood, he batted carefully, scoring one or two now and again when he could do so without risk. Mid-wicket conferences, which Arthur called frequently in order to advise his junior, were quite absent from this innings, which Charles thought odd.

In about an hour-and-a-quarter Arthur completed his century with a straight drive which travelled like a bullet underneath Linda's seat beside the pavilion. Arthur gritted his teeth angrily at this perversity, for he was sure Linda would think he had done it intentionally. Afterwards he lashed out furiously at every ball, hit seventeen runs in a few minutes until he was finally caught by the unfortunate opening bowler with a spectacular effort which prevented the teacups being shattered.

The batsman walked quickly among the genuine applause – and relief – of the fielding side. As he passed his partner who had made twenty, he said briefly, 'Hit out and get out now, Charles. I want everybody to have a go.'

He hurried on to the pavilion. To his intense mortification Linda gave a little scream of delight, ran out and met him thirty yards from the steps, flung her arms round his neck and kissed him.

'Damn you, Linda,' he hissed. 'Do behave. Don't make such a stupid exhibition of yourself.' He put his bat round behind her and slapped her sharply on the bottom with the blade. Even so, embarrassed as he was, he could not help feeling a thrill at the enforced contact with the girl's warm, lively and clinging body. As he tried to remove her encircling arms, which was difficult, hampered as he was by his bat and gloves, he noticed Alison sitting on a bench with a shock-headed young man, both smiling at him and clapping loyally. He drew a deep breath as he pushed Linda aside and entered the pavilion. After removing his pads and accepting the congratulations of his team-mates he went out again, walked past Linda without speaking and stopped in front of Alison and her companion.

'Hello there,' he said with enforced gaiety. 'I thought you said you weren't interested in cricket, Alison?'

'We're not really – oh – er – this is my fiancé, Adrian Brand. Adrian – Arthur Felton, a neighbour of ours.'

'Yes, I know him by sight,' the young man said bluntly, while Arthur said casually, 'Glad to know you, young fellow.'

Alison continued hastily, 'It's a fine afternoon, so we thought we'd support Hartnall for once, and biked over. It only took us an hour.'

Arthur's pleasure at seeing Alison was marred, not only by the presence of the young man whom he regarded as his rival, but also by the fact that Alison would have noticed that Linda's impulsive action was performed as of right and this would reinforce her own expressed opinion that Linda was the obvious choice for Arthur Felton.

The succeeding Hartnall batsmen hit out with vigour and competence, the last wicket falling just before the tea interval at the satisfactory total (from the visiting team's point of view) of two hundred and fifty. Arthur's opening partner, Charles Ratcliffe, by cautious play had carried his bat for forty. Arthur, rather against his will, but feeling that he could not neglect his passenger entirely, had taken his seat beside Linda. As the cluster of players tumbled into the pavilion, Charles detached himself from the group and presented himself eagerly to his captain and his sister, obviously expecting congratulations.

Arthur said coldly, 'For the rest of the season, Charles, you'll go in number eight! When I give instructions I expect them to be carried out.'

The crestfallen youth turned away without a word and Linda said resentfully, 'Was that necessary, Arthur? The poor boy deserved a pat on the back, not a reprimand. What were you thinking of?'

'As long as I'm captain, Charles will obey my orders the same as everybody else. I told him to hurry up and/or get out, and he deliberately defied me. I should be justified in dropping him, but I'm keeping him in the team for your sake, so don't be importunate.'

Linda was silent for she was not sure how to manage Arthur in this authoritative mood, and did not want to lose any of the ground she thought she had gained.

Hartnall won the match easily and Arthur left the ground in a satisfied but detached frame of mind, accompanied by a subdued Linda. She was playing her cards better than she knew, for Arthur thought it quite proper that his attractive companion should feel chastened by his show of authority, even though it was not directed against her. Perhaps Linda was quiet because it was her own young brother who had been reprimanded. All the better, Arthur thought.

As had become a habit, they stopped for a meal on the way home – this time in Derby at the Midland Hotel. Against his wishes and judgement Arthur found himself enjoying these quiet dinners with the lovely girl who sat opposite, but he was sure it was their common love of cricket which made the occasion so pleasant.

'This is getting to be quite a habit, Linda,' he said genially as he sipped the table wine of their choice. 'A splendid meal in a delightful setting and in company with the – er – one of the prettiest girls in Hartnall.'

Linda coughed slightly at the belated qualification.

'What's more Linda, you've behaved yourself very nicely and

that's the important thing. Because of that, and to show I'm not ungrateful or unappreciative, I'm going to let you come along with me to every match for the remainder of the season.'

Linda had great difficulty in restraining her laughter, but she knew that if she so much as smiled she would spoil everything.

'Oh, thank you, Arthur! That's very kind,' she said, with mocking demureness to which Arthur seemed oblivious.

'That is, of course, if I can get away from the harvesting. We've got a lot to get through and it must take precedence over cricket.'

'Don't talk rubbish, Arthur!' Linda replied with spirit. 'You're the biggest farmer in the parish – several parishes, in fact. You employ plenty of experienced men, and if that were not enough, your father's around, and he's a better farmer than you, I'm told. You can easily afford to leave your harvesting for one half-day a week, if anyone can!'

'Thank you for that back-hander! Perhaps you're right, though. I ought to be able to get away. But I think it's more encouraging to the chaps if I stay around.'

'Well, I don't think so at all. If you've got good staff they'll appreciate your trust in them. Your man Marshall, for instance, thrives on responsibility.'

'That's true,' Arthur admitted. 'But I don't understand how *you* can know so much about my men. Through your father, I suppose.'

'There's not much Daddy doesn't know about anybody in this village.'

*　　*　　*

There were several sunny spells in August which allowed the harvest to proceed at an average pace. The Feltons possessed two 12ft combine-harvesters, well maintained by the versatile Dick Marshall, and when both were working together they devoured the crop, acre after acre with insatiable voracity. With their ample staff and their underlying sense of tidiness, the Feltons liked to bale the straw simultaneously. The harvest field was thus a lively and industrious scene; the two combines cruising round majestically, their powerful hum setting a robust background to the gathering of the crop, stopping every now and then to discharge their load quickly and quietly into one of the two tractor-trailers which waited slave-like, on their juggernauts. The pick-up baler travelled at a rare pace, the 'thump, thump' of its ram sounding slightly less deep in the light, dry straw. The shepherd and one or two other helpers were in attendance to set up the bales in small stacks of six or eight, to facilitate collection and reduce the effect of a wet night. In the morning and evening when the corn was not quite dry enough for threshing, all available hands concentrated on picking up a few loads of bales and stacking them in the big dutch barns which had been erected at every steading. Gene King brought his own tractor and trailer and his man to help with this stupendous task, for the number of bales to be moved ran into many thousands.

In such a busy period Arthur was prepared to help at any place in the line where his assistance could achieve the maximum result. In particular, he acted as relief driver on one of the combines or the baler when the regular man was due for a meal-break. He preferred the combine, for the complexity and efficiency of the huge machine – almost a portable factory – fascinated him. The end product of that crop – the grain pouring out of the delivery chute, warm, bold, shapely and multitudinous – gave him a sense of total fulfilment.

There were three fields of wheat totalling about fifty acres on the edge of Oakleigh land where it ran close to the entrance to Hartnall Hall. Sown in one operation, the area was similarly fit for harvesting and a start was made towards the end of the following week. In mid-afternoon of the first day Arthur took over one of the combines while the driver went home to a late lunch. The crop was level, with strong straw which had remained upright and untangled in spite of the wet July. Thus there was no likelihood of blockages and Arthur could sit comfortably steering with one hand except where looping on the corners. Occasionally he would reach out behind him with his left hand into the circular grain tank, fumbling among the golden grain, gloating on the feel of its plump hardness. He was driving along the side parallel to the road when he noticed a wheelchair enter the field through the road gate.

It could only be Colin Clark. In spite of the urgency of the job in hand he stopped his machine and trotted across to the invalid.

'Hello, young fellow! Glad to see you!'

'Hello . . . Arthur,' the young man replied diffidently. 'I suppose it's all right my parking here and watching your machines at work?'

'Of course it is! In the country we don't mind sightseers. You'll obviously keep out of the way of the tractor traffic. Do stay as long as you like. I'll talk to you when my man comes back. I must dash now, though. As you see, the other machine's catching me up,' and Arthur ran back to his idling harvester.

The next time round the field Arthur was surprised, indeed disturbed, to see a female form holding a bicycle and deep in conversation with Colin Clark. He was fairly certain it was Alison and he would dearly have liked to join them but as his man did not return, he could not justifiably quit his machine.

Alison had called at the Hall hoping to see Mr Clark or at least to collect the form she had left on her previous visit. But the woman she had seen, who may have been Mrs Clark or merely a dour domestic help, could not give any information and she cycled on to her next call. Her route took her past the Oakleigh wheat fields and, seeing Colin's chair in on the stubble, she instantly realised that she could press her enquiry to him. She had an instinctive liking for the young man anyway and thought that here was a golden opportunity to combine business with pleasure.

'This is an unexpected thrill,' Colin said with real enjoyment as Alison wheeled her bicycle to his chair. 'Have you dropped in to watch the harvesting, too?'

'Not really. As a matter of fact, I've called in to see you. I was passing and thought the chance too good to be missed.'

'Thank you, Alison,' the youth said, his face glowing at the compliment, casual though it was.

Alison explained her business and added, 'I wonder if you can get this form for me. If I keep failing, it looks as though I'm not doing my job!'

'I certainly won't allow that! I'll ask Dad to complete the form, and if he won't bother I'll get the information and do it myself. What's the form called? A 41C? I'll send it along to your office without fail. No, I won't though! I'd like to see you again. When will be your next trip in this area?'

'Almost certainly Monday.'

'Right, Alison. Call at the Hall and I'll have your 41C ready.'

'Colin, that will be super!' she smiled warmly at him. 'I will report this as a firm appointment, then I am sure to be sent out.'

'Wonderful scene, this,' he waved his arm to include the crop, the machinery and the tractors. 'Must be a tremendous lot of capital involved in this outfit. Before the war all this would have been done by horses and men with pitchforks. Much more picturesque! Not that I know much about it. I was brought up in a town – Derby, of course – but for a time I was an evacuee on a farm in Oxfordshire and gained a smattering of knowledge. I wonder if all this mechanisation is worth while. The cost of this machinery must be enormous, compared with men and horses.'

'It takes a lot of the worry out of harvesting, though,' the girl explained. 'Imagine what harvesting would be like on the Feltons' scale if it was all done up in sheaves. Quite satisfactory in a hot summer if the fine weather lasted long enough. But what if there was a lot of heavy rain and thousands upon thousands of tightly-bound sheaves got wet through? They'd never dry out again – not properly and some of the corn would go mouldy. But it only takes a few hours of sun or wind to dry out the standing corn. The combine can start up and snatch a few acres between the showers, and that amount of corn is safe under cover.'

'But doesn't the straw get wet?'

'Yes, of course, but it lies lightly and soon dries out enough for baling, and if it's baled properly, the rain won't penetrate the bales.'

Colin was impressed.

'You're very knowledgeable!'

Alison laughed at the flattery.

'I daresay most people who've grown up in the country would know as much. My father is a farmer, of course – that is, a dairy farmer. We don't grow any corn now, but I've lived on the edge of the Felton empire all my life.'

'You must think a lot of Arthur Felton!'

'Not at all. I'd hardly met him until a few weeks ago when he called at the office. Mixing with the smaller farmers has never been a Felton characteristic!'

'I'm sure Arthur thinks a lot of you!'

'Then he's no reason to! He's a pleasant chap and all that – got a splendid war record, and thought very well of in the village. In fact, the whole family are looked up to in Hartnall and have been since the year dot. But that doesn't mean he can take up with any girl he fancies – at least, not in my opinion. I've no reason to dislike him, but he just doesn't appeal to me.'

'I'm very glad to hear you say that,' the young man said softly, and Alison immediately worried about the undertones of the remark and wondered how she could discourage such thoughts without being too brutal. She reverted to the subject of Arthur.

'He's a bit silly really, and doesn't make the most of his chances. There's a girl in the village, Linda Ratcliffe, who's been making a set at him for a year or two, but he won't nibble at the bait! She's pretty and she's real classy. Her people lived in Hartnall Hall for hundreds of years.'

'Oh – that family! I know of them, of course.'

'Of course, you know I'm engaged,' Alison blurted out for there seemed no chance of introducing the news gradually.

'Oh yes! I've noticed your ring, and it's very pretty. But you're not engaged to our farmer friend.'

'Our farmer friend, as you call him, will soon be over here to join us. That chap who just came in with a bike is Len Baldock who usually drives one combine. I think Arthur's been relieving him. Have you noticed how he's stared over here every time he drove along this side. He'll come over like a shot, now.'

'You're pretty cute, Alison.'

The bark of Arthur's combine sank to a low mutter. Len Baldock climbed aboard and the machine roared off again, and the late driver strode over the deep stubble towards them.

'Well, I must be off,' Alison said, turning away with her bicycle. 'I've several more calls to make and I'm afraid I've wasted a lot of Revenue time. Still, it's been worth it. Make my apologies to Arthur!'

She mounted her machine and pedalled away rapidly before Arthur could get within hailing distance. So, not wishing to betray his eagerness, he slackened his pace, and crossed the path of the baler, flagging down the machine to have a word with Frank Long, who pulled up with a barely-concealed grin.

Chapter 8

Harvesting was in the air as Alison pedalled out to Hartnall on Monday morning. Not surprising either, she thought, for the weather, although hazy, had that promise of warmth to come later in the day and the sun was already trying to break through. She could enjoy a pleasant day in the country, she told herself, cycling comfortably from village to village, for her task did not demand that she should scorch along as if in a cycling marathon.

She had left the office later than was her custom, for there was a heavier post than usual and this had claimed her attention. Then she listed her calls in route order and sorted the papers for each call in the correct sequence. It was ten-thirty when she left the office, quickly climbed to the top of the bridge, turned left and free-wheeled along the right bank of the Trent until the road veered away at Newton Solney. Morning activities in the fields claimed her attention and, as a farmer's daughter, she automatically appreciated their significance.

In several places the combine-harvester had been unsheeted and the driver, his face still unsmudged with grease, was making the first round of all the lubricating points. On a field which had been threshed a baler was already at work on the bulky rows, its heavy thumping intrusive in the fresh morning air. It was evident that some farmers still preferred the binder, for on another field sheaves cut the previous evening were being set up in stooks by slow-moving, elderly workmen. Further on, wheat sheaves were being loaded quickly and efficiently by two men, while a schoolboy drove the little tractor on from stook to stook.

As she approached Hartnall Hall she found that the Oakleigh wheatfields on the other side of the road had been threshed and all the straw baled, which surprised her, although she recalled that the weekend had passed without rain. Two of the Felton's tractor-trailers were being loaded with bales and as she cycled past the gate, her father and Stan the cowman arrived with their small tractor and trailer, both men smiling at her in genial surprise. Alison welcomed this homely touch, hoping that it presaged a successful day.

She cycled easily down the long avenue to the Hall, which was already beginning to take on a more 'cared-for' look, for she noticed more improvements each time she called. Flowerbeds had been dug over and planted, lawns had been mown, but nevertheless still looked rather more like cleared hayfields than decorative turf. Shrubberies had been weeded and thinned out. She mounted the semi-circular steps, which were noticeably cleaner than on her previous visit, and rang the new electric bell beside the front door. It was opened at once by the middle-aged sentinel she had seen before and Alison wondered if her approach had been monitored.

'I've called to see Mr Colin Clark, by appointment,' she said purposefully and the woman motioned her to enter. Still without speaking, she led the way down a long hall, or rather, corridor, turned into another corridor which ran at right-angles and knocked on the door at the far end. Without waiting for a reply she pushed it open and said indifferently, 'There's a young lady to see you,' and immediately retraced her steps.

'Do come in, Alison,' Colin said with enthusiasm. 'I'm so glad to welcome you to my home. Do sit down – or would you rather come through to my study?'

'What ever you say,' Alison murmured, looking around with appreciation. 'What a delightful room!'

'We've made this a self-contained flat,' the young man said with pride. 'It's only just been finished as you can imagine. You might as well see it all. This is the dining-room, with the kitchen off, as you see. Big enough to do things from a wheelchair and to turn it round comfortably. Through here we have the bathroom and toilet on one side and the study and bedroom on the other side of this small passage.'

'Absolutely splendid,' Alison said with feeling, 'and all your windows look out on to the back park. What a perfectly lovely view!'

'Well, it needs to be if I'm to spend most of my life here,' Colin said, rather wistfully. 'Although I hope to start going to the office soon. If I can't manage it, Dad'll bring me work to do at home.'

'I'm sure you'll be able to go,' Alison said forcefully. 'You're resourceful enough to achieve anything you want, I really believe.'

Colin flushed with pleasure.

'Thank you! Now, here is your 41C, correctly filled in and signed. But you don't have to go at once, do you? Can't you stay a few minutes longer. How about a cup of coffee?'

'Well, I have biked out from Burton and we are allowed a ten-minute coffee break in the morning and ditto in the afternoon. I don't always take them though.'

'Well, how about taking them this time and bracketing them together and staying with me for twenty minutes? Or is that too much of a hardship?'

Alison merely smiled while Colin, working busily from his wheelchair, prepared some excellent coffee.

'This is really delightful,' he said. 'sitting here drinking coffee with such an engaging companion. You're my first visitor, Alison! Living at Hartnall certainly has its compensations.'

'We hope you'll take part in some of the village activities, Colin. There are several things you could help with, you know.'

'Such as?'

'Well, the tennis club needs a new secretary. I'm sure you could take that on. Are you interested in tennis?'

'Used to be.'

'Then come along one or two evenings and get to know the members. The secretary – old Mrs Goodhead – intends to retire at the next AGM. I'd love to nominate you as her successor. Then there's the cricket club – I'm sure they'd be glad to get hold of an efficient young chap to run the club for them. I know I could get one of the leading players to put you up for the job.'

Colin pulled a wry face.

'Arthur Felton, I suppose?'

'Don't make any mistakes about Arthur, Colin. Your father may not like him, and I don't fancy him as a boyfriend, but he's a genuine chap – kind and competent. Likes to get his own way, of course, but don't we all? There's the Repton Dramatic Society as well. Quite a few Hartnall people belong to it.'

'You seem to be opening plenty of doors. I think I might try the tennis club, though,' Colin said, not too enthusiastically. 'Perhaps I could come along with you one evening before the season ends.'

'Of course! That's a smashing idea! I'll get Edith to come along too and you can meet her.'

'Edith?'

'Yes, Arthur's sister. She's really lovely. Most people would say she's the prettiest girl round here . . .'

'She can't be prettier than you,' the young man interrupted with not unexpected gallantry.

'Well, she's not really a girl now – probably about thirty, but she's kind, charming and most accomplished. A bit bossy, perhaps, but then the Feltons are like that. Edith was in the ATS all through the war and finished up as captain. I daresay the old authority still lingers. Her family has quite a romantic history, you know. Edith's grandparents moved into Oakleigh as a honeymoon couple more than sixty years ago. Then about twenty years later, Mr Felton, who was a London newsboy, ran away from home to work at Oakleigh, grew up there and married the only daughter.'

'Quite a success story!'

'Not only for him, but for the family he married into. Their name was Ratcliffe, but of course, not the same family as lived in the Hall here. I think you know about them. Linda often comes to our tennis evenings, I think you'd like her. She's very pretty, but a trifle hard, I think. She's well-bred and well-educated, but not a bit stuck-up. I wish she'd take Arthur Felton off my back. She's terribly keen on him and gets her own way in most things, I understand. I hope she does in this.

'And if you're thinking of farming your own land eventually, you could join the NFU and take part in their activities. I'm sure Arthur would sponsor you –'

'Oh! Arthur again!'

'All right, my father, then. He's a member and no doubt you'll meet him soon, when you come over to see us. But the time's getting on, Colin, and so must I. The Revenue's work must be done. Thank you for the delicious coffee and for showing me your smart flat. I've enjoyed our little chat, too. I'm sure you'll be an asset to the village if you'll only make the first move.'

'Goodbye, Alison. Thanks for coming and thank you for making these exciting suggestions. You're making me think, more than ever, that Hartnall's going to be an ideal home.'

Alison went on her routine calls, pleased to have been the means of bringing a little pleasure into the life of the crippled young man, for she had taken a strong liking to him. Colin was overjoyed too, for he felt that Alison's friendship would lead him back to those parts of normal life from which he had been cut off for three years. He spent the day in a satisfied state of mind, propelling his chair into every corner of the Hall grounds, making notes on his ideas for improvements.

He was still so engaged in the middle of the evening, which was warm and sunny. A good harvesting day, he had no doubt, for he had heard the deep bark of the combines from two directions and assumed that at least one of these would belong to the Feltons. He sat pensively gazing up the length of the front park, appreciating the majesty of the scattered ornamental trees, and the homely sight of the sheep grazing in quiet content over the whole area, level and tidy after having been recently cut for silage. On the other side of the drive the remainder of the front park was equally satisfying, but the lines were harder, for strong black cattle were grazing and the grass, not having been mown, had a tufted appearance. The odd thistle reared itself here and there, but apart from the stock, nothing in the landscape moved. The twin lodges at the drive entrance, hardly visible behind their masking shrubberies, were being renovated and Colin was pondering on this when a black car appeared between them and scurried down the drive. Subconsciously noting that it was a Consul, he turned his chair and rolled through the shrubberies to meet the vehicle. It turned into the side entrance with a splash of gravel as if familiar with the ground and the driver opened the door and swung her legs out as soon as the car stopped. Colin recognised her at once, for Alison's description had lingered in his mind and the family likeness was uncanny. Alison must have worked fast.

'Good evening,' he said gaily, 'Miss Felton, I presume?'

'Now, how could you possibly know that?'

'The resemblance to your brother is quite striking. I'm so glad to see you! Have you come to see me about tennis?'

'Tennis? Why, no. I wasn't aware . . . I've come to talk to your father – about farming, I hope.'

'I'm sure he'll be glad to meet such an attractive farmer. I'm his son, as you will have heard. He is at home – in the drawing-room, I think. Now, would you prefer to go up the steps to the front door, in which case I can't take you, or come with me to my entrance round the other side which is, of course, on the level, and I will take you to him.'

'I'll come with you, of course, and thank you for your courtesy.'

She smiled so charmingly that Colin blushed in confusion but turned his chair and led the way round the house to what had previously been a tradesmen's entrance. Edith complimented him on his new home as she followed him, for she could see his obvious pride in his own domain. Taking her through into the main corridor of the house, Colin guided her to a door near the front entrance, opened it and wheeled himself in.

Mr Clark was seated in one of the deep armchairs, opposite the new television which was switched on, but he was not watching it, for his attention was concentrated on an important-looking folder.

'Dad, I've brought you an exciting visitor. Miss Felton of Oakleigh to talk about farming.'

The man looked up at once, his eyes shining with admiration and lust. He stared hungrily at her shapely legs as he rose to his feet.

'Yes, we have met, Colin, and it was a grand experience.' He walked across and switched off the television. 'I'd much rather you'd made an appointment, young woman, then I could have been prepared for you. As it is you've caught me on the 'op. You're welcome, anyway – you'll always be that, and I'll be disappointed if we can't find pleasanter things than farming to talk about.'

'This is a business call, Mr Clark.'

'Then you should certainly have made an appointment. Sit down, won't you? Perhaps you'd like a glass of sherry? Colin, I daresay you've got things of your own to do.'

'Er – yes, of course,' his son said at once, although his face showed his disappointment. 'Good-bye, Miss Felton. I hope to see you again. Alison King was telling me about you this morning.'

Clark shut the door behind the wheelchair and sat close to Edith, but opposite, for he wanted to see as much of her as he could, and a side view might not be so revealing.

'I don't often have someone as gorgeous as you in my house, Edith. That is your name, isn't it?'

'Yes, but how did you know?'

'One finds out these things – at least, I do.'

'I've called to see you about the park grazing, Mr Clark,' Edith began, feeling she ought to get to the point at once if only to head off Mr Clark's tendency to introduce other topics. 'As you may know, I'm in partnership with my father and my brother and I take an active part in the administration. We farm a large acreage, but the seventy acres of parkland, being so close to home, has been very useful to us and we don't want to lose it!'

'That I can well believe!'

'It's not all one-sided, you know,' the young woman said sharply. 'We buy the grazing each year only up to October 1st, but in the winter we come on the land by courtesy, do the rolling and harrowing, repair any fences and apply fertiliser. Not many farmers would do so on a grazing tenancy. The agent will confirm that.'

'Why didn't you go and see him about it?'

'As we are neighbours I thought a personal approach on a friendly basis would be better.'

'I daresay you've been good tenants. Personal approach, eh?'

He looked at her lasciviously, his greedy eyes taking in every curve of her body, every line of her attractive beige dress. Edith was angrily aware that he was mentally undressing her, but she had visited the Hall for a purpose and did not intend to be deflected from it.

'But this is only August,' he pointed out absently, while his eyes said other things. 'Then there's six months of winter until you need the land again!'

'At Oakleigh, we like to plan things well in advance, Mr Clark. If you'll agree to our having the grazing again next year, we'll pay you for it as soon as the contract is drawn up, and that should not take more than a few minutes.'

'There's more'n one way o' payin'.'

'Yes, indeed. What do you suggest? We could do some tractor work for you, or help you out with labour.'

'I wasn't thinkin' on them lines. Tell you what,' he was almost licking his lips at the thoughts that were coursing through his mind, 'I'll let you have the grass if you'll be nice to me!'

Edith faced him squarely, suppressing her revulsion.

'I hope you don't mean what I think you mean. If you do, the answer's no! Definitely no!'

Clark brought his hand down on his knee with a hearty slap, chuckled hoarsely and pushed his chair back a foot.

'Well, I'm damned! You're a reight 'un! Takin' it as calmly as that. I thought you'd either a' slapped me face or jumped up and stamped out i' disgust!'

'I was in the army, Mr Clark, all through the war and a bit after. I got used to dealing with all types then, I can assure you.'

'I bet you did! I were in the army meself. By God, I wish I'd 'a met you then!'

'Fat lot of good that would have done you,' Edith said to herself, but aloud: 'What about this grazing? I made the effort to come here and want to take something back, or I'll be the laughing-stock of my partners.'

'Have another drop o' sherry.' He refilled her glass without waiting for a reply. 'The fact is, Edith, I'd a fancy to farm the park meself, just for interest's sake, like.'

'That's not unreasonable – in due course, that is. But I understand you don't know anything about farming yet, and you might make yourself the laughing-stock of the village! You don't want that, I take it!'

'No. I bloody well don't! It'll go 'ard wi' anybody as laughs at me! Still, I'd like to start sometime, I think Colin would, too.'

'All right! Why not compromise? Let us have the front park and keep the back park for yourself? There's thirty acres there and it's mostly out of sight from the road . . .'

'That's not very tactful, Miss!'

'. . .You could keep a fair amount of stock there, and plough some of it, I daresay, although it escaped ploughing all through the war. And I promise you that my brother or my father will give you all the advice you need and all the help necessary.'

'What about you coming to give the advice?'

'Oh, come now! I'm a farmer's daughter and an experienced administrator and have plenty of superficial knowledge which I've picked up. But I'm not a full-blown farmer to give advice. Comments, perhaps.'

'I daresay I could get on with your father, but I'm damned if I'll take advice from that big-headed brother of yourn. He really sets my back up! Too bloody high and mighty!'

'Arthur's all right! Knows about all there is to know, I think. But he was a major in the Fourteenth Army, and I daresay that's made him dominating.'

'Ar – I were in the army all through the war meself. Knew plenty o' officers and 'ated every one of 'em. None of 'em had as much experience as me and yet I couldn't get 'igher than sergeant-major. Officers!' He made as if to spit.

'As a matter of fact, I was an officer. I got as far as staff captain and I don't think I want you to spit at me!'

'Ah! You're about the only officer I could 'a got on with. I'd 'a put you in a class by yoursen.'

'Thank you! That's very reassuring! It is agreed about the park, then? We have the two front parks next year at the same price per acre, and give you all the necessary advice on managing the back park. In addition, I'll undertake that, during the winter, we'll harrow and roll your area at no charge.'

'Agreed – and I might tell you, I never go back on my word. I'll get my girl to type out an agreement tomorrow and send it to you, and I'll be glad to have your cheque by return. I'm 'oldin' you to that. Might as well have the money in the bank earnin' a bit extra!'

Edith rose to go, glad the interview was over, for she was bored by his bombast.

'I'd quite hoped we could'a come to an understandin' in a different direction,' he said with another of his repulsive leers as he accompanied her to the door. She ignored his hint and as she opened the door, he said in quite a different tone, 'P'raps you could have a word wi' Colin afore you go. The lad doesn't get many visitors. You know the way to his flat, I reckon?'

'Of course I'll see him. I'd love to get to know him better. A charming boy, with such pleasant manners. Goodbye, Mr Clark, and thank you!' But he had already closed the door behind her.

When she tapped on the main door of Colin's apartments the cheery voice which invited her in was like a breath of fresh air after a particularly sultry storm-cloud had passed on. He could hardly contain his delight at having two beautiful females as visitors on the same day. Recognising immediately the innate sympathy in Edith's character, he unburdened himself of his hopes, fears, plans and limitations. Quickly realising her experience and sense of maturity, Colin felt he could confide in her as in an elder sister. She fully supported Alison's suggestion that he might be secretary of both tennis and cricket clubs.

'I'm chairman of the tennis club and can guarantee you that appointment,' she said firmly. 'My brother is skipper of the cricket team and I'll see that he's on your side there. Go ahead and make plans for both jobs, Colin, and if anyone tries to prevent you, refer them to me!'

They both laughed heartily and as Edith returned to her car, Colin insisted on accompanying her. 'I hope to have my own car in a few days,' he remarked as casually as he could, as she pressed the starter.

Edith replied, speaking clearly above the beat of the engine, 'When you get it, I insist that you come to see us at Oakleigh on your first time out. It's quite a friendly place!'

As she turned and accelerated up the drive, she raised her right arm out of the side window and waved a gay farewell. Colin Clark began to feel that normal happiness was gradually replacing the brooding resentment which had been there for three years.

Chapter 9

When Edith returned in triumph to Oakleigh, her father and Arthur, happy at the completion of another successful day's harvesting, were delighted at her achievement, and said so. Arthur was not even put out when Edith tactlessly recounted Clark's definite rejection of the young man as adviser and insisted on their father's help.

'Suits me,' Arthur said indifferently. 'Every time I see that chap I feel as if I'd like to slug him and that would be most unbecoming – for both of us. I must say though, his son's a pleasant young fellow, although he's a cripple. He impressed me very favourably.'

'Yes, I've just left him. He's quite charming in every way, and I think he's a capable bookkeeper. At least, he's going to do that at his father's business. I'm sure he'd like to help in the village too, and he could make you a good cricket secretary, Arthur.'

'Hmm, that'd need some thinking over! We need somebody really keen and competent. Young Worthington would be glad to be shut of the job, I believe. Tell you what, we'll have the annual general in October and see what the feeling is. Plenty of time for a new chap to settle in, if we do change.'

'In the meantime, you two men, there's something even more pressing which you appear to have forgotten about. I hope you're well up with the harvesting. Don't forget we've to go to Aunt Betty's for the wedding on Saturday. I feel we ought to stay a few days as we haven't visited them for so long.'

'That's not possible for us,' her father said tartly. 'You can stay if you like, but I don't know how we shall manage here without you. Why can't they wait until after harvest?'

'They probably have, Dad,' Arthur said. 'They're usually at least two weeks earlier than us, and we haven't got much left. We'll be able to get away all right. Dick's quite capable. I'll have to miss cricket though – I forgot about this damned wedding being on Saturday.'

'I hope Robin doesn't know you feel that way,' said Edith severely. 'Most ungracious. I must say you seem to be taking a greater interest in cricket this season. Is it because of . . .'

'I don't think so at all! I am the captain!'

'And have been since the war!'

'Still, it's a home game and against a very moderate side. Hartnall should win easily, even without me. Linda doesn't know though. Still, no doubt you'll be in touch with her about it. You seem to take the major part in organising our comings and goings to cricket matches without consulting me.'

'Nonsense! I only know Linda thinks the world of you in spite of your bad manners, and I think you should settle with her.'

'You're talking the nonsense. I'm interested in Alison who's a sweeter kid altogether.'

'Maybe, but Linda's more your type. I think she's determined not to give you up, so you might as well accept the inevitable!'

Arthur spluttered with indignation which increased when their father joined Edith in hearty laughter. But Robert Felton looked grave and thoughtful when the merriment subsided.

Edith went on, 'You know what Grannie Ratcliffe used to say. "Lord, give me the strength to change what can be changed; to endure what can't be changed; and the wisdom to know the difference!" So you might as well endure it, Arthur.'

'What nonsense you women think up! Perhaps I can't change Linda, but I could change myself and I don't intend to do that. Anyway, I don't remember Grannie saying that, and I'm sure you can't, since you were only a day old when she died!'

'Mummy told me, silly, ever so many times.'

'Ah, your grandmother was a wise woman. I've heard her say that often – generally when your grandfather was a bit too overbearing. She was as gentle as she was wise.' Robert Felton sighed deeply. 'She was only fifty-five when she died. Blimey! That's exactly my age now!'

'Well, don't get morbid about it, Daddy. You're good for a long time yet! We'd better talk about this wedding. It's set for twelve o'clock so we shall have to start from here fairly early.'

'Will you take your own car, Sis, if you're coming back separately?'

'No fear. Blow that! I'd rather go in your car. I prefer to be driven than drive, anyway, and it's faster in the Jag. I'll come back by train and you can pick me up at Derby.'

'Well, for goodness' sake make firm arrangements about our meals!'

'Is that all you can think of at this time, Arthur? Of course, I've done so. Mavis will take over, and I expect she and Mrs Long will share the management, and Jessie Allsop will come in as an extra every morning when I'm away. I've arranged it so you won't even know the difference!'

'No one's likely to beat you for efficiency,' her father said proudly. 'but don't stay away too long. I'll be glad to see Betty again myself. You know,' he said reminiscently, 'the years roll back when I think of her. She was an indispensable member of this household for nearly five years. Now she's been away about twenty-seven – got twins of twenty-five and a daughter of twenty-one! Life's ticking away for all of us!'

'Oh shut up, Dad! Aunt Betty must be thrilled to get one of her family off her hands at last. Funny how those two lads have diverged since the war! They joined the RAF together, both reached Flying Officer rank at about the same time, and were demobbed the same week. Since then Robin has become absorbed in Edwin's business and Desmond – well, he thinks of nothing but the farm, and quite right, too!'

'Marrying is a catching complaint when it starts, Arthur. Perhaps Desmond will pick up a girl from a farming background and marry her before we know where we are.'

'That's not very likely,' Edith said scornfully. 'He's too precise for most farming people.'

'He's a top man at the job, though,' her father reminded her.

'A good thing he is,' commented Arthur. 'I shouldn't want a relation of mine to be a mug at anything!'

'I hope he's not as conceited as you are about it,' Edith said, determined to have the last word.

Dick Marshall, knowing of the wedding and still having a soft spot for Mrs Betty, whom he had known when she had first come to Oakleigh as a sixteen-year-old, had volunteered to polish Arthur's car on Friday evening. There were no combines at work that evening, but there were still plenty of bales to pick up; Dick felt that his presence could easily be spared from that chore especially, as to his surprise, both gaffers turned out to help. 'Must have a guilty conscience or summat,' he grumbled to himself as he applied sponge and polishing cloth.

He even brought the gleaming car round to the back door (the front door was seldom used at Oakleigh) at 7 am, walked into the kitchen and officiously demanded the luggage, which he stowed in the boot, wondering why the hell they needed so much for one day, then opened the rear door for Edith, just like a chauffeur. He was sufficiently rewarded when the old gaffer said, as he took his seat beside Arthur, 'It's all yours, Dick. See you tomorrow – maybe.'

'Which way this time, Arthur?' the old man continued.

'Ashby, Leicester, Market Harborough, Northampton,

95

Buckingham and Aylesbury. It's the way I know best.'

'Do it in two hours, do you think?' asked Edith from the rear.

'By gum, I don't know. It's over a hundred miles and not exactly Roman roads all the way. Say two-and-a-half. We'll still be there in plenty of time.'

The Jaguar drew into the little drive of the Chiltern manor house soon after nine-thirty. There was much embracing, greeting and cross-greeting, for the two families had not met for nearly a year. After coffee in the morning-room, the party split up, Edith moving with Aunt Betty and Cousin Caroline into the drawing-room for a feminine conference. Desmond Salt, the farmer twin, insisted on taking Arthur out to show him the samples of grain in the modern store and the pedigree beef herd, while Edwin Salt and Robert Felton, who had both fought in the first war and materially helped their country in other ways in the second, remained in the morning-room. The bridegroom-to-be, Robin Salt, having nowhere to go, remained with them. Perhaps he was a little peeved at the desertion of his brother who was to be his best man, but he was well aware of Desmond's efficient quality and had no fear that anything vital to the ceremony would go wrong.

As always, Arthur was much impressed by his cousin's husbandry – the several groups of pedigree Aberdeen-Angus cattle grazing in neat paddocks, sometimes with a horse or two, adjoining the house and steading; further afield the commercial beef cattle, grazing in much larger batches in more extensive fields, short-term leys which had been kept neatly trimmed so that no growth was wasted; grey-faced ewes picking a living from the recently-cleared stubbles. Here, Desmond explained with pride that all the lambs had now been despatched to the grading centre. Two tractors, each with a three-furrow plough, were busy turning over with speed and precision what Arthur, used to the reddish soil of the Trent valley, considered shallow, greyish and low in fertility. Returning to the spacious buildings, they inspected the grain in the huge bins and found it clean, dry, plump and plentiful.

Arthur wondered how the farm performed in a financial sense, for he knew the pedigree cattle were a hobby and an expensive one at that, if Desmond kept to his declared intention of exhibiting at the summer shows. He made tentative enquiries. Desmond grinned.

'If we bracketed the Angus with the general farming I daresay we'd make no profit at all,' he explained. 'Maybe we'd be in the red. Some breeders with other businesses like to do that, to save themselves income tax, or so they think. But that wouldn't suit my book. I like to be known as basically a commercial farmer so I can talk with other farmers at their own level. Of course, I have the advantage of extra capital if I wish to draw on it.'

'Where do the pedigree cattle come in, then?'

'They're owned by the family business and will be exhibited under the name of the firm. All the costs are set against the factory which also pays the farm a rent for the grazing ground. Of course, it reduces the profit from manufacturing, but that's acceptable because the percentage is very small. It's better than trying to lose the pedigree expenses among our sheep and corn. I've worked out a good system, Arthur, and I'm proud of it.'

'Doesn't Robin take any interest in the farm since the war?'

'No – he didn't before, anyway. Neither does Dad now, except for riding around. Mum and I do the farming, although she leaves all the decision-making to me now.'

'The wedding today won't make much difference to the set-up then?'

'None at all. Robin and Diana have bought a suburban-type house just outside Bradenham. The firm's doing quite a bit of exporting now and that will be his province, so I daresay they'll be making trips abroad, for you can bet that Diana won't want to stay at home while he's globe-trotting.'

'Well, that's how it is when you're married, I s'pose. What about you? Aren't you setting up to be a bridegroom soon?'

'No! It seems to me your family should be the next to stage a wedding. You're a fair bit older than us!'

'Me, do you mean?'

'Yes – or Edith.'

'I'm not in any hurry, Des. Why should I be? 'Course, I can pick up a girl any time and get what I want, if I want it, but farming and cricket just about fill my life. Marry at any time I like, I reckon. There's one little girl at home I'm keen on, but she's very young and, so far, not very keen on me. I shall probably keep trying with her, though. Edith? I don't know! She's still mourning that chap Green and takes no interest in anybody else. My God! She'd make somebody a fine wife, but she's destined herself to be an old maid, I doubt. She'll be thirty in November, you know.'

Desmond Salt looked glum and made no reply.

They returned to the house hurriedly, for the groomsman had decided that he had not allowed quite enough time after all. He hustled his groom upstairs while Arthur joined his father and uncle for another run-through of farming topics. Caroline had departed in her own car to the bride's home at High Wycombe, to dress with her fellow bridesmaid. Betty and Edith had been jogged out of their comfortable feminine conclave to join their menfolk.

'You've put quite a bit of weight on, Betty,' Robert Felton said tactlessly to his sister during a lull in the chatter.

'Have I, indeed?' Betty said indignantly. 'It may be obvious to you, Bob, but not necessarily to other people, so there's no need to blurt it out like that!'

'Why, does it matter?' Bob asked, puzzled, or pretending to be.

'It doesn't matter to me,' Edwin Salt said gallantly, walking over to his wife, putting his hands on her shoulders as he faced her affectionately. 'Betty's just how I like her and always will be.'

Certainly his wife was not the slim, dainty girl he had married at Hartnall church twenty-eight years before. But she was pleasantly covered and did not look short unless her towering husband or sons stood close beside her. The thick black hair was as glossy as ever and for a matron of forty-eight with three grown-up children she was more than comely.

'I don't see what you're grumbling about,' protested her brother. 'I didn't say anything out of place. In fact, Betty, I think you look marvellous. Not a grey hair on your head and your skin is as fresh as . . . as . . . as the morning, or as er – milk. Yes, as fresh as milk!'

'Dear old Bob. You always mean well,' Betty said good-humouredly, kissing him on the cheek. 'I'm sure there's no end to the compliments you could think of, but I think we ought to get out to the cars now. I hate being rushed, or late for anything.'

The church was only a few miles away at High Wycombe and they were there in plenty of time. Arthur saw to that, for he liked being late even less than Aunt Betty. The bridegroom and his man, together with their parents, sat in the small front pew and the three Feltons in the second row. They could all have easily been accommodated in one pew, but Robert and Arthur, being farmers, liked plenty of room, and Edith was of the same mind.

As the ceremony proceeded, the Feltons watched with a detached interest. Arthur idly compared the twins, both tall, lithe young men with their mother's dark hair, but Desmond the farmer seemed more wiry, his face was more tanned, his hair more crisp, his whole form more stable than his desk-bound brother. Farming was clearly the life for him.

Robert Felton seemed mesmerised, not by the lovely bride, but by her equally lovely chief bridesmaid, Caroline Salt. He took in his breath sharply for, unless his memory was failing, the girl was the replica of her mother as a bride, whom he had given away at her wedding in Hartnall church; small, dark, with delicate features and ivory complexion. Then he glanced at his daughter who sat beside him, beautiful, strong, thoughtful and comforting. A lump came into his throat, for if her hair had been the faintest tinge lighter in colour, Edith would have looked the counterpart of her mother at the same ceremony. The congregation, which half-filled the ancient church, rose to its feet to sing the first hymn with gusto. Fortunately it was a popular tune which Bob knew well, and he was able to put Meg out of his mind and join in.

Edith had eyes for nothing but the wedding group. She appraised the bride, silently complimenting her on her choice of outfit, her impeccable preparation of it, her good looks and her quite obvious happiness. Edith, too, recognised Caroline as being almost identical with her childhood memories of her adored Auntie Betty. The other bridesmaid – the pretty sixteen-year-old sister of the bride – called for no conclusion, except that she looked too demure to be true.

Her gaze kept straying to the bridegroom and the best man, and each time her eyes lit on Desmond she was conscious of a recurring tight feeling at her breast which she could not explain. Looking at him unawares gave her the same sort of secure enjoyment as, when having bought a new car, or a horse or a piece of furniture, she felt the need for a frequent peep at her new acquisition. It was not that she felt she had acquired her cousin, but she certainly seemed to be seeing him in a new light. Other than in early childhood, they had not met many times in their life, for he had been at school when she had joined the Colours in 1940, and since the war the interchange of visits had been a rarity. Aunt Betty had visited Oakleigh several times, for she still remembered it as the idyllically-happy home of her teens, but she did not expect her grown-up sons to accompany her.

The wedding group moved away from the altar and Desmond, with a sort of telepathic communication, focussed his gaze on Edith in a bold and comprehensive stare. The girl blushed deeply, a reaction which she had never been able to control, bit her lip with annoyance and muttered not very refined curses to herself as everyone drifted outside. It was a bright warm day – far too good for post-harvest weather, Arthur was heard to remark gloomily to his father – and after the signing of the registers the key figures joined the main party outside the church for the photography and the public kissing.

The groomsman did not deny his right, nor was he prepared to shirk from his traditional duty of kissing the bridesmaids. However, since one was his own sister, he could not anticipate any particular thrill in performing this pleasant mark of affection. He could have kissed Caroline any time, but to what purpose? The other attendant, Diana's even younger sister Helen, although pretty, was also of negligible interest. He seized her, smothered her face with vigorous pecks, then put her down, rather roughly. Without pausing, and ignoring everybody, he strode firmly over to Edith, seized her in his long arms and kissed her lengthily, as if he were a film star and she his leading lady at the conclusion of a particularly erotic film. To her own astonishment, Edith found herself returning the embrace, hugging him tightly with her own not inconsiderable strength.

Arthur sauntered over and nudged Desmond in the ribs.

'What the hell's this?' he said mischievously, 'Clinching is not allowed. Break it off!'

Desmond put out a large shoe and pressed hard on Arthur's toe, and his cousin limped off, swearing under his breath. Then official duties claimed the best man as the whole party split up and boarded their various cars to return to the reception hotel. After the luncheon, the toasts and the cutting of the cake, Desmond despatched the newly-weds with hurried precision and, disregarding Arthur's quizzical gaze, made straight for Edith's side.

'Thank God that's all over!'

'Don't sound so relieved. If you take a job on, you shouldn't allow yourself to get fed up with it halfway through!'

'Everything went off all right, didn't it?'

'Perfectly.'

'Then don't criticise my feelings of completion. I say, it's a bit crowded here! Can we move over to those easy chairs among the palms?'

Edith got to her feet with an alacrity for which she secretly reproved herself.

'What's all this about?' she said when they had settled themselves down in partial seclusion of which the other guests had only a restricted view.

'I just want to talk. I suppose I can talk to my cousin, can't I?'

'It's taken you a long time to want to. Twenty years, I guess!'

'I suddenly feel as if I'd known you well all my life.'

'Indeed?' Edith said, hiding the fact that the feeling was mutual.

'Will you marry me, Edith?'

'No!'

'Why not?'

'The whole idea's ridiculous. Robin's wedding must have turned your head. We don't know each other really. Anyway, I came here to attend a wedding, not to arrange one for myself!'

'I admired you so much in the war, when you were a captain and I was only a flying officer, and respected you, too.'

'So you should have: (a) you were only a boy; (b) the army is senior to the Air Force; and (c) I'm a good bit older than you.'

'Not very much! Only four years!'

'It's too much for what you're thinking of.'

'Nonsense! You'll always be young, Edie. You're the personification of youth! Your whole outlook and approach to things exudes youthfulness!'

'Don't call me Edie,' she flared, after carefully waiting for him to conclude his peroration. 'You ought to know I hate being called that!'

'Sorry, I didn't know.'

'Well, you'd better remember that!'

Desmond hurriedly made a mental note and preened himself he was making at least some headway with this strong-minded young woman. He decided to carry on with the good work.

'I think I've loved you all my life in spite of your bossy ways!'

'Oh, thank you!'

'Well, you always used to boss us about whenever you stayed with us in the school hols or when we came to Oakleigh.'

'Naturally. You needed it. Your mother spoiled you all outrageously.'

They sat silent for a moment or two, Edith comfortably on the defensive where she intended to remain. Desmond made tentative movements.

'Desmond! Stop that damned fumbling! How dare you?' She nearly added, 'this is not the place,' but stopped herself just in time.

'You can't blame me for trying,' Desmond protested and summoned the waiter for more drinks.

Edith scanned him searchingly. Every line of his handsome face showed him to be in earnest, and he breathed hard with emotion. She recognised similar feelings within herself but had them under tight control. Perhaps she should give him a little encouragement, though. She decided it would be of a practical nature.

'When you do get married, cousin,' she said carefully, 'where will you live? Stoneleigh belongs to Uncle Edwin and Aunt Betty. It's their home.'

'Of course it is! But we've taken on another farm you know, where the pedigree cattle will be housed in the winter. Westmead Farm, it's called. There's a grand farmhouse there – not too big. Just right, in fact.'

'Oh, and who lives there now?'

'Our herdsman, Nicholson, but he wasn't very keen on going in there, so we're building him a bungalow near the steading. Do say you'll marry me, Edith. I may never get another chance to talk to you as intimately as this. Perhaps I shan't see you for months!'

'Rubbish! I'm staying for a few days!'

'Are you, by God? Mum didn't tell me! That's smashing! If I've got a few days to work on you, I might achieve something. Tell you what, I'll take you all round and show you everything.'

'Of course, that's what I'm staying for. And I hope to ride with Aunt Betty too – I've brought my riding kit. That's if you can find me a horse.'

'You can have mine. Wait a minute, though. I shall be coming with you, so I'll want him myself. You can have Dad's or Caroline's. If they want to ride, they can use one of the others. Everything's going to be perfect, and I'll propose to you every day!'

'You'll do no such thing. You may ask me again in three months.' She stopped suddenly for she had been about to add, 'and I'll say yes then,' but restrained herself. Edith knew her own mind, as always, but was not sure that her handsome suitor was similarly stable.

'Three months? Hmm ...' He made a rapid mental calculation. 'Mid-November? Yes – we should have all the winter corn sown by then, the sugar beet off and the cattle housed. Yes – that'll be fine. We could have the wedding early in December which is a slack month, anyway.'

'Are you sure you can spare the time from your farming to get married?'

'Absolutely! Getting married is as important to a farmer as – er – turning the – or taking on another farm. Yes, definitely as important as taking on an additional farm. Ah, music! Let's dance, Edith.'

He offered her his hand but she was on her feet first.

'Desmond Salt! If I wasn't sure you had your tongue in your

cheek when you made that last statement, I'd have hit you! Yes, you'd better grin!'

'One thing worries me, though,' he confided as they waltzed smoothly over the uncrowded floor. 'How am I going to survive without seeing you for three months?'

'What rubbish are you talking about now? I didn't say anything about our not seeing each other! I know the way here, and you haven't forgotten the way to Oakleigh, I hope!'

He crushed her in to his body.

'I can't think what's come over Edith and Desmond,' Arthur commented to his father from the wings. 'They're spending a lot of time in each other's company, and acting very strangely.'

'Had too much to drink, I suppose,' his father replied indifferently. 'Like most of the other folk here, I reckon. You'd better be careful how much you drink, lad,' he said as an afterthought. 'I don't want to end up in the ditch on the way home.'

'No, I wouldn't want the Jag to end up in the ditch, either. Don't worry, Dad. We've got all the weekend in front of us. I'll nod off for a couple of hours before we leave Stoneleigh.'

Chapter 10

It was midnight before Robert and Arthur Felton finally said farewell to Edwin and Desmond Salt, their womenfolk already having retired after, as they described it, a tiring and emotional day. Robert complained about the night drive, but Arthur assured him he preferred to drive at night when there was less traffic about. He was fresh and alert after his armchair nap, and they set off in the light of the harvest moon.

'I'm a bit worried about Edie, Dad,' Arthur confided before they had moved out of the sphere of the wedding celebrations. 'It seemed to me that Desmond had his eye on her. He was acting damned peculiar.'

His father chuckled.

'I pity anyone, cousin or otherwise, who tried to get fresh with Edith when she wasn't in a receptive mood. I reckon her six or seven years in the army will have left her tough and capable in any situation. Let's concentrate on getting home. I wonder how Dick has got on with those last two fields of barley?'

Driving easily and conversing most of the way, the Feltons did not arrive back at Oakleigh until well after three o'clock. The farmhouse seemed dark and forlorn, for they had never quite got used to coming home to an empty house. The fire in the kitchen range was slumbering which added a little touch of homeliness to the slight chill of the late-August morning air. Father and son lingered over giant mugs of tea, several times refilled, and piles of wholemeal biscuits.

'It's gone four o'clock,' Robert Felton said at last. 'We'd better get to bed or we'll not want to get up in the morning.'

'Hell, I don't know that I want to get up early. It's Sunday, Dad! Leave the work until we're called for. I'm sure Dick has it well in hand. If there's anything wrong, he'll be here to wake us up at the same time as the cowman. It's my bet he'll have finished the barley and made plans to start on the spring wheat to-day.'

'In that case I must certainly be around,' Robert Felton said, with some pretence of agitation. 'I'm not sure that wheat's fit for combining, and I want to see it before he starts.'

'It was fit three days ago, so it must be fit now,' Arthur replied. 'Anyway, there'll be a heavy dew tomorrow, or rather, today, so the combines won't roll until eleven o'clock at the earliest. See you at the field!'

He may well have decided to sleep late on the Sunday morning, but the acting housekeeper, Mavis Marshall, decided otherwise. Soon after eight o'clock she rapped hard on his bedroom door.

'I'm just cooking the breakfast, Mr Arthur. Come down in ten minutes if you want some!'

Cursing sleepily, Arthur tumbled out of bed, had a hurried wash, omitted to clean his teeth and pulled on a shirt and flannel trousers before stumbling downstairs to find his father already eating. Dick's wife placed a huge basin of steaming porridge in front of him and a capacious mug of sweet strong tea, followed by a plate of bacon, eggs and potatoes, piled on with a very heavy hand.

'I must be off now,' she said gaily as she bustled out. 'There's plenty more tea in the pot. Elsie Long will be in presently to do the washing up.'

'It'll be a good thing when Edith gets back,' Arthur grumbled with his mouth full. 'I don't like these haphazard meals.' He paused, broke the yolk of a third egg and continued. 'This is an old-fashioned breakfast! A troughful of porridge, a tray full of bacon and eggs, and nearly a bucket o' tea.'

'You seem to be wrapping yourself round it, nevertheless, so I don't know what you're grumbling about. When are you going to stop eating?'

'No good wasting it when it's been cooked,' Arthur replied stubbornly. 'Mavis needn't think she can stall me!'

Breakfast over, they left the house and hurried out to key points on the farm – the grain storage bins, the straw barns and the stubble fields. Both men seemed faintly surprised to find that the farm had not suffered unduly from their absence, although they had been away for a whole day! They were now on the last leg of harvesting. The weather was sufficiently kind to enable the last crop – forty acres of spring wheat – to be harvested in average condition over the next few shortening days. After the combines had been dusted and stowed away, the whole of the staff was available for bale-hauling and by the end of the week that formidable task was nearing its end.

Throughout the whole week Arthur and his father sadly missed Edith, not only for her household management, but also for her secretarial work, most of which fell to Arthur, which he performed with an ill grace, laying aside all but the most urgent documents.

'Thank goodness Ede's coming back tomorrow. I hate standing in for anybody else, especially at paperwork.' They were sitting down on Friday evening to an ample but hastily-prepared meal. 'I suppose you can meet her off the train? I shall be at cricket – the last away match this week.'

'Taking Linda?' his father asked casually.

'Might as well,' Arthur replied equally casually. 'She's got used to behaving herself now and she's quite good company. It'll be her last opportunity this week, though.'

'Bring her home if you feel like it, Arthur. Her father and I have been at loggerheads more or less for forty years, but whatever mischief he may have done, there's no reason for the bad feeling to be carried down to the next generation.'

'I never thought of it like that, Dad. It hadn't occurred to me to bring her in. I always assumed she'd call to see Edith if she wanted to visit us. I'll give her a ring and see how she's fixed.'

The telephone rang while they were still at the meal and Arthur, hurrying to take the call, was faintly disappointed to hear his sister's voice.

'Oh, Arthur, I shan't need you to pick me up tomorrow, after all. Desmond is bringing me back in the Mercedes.'

'Huh! Doing the thing in style, aren't you? What's the reason?'

'I suppose a cousin can visit us, can't he? Don't be boorish! We'll leave here after lunch and be at Oakleigh by teatime.'

'OK, I'll tell Dad. I'll be at cricket, of course.'

'Hope you have a good match. Give my regards to Linda!'

Arthur put the phone down with an angry snort.

'Desmond's bringing Edie home about teatime tomorrow, Dad. I wonder what the devil he wants.'

'Probably got some business up this way, although I can't think what. I suppose he'll stay the night. I'd better leave a message for Elsie Long to get the room ready.'

'I suppose he'll want to pry all over the place,' grumbled Arthur.

'Pry be damned! Of course he'll want to go all round. He took you all over their place didn't he? What have we got to be ashamed of?'

'Nothing, really. We haven't all the frills and polish he has but we're tidy enough on the whole, and basically no less productive, I'm sure. I'd better ring Linda.'

When he did so, Major Ratcliffe answered. Linda had not yet arrived home from Derby, he said.

'Major, will you tell her that I'll pick her up at one-thirty if she wants to come to the match with me?'

'I'll certainly give her that message, Felton. I'm quite certain she will come with you. I heard her say last night she was looking forward to it.'

Arthur gritted his teeth and put down the phone rather abruptly.

Saturday morning was hot and clear, and after breakfast Arthur and his father pitched in with the bale-collecting gangs until noon. There were several fields still to clear and the hour or two's urgency engendered by the presence of the two gaffers made little impact on the whole. However, they went home quickly with a sense of satisfaction and Arthur ate a huge salad lunch, liberally dished up by Mavis Marshall, then went upstairs to bath and change for the cricket match. He had plenty of time, so enjoyed a long soaking, then dressed leisurely and went downstairs.

Hearing familiar voices in the sitting-room he looked in and to his surprise and annoyance saw Linda chatting gaily to his father who looked at his most genial. Arthur swallowed hard at the sight of the girl, for she looked especially lovely, wearing a smart grey flannel blazer over a lemon-coloured linen dress with a pleated skirt. He thought he had never seen her so attractive but he said coldly, 'Hello, Linda! What are you doing here?'

His father answered him.

'Arthur! Don't be so awkward! Miss Ratcliffe . . .'

'Do call me Linda,' murmured the girl sweetly.

'Well . . . er . . . Linda has driven round to save you the bother of picking her up. So charming of her! We've had such a delightful chat.'

Arthur felt that Linda was attacking him from the rear and glorying in it.

'Indeed,' he said. 'Well, come on Linda, it's time we were off.'

'Do call and see me again, my dear,' Robert Felton said with genuine warmth. 'That's very nice of you,' he added as Linda kissed him gently on the cheek, while Arthur silently gnashed his teeth. As they got in the Jaguar, Linda was pleased to note that there were several men in the rickyard still moving bales who saw her leave the house with the young gaffer.

'What do you think you're up to, Linda, making up to my father in that transparent way?' Arthur said as they swung out into the road.

'I wasn't "making up to him" as you call it. He's a darling old man and I'm fond of him. Everybody likes him in Hartnall. Even my father has a great respect for him. Don't be mean, Arthur. This is our last away match.'

They were going to Tutbury, a small old town just over the Staffordshire border. The team was a strong club side, not the strongest that Hartnall had met that season, but far better than the village sides which filled most of Hartnall's fixture list. Arthur invariably did well against strong opposition in good conditions and he confidently expected to do so today.

He won the toss and as the wicket seemed firm and true he had no hesitation in deciding to bat, and eagerly walked out with his former opening partner who had been reinstated in that position during Charles Ratcliffe's temporary demotion.

As the field settled into its positions Arthur felt he could make a lot of runs in these ideal circumstances. In fact, the wicket was damper than it appeared. The opening bowler took a longish run-up and delivered a fast good-length ball on the middle stump. Calculating its length perfectly, Arthur swung his bat to drive it straight back past the bowler. To his utter chagrin, the ball did not rise as he had expected and played for, but shot along the ground like a bullet, crept under his bat and ripped the middle stump out of the ground.

In dead silence he walked back to the pavilion, furious in spite of the opposing captain's 'hard luck, mate', for he knew that it would look as if he made a rash stroke whereas he had covered the line of the ball exactly. His team were outwardly sympathetic, for it was the first time that season that the skipper had failed. Disheartened but not dismayed, the other Hartnall batsmen batted with varying success and easily achieved the respectability of a three-figure total.

Needing comfort, Arthur joined Linda to watch his colleagues bat, but she was so glum at his failure she did not quite fulfil his need. He noted with some dismay that the pitch had firmed up under the hot sun and making runs had consequently become easier.

'If we are to win this match,' he said to his team at teatime, 'we must save every run and not put down a single catch!'

'Easier said than done,' someone muttered, but they followed his edict loyally and the wickets fell regularly, but the runs mounted.

The scene was set for an exciting climax. The last two batsmen were together and Tutbury needed three runs to win. Arthur flung the ball to Reg Bentley, the opening bowler who had been resting for several overs. He was much too fast for the number eleven batsman who was facing him. He pushed out his bat vaguely and made contact, but the ball cut off the outside edge with the velocity of a ricochet. Arthur, at second slip, jumped wide to his right, grabbed the ball with both hands, then let it through as he pitched to the ground, while the ball sped to the boundary. Hartnall had suffered their first defeat of the season.

Arthur was not used to failure on the cricket field and the thought that he had erred twice in one match and caused his side to lose the game grieved him. He and Linda had dinner at the Dog and Partridge, an old coaching inn in the centre of town, but even these charming surroundings did nothing to lighten their conversation, and compared with previous similar occasions the evening was quiet and colourless. Linda was full of sympathy but wisely did not try too hard to jog him out of his melancholy frame of mind. An idea formed in her mind, but she could not put it into operation among the crowding beams and oaken fittings of the ancient inn.

They set off again in a subdued mood which even affected Arthur's driving, for the powerful engine was doing little more than ticking over. As they crossed Egginton Common Linda said gently, 'Arthur, do pull in for a while. Let's see if we can talk ourselves into a happier mood. I know a duck and a missed catch in the same match is pretty rough, but it's not the end of the world. We have a few more games this season.'

'No more away games though,' Arthur said, which Linda knew only too well. Then he surprised himself and thrilled the girl by adding, 'and no more drives home in the gloaming.'

He pulled the car off the road into a gateway which led into a small copse. It was just after eight o'clock. The sun was sinking behind the wood, its strong rays filtering through the branches, giving the lingering daylight a reddish tinge. Arthur leaned back with a sigh and so did Linda, but she contrived to fall against his shoulder and then put her hand on his forearm.

'I've had a good season until to-day,' he remarked thoughtfully, 'so I mustn't get too dispirited, especially with a lovely girl like you beside me!'

He looked at her closely. God, how attractive she was! He absorbed every detail – the pretty bare legs, now fallen casually into the hint of a sprawl; the tasteful yellow dress, the delightful curve of her throat; the modest jewellery; the delicate, comely features, the superb mass of glossy hair; but above all, the radiant eyes which twinkled a bold invitation. Why not, he thought, and turned to face her. Linda turned at the same time, bringing her face so close to his that her perfume almost intoxicated him.

'I'm wearing french knickers,' she murmured in his ear, adding the faintest of giggles.

'Yes, I've found them,' he responded instantly. She sighed with pleasure, wriggled, and a bright yellow garment appeared round her ankles. She slipped off her shoes and kicked her feet free, opening her limbs to receive him.

In about a minute they parted, Linda triumphant but loving, Arthur with a sense of accomplishment. It was hardly a conquest he told himself, for she had offered herself as boldly as a nice girl possibly could. Linda shook herself, then bent down to retrieve her underwear.

'Don't put those on again yet,' Arthur said at once. 'I might not have finished with you!'

'Oh Arthur!' she exclaimed and to his surprise she blushed crimson as she smiled her willingness. 'I'd better take my dress off, then,' she added, 'or it will get as creased as a sack apron.'

She looked so utterly desirable that the man's ardour quickly returned and they joined again in a less violent but more extended embrace.

As Linda's car was still in the yard at Oakleigh, she naturally had to accompany Arthur home. When they drove into the yard she was impressed and thrilled by the sight of Edwin Salt's Mercedes standing there, for Desmond, wishing to offer Edith the acme of comfort, had borrowed his father's car for the trip. Linda's pleasure did not end there, for Desmond and Edith returned at that moment from a stroll round the home field, and Edith took the opportunity of introducing her cousin. As a sequel, they all went into the farmhouse for drinks and Robert Felton was surprised and delighted at this sudden influx of company. Linda was beside herself with delight for she took it for granted that she had now been accepted as a friend of the family, although with the secret of their recent behaviour (or misbehaviour) in her mind she saw herself as something much more positive than that, but she soon realised that Arthur did not accept her assessment of the situation. He was much less ecstatic, for after the thrill of the moment his ardour was cooling. He was already thinking of Alison and wishing Linda away.

After a very pleasant hour Linda got up to go and Arthur had to escort her to her car as matter of course. In the warm darkness she was prepared for an amorous and positive goodnight kiss and was disappointed when Arthur sent her off with a perfunctory peck on one cheek. 'I might have been his sister,' she grumbled to herself as she drove back to Home Farm.

Desmond Salt was utterly happy to be staying the weekend at Oakleigh, which he had not visited for some years. He had developed a remarkable affection for his lovely cousin – romanticists would say he had fallen very heavily in love. He was convinced she returned his feelings, but with her totally practical approach she declined to reveal her thoughts until the young man had consolidated his attitude.

So Desmond went happily to bed, unaware that the guest-room he occupied was that which had been allotted to his mother when she had arrived at the farm as a sixteen-year-old girl, over thirty years before. The three main bedrooms of the farmhouse were naturally occupied by Robert, Arthur and Edith, and the upper floor – now no longer needed for domestic help and farm lads – had been made into guest-rooms.

Desmond was even more pleased the following morning when he joined the Feltons at breakfast. A farmer himself, he recognised the validity of a farmhouse breakfast – early and plentiful. Not for him the dainty tray in his bedroom, which Edith would have provided had he so opted. He clumped firmly downstairs, hungry for the unchangeable Oakleigh breakfast of porridge and bacon and eggs, plus other odds and ends if needed.

Edith, even when at her household duties, never failed to be neat and attractive in her dress and perhaps for Desmond's benefit she added an extra touch of smartness. He was dazzled by her comeliness and competence and thought how marvellous it was that this feminine paragon would soon be sharing and supervising his own household.

As might be expected, the visitor was claimed after breakfast by Arthur and his father for a tour of the Felton acres. The young man could not fail to be interested, for his own farm life owed its existence to the fact that his father had been the pupil of Robert Felton and old Arnold Ratcliffe immediately after the First War, and his mother had been courted and married at Oakleigh.

On the farm tour they concentrated on the lines which were of mutual interest, and the pauses for explanation and discussion were so many and so long that the morning passed quickly. Arthur and Desmond were engaged in a deep argument as to the economics of grass-fed as opposed to yard-fed beef, when Robert suddenly looked at his watch.

'It's nearly one o'clock, you two! We'd better get back quickly. Edith won't be pleased if we're late for the lunch she's been to so much trouble to prepare!'

'Not all alone, I hope?' Desmond said anxiously as they scrambled into the Land Rover.

'No, she has one or two of the chaps' wives in to help. They appear to take it in turn, and I daresay they're glad to earn a few shillings extra. Edith's a wonderful organiser and they'd do anything for her,' Robert Felton went on, quite unaware that he was talking to her husband-presumptive. 'She's efficient in everything she does, is Edith, and charming with it, but oh, so stubborn!'

Desmond was embarrassed at being the recipient of these confidences while unable to appraise the speaker of his own hopes and plans, but he felt he had to say something, so he murmured, 'She's a rare young woman.'

However, he unconsciously put so much feeling into his words that Arthur looked across at him from the steering-wheel in some surprise.

Edith, preparing to reprimand her menfolk for their near-lateness, was much mollified by their transparent haste and presided over the meal with her usual charm. To Desmond, who could not keep his eyes off her, she seemed a veritable queen, but less so to Arthur when she remarked casually, 'Linda was on the phone this morning.'

'What did she want?'

'She didn't say, but asked me to ask you to ring back.'

'I've nothing to say to her. The next match is still a week away. She can tell me then.'

Arthur looked so angry that Edith forebore to comment on such unwarranted ill-manners.

The domestic helpers having departed for their own homes before the meal, Edith sent her father into the sitting-room for his usual Sunday afternoon nap, instructed her brother and their guest to attend to the washing-up (which Arthur did very ungraciously) while she went upstairs to change into her afternoon clothes. She thrilled Desmond by returning in a tweed skirt and woollen jacket and wearing brogues, so he took his cue by suggesting she should show him over the river meadows which had been left out of their morning tour.

As they walked down the drive together, Desmond felt at that moment prouder of his companion than of the whole of the farm he had left behind. Crossing the road, they entered the pasture where the young dairy stock were grazing in sleek contentment. They looked curiously but warily at these two intruders of their summer home. The bright warm sun was obliging them to seek the shade of the scattered oak trees. These old pastures had not been trimmed, and stalky buttercups stood here and there, in singles and bunches like drowsy sentinels.

The couple reached the Trent and wandered along its bank, admiring the shallow, rippling drinking-places, respecting the swirls and eddies of the deeper stretches. In this remote spot the river looked peaceful, attractive and romantic. At least the young man, whose farm did not boast a river, thought so, and stole a glance at his companion. But Edith had grown up by the Trent and though she still appreciated its beauty, the romance had long since faded.

Desmond, his eye fixed on a secluded clump of willows ahead, put his arm round her waist and pulled her to him.

'Edith! This three-month delay business is damned nonsense! Why can't we get engaged right away? I really love you and I shan't change my mind. We Salts don't, you know!'

Edith knew the train of his wishful thinking and had no intention of gratifying it.

'I believe you Des, and I'm going to allow you to buy me a ring, but that's as far as we're going. Everything else will wait until after the wedding!'

'Oh hell! Can't we bring the wedding forward then?'

'Restrain your impatience! You suggested December as a suitable month and now I'm holding you to it. The house isn't even vacant yet.'

'True, and there are a lot of alterations to be done. They ought to be put in hand soon.'

'Have you forgotten that the building industry is still fully controlled and all materials only supplied under licence?'

'These things can be circumvented.'

'Maybe, but I'm not sure I want a lot of alterations. It's really a delightful old place. Of course, the outside needs looking to and the rooms will all have to be redecorated, but any big changes ought to wait until we've been in there a few months. Then we shall know exactly what we want!'

'A bit inconvenient having structural changes while we're living there.'

'We can stay with your parents for a while.'

'I thought you didn't want to do that!'

'I didn't want us to stay there as newly-weds. I don't mind later on. I'm very fond of your mother!'

'Whatever you say, my dear. My word, it's hot this afternoon. Can't we sit down under the willows for a spell?'

'No, we cannot!' She steered him away from the river and temptation. 'We'll have the wedding early in December and that will give us time to get back from the honeymoon before Christmas.'

'What honeymoon?'

'We must go somewhere! I can afford it if you can't, and since December weather is generally miserable in England, I suggest we go where there's some sun. Say a cruise to the Canaries for a fortnight!'

Desmond appeared to think deeply.

'Well – yes,' he said at length, 'I think I can manage to leave the farm for a fortnight, as it's December!'

'Desmond Salt, one of these days you'll have your tongue so far in your cheek, you'll bite through it! But to continue – at Christmas we'll spend one day here at Oakleigh and the other day with your parents.'

'My God, you've got it all worked out, haven't you? Here was I, thinking you were teetering and you intended to say yes all along!'

'Of course!'

He threw his arms round her and in spite of her weight of eleven stones, swung her well off her feet.

'Edith, I think you and I are going to be the happiest couple in the world!'

'Did you say happiest or heaviest? Put me down, please, your grip is squeezing me out of breath! Thank you! You know, Des, I've always said that any couple, with only average feelings, but with patience and tolerance, can make a success of a marriage if they want to. I'm sure we're going to do a thousand times better than that!' She pushed his hand away. 'None of that! You won't find me wanting on our wedding night, I promise you!'

They wandered back to Oakleigh, through the silent kitchen and found Robert and Arthur in the sitting-room, drowsily watching television. They became wide awake when Edith broke the news.

Her father said, 'Your mother would have been pleased, and what pleased her, always pleased me!'

Arthur said, 'Well, I don't know! Good luck to both o' you and happy farming. Dad, we've got to dig up a hell of a lot of money from somewhere to buy Edith's share of the business.'

'What utter rot!' Edith replied indignantly. 'Sell my share of dear old Oakleigh? Not bloody likely!'

Chapter 11

The shock of Edith's engagement was great but by the time Desmond left for home in the late evening, Robert Felton and his son had become vaguely used to the idea. They saw no cause for immediate changes in their habits; December was a long way off and there would be plenty of time to sort something out. In the meantime, the farm would occupy most of their attention, for a busy time of year was creeping up. There was much ploughing to be done, winter corn to be sown, potatoes and sugar beet to be harvested; but first the rest of the straw bales had to be collected. Both of the Feltons flung themselves wholeheartedly into the job, working until dusk every evening, filling every empty shed and barn, as well as building numerous rectangular stacks.

Arthur contrived to be out of the way whenever Linda telephoned, which was once or twice every morning. Edith sensed the disappointment in the girl's voice and, although unaware of the extent of the emotional development, she was annoyed with her brother for his casual attitude to a very pleasant and affectionate girl. Newly engaged herself, she would have looked with favour on an understanding between her brother and Linda, in spite of what she imagined her father's reaction would be to a union between their two families.

Nothing was further from Arthur's mind than the thought of a promise to marry Linda Ratcliffe. He was angry with himself for succumbing to temptation and brooded on the matter until he convinced himself that he had been unfairly treated.

'Damn the girl,' ran his thoughts, 'egging me on like that.' He supposed he was partly to blame, though, for giving way to her. It had certainly been unpremeditated on his part and almost certainly intended by Linda. He had not been prepared either, for he had not been in the habit of carrying packets of three since he had left the army. After the war, farming and cricket had absorbed all his interest and energy. He had partly made up for it on Saturday, though. The little baggage had been so seductive he had offered and been accepted three times. She'd been a virgin, too. He certainly hadn't expected that! Of course, it had been a satisfying experience. How could it be otherwise with a girl so lovely, so clinging and so ardent as Linda? He believed the young devil had done her best to get herself pregnant, for she just wouldn't let him go. Naturally, if that happened there was only one result possible. He would marry her very quickly, for he had no intention of allowing himself to be the target of sniggering in the village nor would he wish to subject Linda to such humiliation. He paused in his thought for a moment, pondering on what marriage to Linda would be like. Strangely, he could find nothing against it except his own inclinations. He still hankered after Alison and decided to try harder, even if it meant manufacturing opportunities to see her. He would have to be watchful that Linda did not try to ensnare him with a false pregnancy, but quickly decided she was not the sort of girl to do that. She had her pride – plenty of it!

There was really no need to concern himself unduly. Taking a girl in a car was not so rare after all, even if she was a virgin. They were all virgins to begin with, anyway. Some young fellows made a hobby of it. He personally did not approve of such promiscuous behaviour. There were certain limits! He decided that when he saw Linda again, which would not be later than the next cricket match, he would behave normally to her as if the event of Saturday had not taken place. In the meantime he would find a reason for contacting Alison.

With no other work to distract the staff, the remainder of the bales came in with a rush. Every man and every trailer from Oakleigh was engaged and Gene King brought his tractor and his cowman for a few hours every day. The job was finished on Wednesday evening and after the evening meal on the following day, Arthur drove round to Hilltop Farm to settle the account. He knew well enough that it was not customary among farmers to pay bills before they had been presented, but Arthur needed an excuse which was not too transparent and here was one to hand.

Mrs King appeared at the back door before he had time to knock. She was very gushing, Arthur thought.

'Come right in, Mr Felton. How nice to see you!' Arthur strode into the kitchen which, as in most farmhouses, was also the living-room. There was a comfortable armchair each side of the inevitable cooking range, and a sofa under the window on which sat Alison, busily engaged in sewing what appeared to be underwear. The very picture of domesticity, thought Arthur to himself and his heart warmed to the girl. Mrs King offered him the armchair which was indirectly opposite her daughter. Had he sat in the other chair he would have had his back to her, which was clearly undesirable, as Mrs King silently agreed.

Gene King emerged from somewhere and sat in the other armchair, so Arthur could discuss his business and keep an eye on Alison at the same time.

'Glad to see you, Arthur,' the farmer said. 'Will you have a drink with us?'

'Well . . . no, thank you, – I only just . . .'

'We've got some rare parsnip wine – just started on the 1947 bottles. Mother's a dab hand at wine-making.'

'Well, just a little, then,' Arthur said and looked askance at the large glasses – almost tumblers – with which Mrs King adorned the table, and filled to the brim.

'Here's to the start of another farmin' year, Arthur – it's none so far off – and may the weather be better than this year.'

'I'll certainly drink to that,' his visitor replied and conveyed the glass to his lips, gingerly, to avoid spillage. To render the glass easier to handle he took a large sip and felt the liquid coursing down his gullet like hot, sweet oil. He decided he would get to the business of the evening while he was still sober.

'We're very grateful for your help with the bales, Gene, and I've called to settle up.'

'Well, we're glad to see you at any time, but there were no need to be in such an all-fired hurry. I haven't paid your bill for baling that hay for us, and I reckoned the straw-shifting would just about work that off!'

'No, no, I'm sure there's a good balance due to you. Did you have a bill for the baling?'

'Oh yes. Your sister were right on time. 'Er allus is, I understand. Bill arrived on second o' the month.' He reached up and took out a folded paper from behind a toby-jug on the mantelpiece. 'Here y'are – 920 bales at sixpence – twenty-three pounds.'

'I'm sure we owe you more than that. What do you reckon your time and tackle was worth?'

'I just don't know – wasn't too interested. Just wanted to help you get 'em under cover.'

'All right! Now, the tractor and trailer must be worth ten bob an hour at least. Do you agree?'

'That sounds liberal.'

'And two men at three bob an hour each – is that enough?'

'Plenty!'

'And you must have come at least twenty times. Say five hours a day – that's a hundred hours at sixteen shillings – eighty pounds Gene!'

'Ah, but we 'ad some straw ourselves, early on. Dick said it'd be all right as you'd plenty. So one day we filled up the empty bay in our barn. Your two trailers and mine came in twice. That's six hundred bales.'

'OK I didn't know. Dick didn't mention it to me. He probably gave the particulars in at the office. Fair enough. Six hundred bales – ten tons at four pound a ton – £40, plus the baling, £23 – that's £63 altogether. Your account comes to £80 so I have to give you seventeen.' He pulled his cheque-book from his inside pocket.

'This is rare good luck,' King said. 'I was quite prepared to pay you summat.' He stowed the cheque away behind the toby-jug. 'This calls for another drink. Fill the glasses up, Mother.'

The potent wine began to take effect on Arthur's mental processes. Halfway down the second glass he announced that he would himself propose a toast. Groping to his feet, he held his glass out to the full length of his arm and, looking dazedly at Alison, he cried, 'Here's to Alison King, the prettiest girl in Hartnall.'

Her parents responded, smiling happily, but Alison flushed and said crossly, 'Don't make yourself ridiculous, Arthur. It seems as though Mum's wine is going to your head!'

She gathered up her sewing and left the room, to her father's obvious displeasure. Arthur drank another tumbler of wine which made him feel even more muddle-headed, but he was sober enough to realise the sort of figure he was cutting. As Alison had left the company he saw no further point in remaining, so he drained his glass and announced his departure. As he rose to his feet Alison reappeared, minus the sewing basket. One look at her assured him that if he reversed his decision to leave, he would be unpopular.

'Ah, Alison!' Said Gene King, 'Arthur's just going. Show him to the Land-Rover.'

'I'll show him out, certainly,' Alison said distinctly, 'but I'm sure he can find his own way to the Land-Rover and I'm equally sure he's not fit to drive it home. Come on, Arthur.'

The young man pulled a wry face at Alison's parents which caused them to smile, but uneasily. He followed the girl sheepishly.

'You're making an exhibition of yourself tonight, aren't you?' she said crossly. 'Haven't you tasted home-made wine before?'

'None of your mother's! It was as powerful as peach brandy.'

'And you're as drunk as if it were. You'd better not drive home. You're not in a fit condition.'

'I'm fit enough to drive if the roads are empty. But as there may be a car or two about, I'll leave the Land-Rover here and walk. Will that please you?'

'It's more sensible, anyway. Goodnight, Arthur.'

'You don't have to go in, surely? Can't we talk awhile? We can sit in the Land-Rover.'

'I'm certainly not going to sit in any car while you're in that condition. What have we to say to each other?'

'You're not very approachable, Alison. Have you seen young Clark lately?'

'I have as a matter of fact – twice,' Alison said, brightening up immediately which Arthur did not fail to notice. 'I've called to see him twice and he's been here once. He's got his car now, you know, and is getting in a bit of practice.'

'Edith invited him to visit Oakleigh, but he hasn't been yet,' grumbled Arthur. 'Can't do anything right for some of 'em. Edith's got herself engaged, as you'll see in the paper tomorrow, so that will cause some disruption in our happy home or, rather, the wedding will.'

Alison thought this news exciting, but she would not show it, for she was anxious to be rid of her visitor. She merely said, 'Who's the lucky man?'

'Chap from down south. A distant relative. You wouldn't know him.'

'And the wedding – when's that?'

'I don't think it's fixed yet. The date'll soon get around when we're sure.' He wobbled slightly.

'You'll need a stick to walk home in that state. I expect there's one in the back, isn't there? I'll get it and take out the ignition keys at the same time.'

She brushed closely past him – too closely, for on a sudden impulse he seized her with both arms and smothered her with kisses, on her lips, cheeks, ears, then down her neck and as low as he could down her breast. The warmth of her lithe body, her perfume, and her vigorous struggles, awakened his innermost feelings which he did not bother to control. Alison was physically aware of this and it made her even more furious.

'Damn you, Arthur,' she stormed. 'You drunken bastard! Let me go or I'll knee you in the groin! I will, by God, I will!'

He released her as if in hurt surprise.

'Oh come now, Alison! Was all that necessary? Just a little kiss!'

'You were thinking of a lot more than kissing,' she panted. 'Don't think you can maul me about just as you like, Arthur

Felton. There are plenty of girls round here who would be glad of it, but I'm not one of 'em. Here's your stick. I ought to beat you over the head with it, and I would if you weren't drunk. Clear off now, and when you're sober, you can come back and apologise.'

She ran off in the direction of the house, which now showed lighted windows. Arthur, even in his stupefied state was thankful that the closing dusk had shrouded the scuffle from would-be viewers in the house. He gripped his stick and plodded out of the yard, weaving slightly.

He was in no hurry and decided to follow the lanes, although it was all of two miles – nearly twice as far as over the fields. His route took him past the entrance to Hartnall Hall. He paused for a moment, thinking foolishly that he would like to see the lambs fattening in the front park, then remembered it would be too dark, so he swayed on up the slope. The hedges were high and thick and effectively prevented him from seeing oncoming traffic. However, it was now dark enough for headlights and he expected to see the reflection of their glare. He continued to walk unsteadily in the centre of the road.

His hearing was not as perceptive as it should have been, for suddenly he was aware of a huge car spurting towards him round a wide bend, showing side-lights only and fully spanning the centre of the road. Arthur shouted involuntarily, flung himself to his left into the ditch, and the offside front wing just touched his knee. As the car braked, the headlights came on, then went off again as it scraped to a halt eighty yards down the road.

Arthur scrambled out of the ditch, half sobered by his fury. His clothes untidy with cleavers and broken grass, he strode down to the car which he now recognised as George Clark's Bentley. The driver squeezed out and slouched back up the slope to meet Arthur who shouted when he was still twenty yards away. His words were barely coherent as they tumbled out of his mouth.

'You bloody fool! You lunatic road hog! What the hell d'you think you're up to, charging along in the middle o' the road in this winding lane? And no headlights either! You're not safe to bloody well drive!'

'Oh, it's you, is it?' Clark said sourly. He could see Arthur was shaky on his legs. What the 'ell were *you* doin' i' the middle o' the road? Drunk by the look of you. I should have thought an important man like you would have knowed enough to walk i' the gutter in these narrer roads. You don't seem to be 'urt. Serve you bloody well right if you 'ad been!'

They were face to face now, and Arthur was strongly conscious of the other man's beery breath. He tried to speak calmly although he felt his anger was becoming uncontrollable.

'I may be drunk, but at least I was on foot! You were drunk and driving to the public danger. My God! If I hadn't jumped, you'd have gone right over me, you drunken swine!'

He lashed out with his right fist and hit him full in the mouth. Clark was too heavy and stocky to fall easily but he staggered backwards until he was supported by the rear of his car.

'You bastard,' he spat blood from his injured lips. 'I'll teach you a lesson that you won't forget, you cocky farmer!'

He stepped forward solidly and swung his fist in a savage arc. Arthur tried to parry the blow but his reflexes were too slow in his befuddled state of mind and Clark's fist caught him on the side of the jaw and sent him crashing to the gritty road. Clark stood back while the farmer clawed himself to his feet, vowing to give Clark the hiding of his life. He did not anticipate any difficulty for he was taller, quicker and ten years younger. But as he moved forward the reflection of a pair of headlights lit up the sky as they rounded a distant bend. It might be a local car he thought, and paused, for he had no intention of allowing someone who might know him to be entertained by the sight of Arthur Felton engaged in a brawl. He panted hard to contain his fury as he faced his adversary.

'This has gone far enough, Clark. It's no way to settle an argument, although by God, I've no fancy for being run over by a boozy neighbour. Keep your lights full on i' these lanes, like this car is doing, and people can get out o' your way.'

'I can understand you being upset and frightened,' Clark said slowly as he wiped the blood from his mouth with his handkerchief. 'I s'pose I should have had full lights on. You don't look too good. D'ye want me to drive you back to your farm?'

'No thanks, I'm safer walking than riding with you,' Arthur said and strode off without another word, raising his hand in acknowledgement of the driver of the other car who, unidentifiable behind his glaring lights, nevertheless gave a friendly toot as he skirted by.

Arthur walked home, frequently stroking his tender jaw. He wondered if the bruise would show at home and hoped not, for he was not in the mood for explanations. Quietly, he entered the house through the back door and was relieved that the scullery and kitchen were empty. The sound of the television in the sitting-room suggested that his father and sister were in there. Removing his shoes he walked quietly along the hall and upstairs to his bedroom where he quickly tumbled into bed to sleep off the effects of Mrs King's wonderful parsnip wine, her daughter's intransigence, and his perilous encounter with another semi-drunkard.

He felt no ill effects the next morning, apart from a slight stiffness of his jaw as he ate his breakfast. To enable the documentation to be effected, he told Edith of his financial settlement with King and received what amounted to a sharp reprimand for his totally unbusiness-like approach.

'You'd have been better at home last evening,' she added. 'Linda was on the phone again.'

'I'll see her at the match tomorrow,' he said doggedly.

He was beginning to feel wary of meeting her again after ignoring her telephone messages, but he could hardly go through a whole cricket afternoon without some contact, for as usual, she would be there supervising the teas, so he decided to seek her out while Hartnall batted. To achieve this, he would get out quickly and spend the rest of the innings in quiet conversation with her.

To avoid meeting her before the game started, he decided he would arrive later than usual, so to give an appearance of unavoidable delay and haste, he changed into cricket flannels before leaving home and arrived at the ground to toss the coin just as his team was about to send out a search party. The visiting captain called incorrectly, and Arthur marched out eagerly with his opening partner.

He played a forcing stroke to every ball bowled and scored off most of them. Stanley White, his partner at the non-striking end, looked open-mouthed while he wondered what was in his skipper's mind. However, he backed him up loyally to give Arthur the strike. Whenever Arthur scored a single or a three, unless it happened to be the last ball of the over, Stanley quickly notched a single to allow his captain to face the bowling again.

It was too hectic to last. Facing the last ball of the fourth over, Arthur hit the ball hard along the ground to mid-on. Although it was clearly not his call, Stanley, wishing to prolong the good work, shouted 'Come on,' and ran recklessly down the pitch. Against his better judgment Arthur complied, and sprinted to the other end at his best speed, but the fielder gathered the ball cleanly and with praiseworthy accuracy demolished the wicket while Arthur was still two or three yards out. He continued running and headed straight for Linda who sat alone on a bench beside the pavilion.

She looked at him accusingly but with sorrow in her eyes.

'What got into you to-day? Thirty-eight runs in just over a quarter-of-an-hour, run yourself out on a ridiculous call, then carry on running nonchalantly as if you didn't care! That's no way for an opening batsman – and a captain – to behave!'

'I wanted to get out quickly so that I could talk to you!'

'In cricket you should put the interests of your team first, as you well know. All this week you've deliberately refrained from telephoning me, so what have you to say now that's so important?'

'I want to know what you have to say to me. We've got an hour at least – perhaps two – in front of us.'

'I thought that after Saturday we should go right on from there – become engaged and all that. A girl doesn't give herself to a man unless she loves him!'

'Oh Linda! You can't be so naive as to believe that! Not in 1950! If a man and a girl embrace in a car, it doesn't mean they have to get married!'

'It does with me. What's the matter with you, Arthur? Didn't you enjoy it?'

'Of course I did. How could it possibly be otherwise. Anybody would, with such a lovely and enticing girl as you. I didn't know I was the first . . .'

'Thank you!'

'Well, how could I know?'

'You should have guessed, or assumed so.'

'I ought – I agree and I'm sorry. I'm sorry, too, that I wasn't prepared. I should have had a sheath with me.'

'Indeed! So you weren't prepared? I suppose I may take that as a compliment?'

'You can't really be serious in your attitude, Linda. I was just carried away by my feelings and the conditions. I'm sorry if you think I took advantage. But I might want to marry some one else – it's not unusual.'

'You won't find anybody to love you as steadily as I do, Arthur,' Linda said mournfully. 'And whom do you propose to marry, may I ask? Alison King?'

Arthur was beginning to feel uncomfortable, but he stubbornly refused to evade the issue. 'As a matter of fact, yes!' The close contact with Alison on the previous Thursday evening had strengthened his resolve.

'Does Alison know about this?'

'Well, no. I haven't pushed it yet. But she'll come round. Girls generally know which side their bread's buttered!'

'Don't be so utterly conceited! Alison's not for you, Arthur. Not your type!'

'And you are?'

'Yes, I am, and you're the only one who doesn't accept it. You're too stubborn and pig-headed. Suppose I'm pregnant?'

'I have supposed that! By jove, you tried hard enough, didn't you, you young madam! Yes, you should blush! But I don't think you've conceived.'

'And if I have?'

'If you're pregnant, Linda, of course I'll marry you like a shot. I'm not going to have mischievous tittle-tattle circulating the district about Arthur Felton! By God, no! Nor about Linda Ratcliffe, either.'

'Thank you for including me as an afterthought! But aren't you afraid I'll tell you I'm pregnant even if I am not?'

'No. You wouldn't do that!'

'You're right, I wouldn't.'

Linda sighed, but strangely, feeling the heavy disappointment in her heart lift ever so slightly. She had hoped for so much in return for Saturday's surrender, but she realised now she had been far too optimistic. The position between her and Arthur was totally unchanged, but the effect of the one intimacy might add its own undertones.

'I'm sorry about it all,' Arthur was saying. 'I promise it won't happen again.'

'What, never? Don't you like me well enough?'

'I like you too well to use you as a means of relieving physical tension. If I did so, there wouldn't be any possibility of your becoming pregnant! But I can get physical satisfaction anywhere.'

'How utterly sordid!' Linda turned her head away.

'If I ever make love to you again, Linda, it'll be because I'm going to marry you. But it won't happen again. That's quite definite!'

Linda sighed, for although she was determined to do her best to see that Arthur's resolve was not definite, she hadn't much to be cheerful about. Wisely deciding to change the subject before Arthur announced any more rash vows, she said, 'I must congratulate Edith on her engagement.'

'Oh, you saw it in the paper?'

'Yes. I'll come back with you after the match and tell her personally.'

'Can't you phone her? I might not be going straight home!'

'Yes, you are. You came here in flannels, remember, so you could rush out on the field without speaking. You'll have to go home to change before you can go out.' She added mischievously, 'I may even stay to supper.'

'Well – er – I don't know. Edith might not . . .'

'Edith's a charming and competent hostess. She wouldn't bat an eyelid at having an unexpected guest for supper.'

'I didn't mean that,' Arthur lied. 'I was going to say that Edith doesn't spend twenty-four hours a day, seven days a week, ministering to our comforts! She has interests of her own. Dad and I might even have to provide our own supper!'

'That's all right! If Edith's there, I'm sure she won't mind. If she's not at home, I'll take pot luck with you and your father, who won't mind either. In fact, I could get supper for all of us.'

'Linda! By God, I could spank you! Preferably with this bloody bat!'

Red and angry, Arthur got to his feet and stalked towards the pavilion, swinging his bat forcefully, as though preparing it – and his arm – for that very purpose.

Chapter 12

Edith took the letters from the hand of Harry, the postman, at the back door and walked across the scullery to her office. Harry stayed to exchange morning chat with Mavis Marshall who would no doubt offer him a cup of tea from the half-empty pot which still stood on the Aga. There was a letter-box in the external office door specially designed for the farm mail and since it was approached from the front of the house, was consequently nearer to the farm drive, but Edith had long since given up expecting the postman to use it. Harry and his predecessors had been delivering the Oakleigh letters to the breakfast table via the back door and the scullery for over sixty years and had thereby enjoyed thousands of cups of tea in total while doing so. They saw no need to save a few yards by delivering the letters to a new-fangled door which could not provide a morning cup of tea.

There had been a slight frost overnight and the air in the office was quite chilly so Edith switched on the electric fire before she made herself comfortable at her desk and started slitting the envelopes. There were only a dozen or so and, as it was the beginning of the month, they were mostly bills and she quickly sorted the contents into four lots – bills to be paid, bills to be queried, letters needing replies, and the remainder. She was disappointed again not to find a letter from George Clark agreeing to the grazing tenancy which she had arranged. He had promised to deal with it the next day, but several weeks had now passed, so she made a mental note not to trust Clark's promises again. She hoped the agreement would turn up. If it did not, her little triumph would crumple and her two partners would not hesitate to show their contempt.

The slight movement of Harry's departure on his bicycle caused her to look up and as she did so a huge car glided up amid a broken rattle of chippings and stopped in the farm gateway. George Clark got out stiffly and gazed about him.

Edith reflected that most people would have driven through into the yard and approached the back door, as was the usual custom with farmhouses, but Clark opened the garden gate and followed the flagged path to the front door. The office door was further along, facing the end of the path and a little thought

126

should have sufficed to recognise it as the business entrance, but Clark knocked vigorously on the front door several times. Mavis, in a great fluster at being called on to open it so early in the day, pulled back the bolts noisily and peered through.

'Is Miss Felton in?' the man asked the servant bluntly.

'She's in the office – the door at the end of the path,' Mrs Marshall said shortly, closing the door without waiting for a reply.

Edith had unlocked her door and when she heard Clark's bold knock she invited him in without moving from her chair.

'Good morning, Edith,' he said, entering the room and sitting down in a chair by the wall. 'You've a comfortable office here! Very nice!'

'Good morning, Mr Clark. I'm sure you didn't come here simply to pay compliments.'

'No, I didn't, and you don't have to be sarcastic, young woman. I came to bring the contract we agreed on.'

'You mean the one you were going to send me the next day?'

'There you go again! Won't give me a chance to explain, will you? I really meant to do it the next day, but my girl was ill and didn't turn up for a few days. Went straight on her holiday after that and only came back yesterday. So I haven't wasted much time have I? 'Ere's the papers. If you'd sign one and give it me back, you can send the cheque through the post.'

'You can have your cheque now, Mr Clark. It won't take more than a few seconds.'

'Can you sign cheques yourself, then?'

'Of course! At least, I can countersign them.'

She wrote quickly and handed the cheque across to him. He glanced at it automatically and put it in his inside pocket.

''Ow's your brother gettin' on?'

'Arthur? All right as far as I know. Why should you ask?'

''E didn't tell you about that little mix-up the other night, then? 'E were walkin' 'ome one night last week – Thursday I think it were – 'alf p–, 'alf drunk i' the middle o' the road. I came round the bend pretty fast and scared him into jumping into the ditch.'

'Indeed! Were you quite sober yourself?'

'Soberer than 'e were, any road. 'E were so mad 'e welted me i' the mouth. I didn't think 'e 'ad it in 'im.'

'I certainly didn't think he had it in him to brawl with you! He's gone down considerably in my estimation!'

'Don't take it too much to 'eart. No 'arm done. And while I'm

127

'ere I'd like to wish you the best on your engagement. Hope you'll be very happy!'

'Thank you. I'm sure I shall be.'

'I reckon you will. You're the right sort. Y'know, when a woman's married, she gets used to goin' to bed wi' a man and can't do wi'out it. If you ever want a change, well, I'm not the chap to say no!'

'I'm sure you're not! But as a married woman, I'm not likely to accept your invitation. Nor, I may add, should I do so as a single woman. But are you not married yourself?'

'Oh, ar! But the missis is a poor sort of a thing these days. 'Er wouldn't get in the way. We could arrange to meet somewhere else.'

'You'd better go, Mr Clark,' Edith said, smothering her disgust. 'Your car is blocking the gateway.'

'Is it? So it is. I'll go then. It's been grand seein' you. Don't forget what I said.'

'Shut the door behind you, please.'

Clark's visit quite spoilt Edith's day. Whenever her mind wandered from the present to dwell on her wedding, which was not infrequently, she felt vaguely contaminated by the fellow's suggestions.

A visit from Colin Clark a few days later quite dispelled her melancholy. After proudly showing her his new Riley he offered his own good wishes. He added wistfully, 'But I'm sorry you're going so far and for good. I'm sure we could have been wonderful friends.'

Before he left, Alison called, taking a long evening walk from her home. She told Edith that everybody was overjoyed for her, but equally sad at the thought of what her absence would mean to the village. Colin, anxious to display his driving ability gallantly offered to drive Alison home and she accepted instantly, much to Arthur's private disapproval.

The feelings expressed by Alison were general among Edith's friends and neighbours. Even Mrs Foster sent her a note which, to save postage, she handed to Len Baldock who was ploughing the adjacent field. After the usual good wishes, Edith was amused to read that the sender hoped that the reception would not cost her father too much, as money was so hard to come by these days, and ended up with various suggestions for economy, such as the use of smaller plates and the smallest glasses which could be found. 'You will need many things for your bottom drawer, of course, and I want to remind you that splendid articles can be found at jumble sales, and would cost very little. I propose to send you as a wedding present an old toby-jug. It is broken, but the piece is there, and if carefully repaired, it could pass for an antique.'

Major Ratcliffe was most eloquent in an extended chat over the telephone, speaking in glowing terms of their long acquaintance – he called it friendship, which was not quite accurate.

Dick Marshall was the saddest of all her well-wishers.

'By gum, I'll be reight sorry to see you go, Edie,' he said when he called to see her about some farm administration. He was the only one allowed to call her that without getting his head bitten off. 'Ah can remember right easy the day you were born. We'd some rare times together when you were a growin' wench. Remember? An' when you drove the tractor for me i' the cornfields, the year your grandad died? Now it's all over! You'll not live at Oakleigh again, and I feel right bad about it.'

'Do cheer up, Dick! Why, your own oldest girl is getting married next year. I hope you won't feel so badly about that.'

'Ar, but 'er won't be going so far,' Dick grumbled as he walked slowly away.

'I insist on coming to the wedding,' Edith called after him.

Linda had offered her own congratulations at the merry supper party the previous Saturday evening. Arthur had brought her home to Oakleigh, but seemed strangely dejected over it. Robert Felton, in spite of his antipathy to Linda's father, made no secret of his pleasure at seeing the daughter.

With the end of the cricket season at hand, Linda was depressed to think that her opportunities to meet Arthur would be limited or perhaps non-existent. Early in October she flaunted tradition by accompanying her father to the cricket club's annual general meeting. She was the only female present. Of course all the members except Arthur were delighted, and he, being captain, could hardly show his disappointment openly. The retiring secretary willingly surrendered his office to Colin Clark who, although not present, was proposed by the captain and seconded by the president, Major Ratcliffe. The outgoing secretary promised to give the new man as much help as necessary during the first year, and Linda volunteered to convey the news to him, a proposal which was accepted with much acclaim.

Holding steadfastly to her course, Linda boldly decided to pay a social call at Oakleigh every week or two, hoping to see Arthur, or at least hear about his doings. She knew he did not often leave home in the winter evenings, apart from NFU meetings and other farming functions and committees, dates of which were known in advance. He always patronised local events in the village hall, but with the spread of television these were becoming less frequent. When she did manage to catch him at home he was pointedly unenthusiastic, although normally polite, for his father would not have tolerated rudeness to a guest, particularly a girl so approved by himself, so Linda subdued her feelings. Whereas she had been vivacious and bubbling with mischief, now she was demure and sedate.

Edith took her to task over this. 'If you give up so easily Linda, you're a fool,' she said bluntly when the two young women were upstairs together looking over some of Edith's feminine preparations. 'You must keep trying. But I must tell you this. If you can't get Arthur by being cheerful, you certainly won't get him by being miserable. Your liveliness is just what Arthur needs. He's too much of a sober-sides. That's one reason why Alison's not the girl for him even if she wanted him, which she doesn't. She's too quiet and steady, and Arthur definitely needs livening up.'

'You think I should keep trying then?'

'Of course, Linda. *Never* give up – at least, never until you see Arthur at the altar with another woman, and if you allow that to happen, you're not the girl I think you are.'

'I always feel more confident when I'm with you, Edith, and that's a fact.'

'One thing I must say, Linda. I'm concerned about my father. When Arthur does get married his wife might think it appropriate that Dad should leave the farmhouse and buy a cottage somewhere – perhaps in the village. I wouldn't like that, Linda, and Dad wouldn't either. I think he would pine to death. He came to this house forty years ago, courted my mother here and married her, and Arthur and I were both born here, as you probably know. It's been his whole life, Linda, and it would break his heart to leave it. Still, he might offer to do so if he thought it was in the best interests of the farm and of Arthur.'

Linda clasped Edith's forearm.

'Edith, I'm very fond of your father. I almost love him already. He's one of the finest characters I've met. If I marry Arthur . . .'

'You mean 'when' don't you?'

Linda gave one of her old-time giggles, then said fervently.

'I'll look after your father as well as your mother looked after your grandfather, and that's still talked about in the village. I still remember the old man myself, quite clearly, although of course I was at school most of the time.'

'I was sure you'd feel that way Linda, but now you've said it I feel satisfied and confident. By the way, I'd like you to meet Desmond. He comes up here every second weekend, to make sure I haven't eloped with somebody else. Sometimes, on the alternate weekend I go down there, although I don't care for driving all that way and there's no direct train service. Come along to supper, say about seven o'clock, and spend the evening with us.'

'I'd love to! Will Arthur be there?'

'I'll see that he is, never fear.'

Arthur had not seen Alison since the incident of the parsnip wine and could think of no opportunity of meeting her. When Edith remarked casually that Linda was coming to supper on the Saturday, Arthur merely grunted and then said, 'Why not ask Alison as well?'

'I did,' replied Edith at once, 'but apparently Alison and her young man are going to Manchester to see Derby County play the City, and won't be back until quite late.'

Arthur grunted again and fell silent.

The party was a success. Edith had organised the meal impeccably, arranging for Jessie Allsop, wife of the cowman, to help with the serving and the washing-up. Linda, overjoyed to be invited to such an intimate gathering, was in her most sparkling mood. Desmond Salt, who could exert all the social graces when he chose, was captivated by her. No doubt feeling that with the lovely Edith safely landed he could afford himself free latitude, he was utterly charming to Linda and monopolised her attention, taking total possession when they attempted a few steps of dancing.

At first Edith was pleased at this development but when it persisted she became short in her answers. Arthur was also shaken out of his lethargy. His indignation mounted as he began to think it was damned cheek of Desmond to make free with someone else's girl, especially when his own fiancée was in the room. Putting on his best drawing-room manner, Arthur quickly set about winning Linda's company. The girl, having achieved her aim, quickly responded and as Edith soon regained her normal even temper, the evening ended on a splendidly convivial note. Possibly the happiest of them all was Robert Felton, who came out of his self-imposed shell, timidly at first, but later with enthusiasm. His son and daughter were delighted, for this was the first occasion since their mother's death that he had fully relaxed.

As the wedding day moved nearer, Edith urged her two men to make proper arrangements for their comfort when she was no longer at Oakleigh. Her father was unprepared to face the finality of her departure and would not consider at this stage the appointment of a housekeeper. Arthur was also anxious to minimise any changes in their home life and agreed with him. As a stop-gap Edith arranged for Mavis Marshall to act as a part-time housekeeper with Elsie Long and Jessie Allsop sharing the housework. Arthur was sure he could cope with the office work, provided Edith explained her system, preferably more than once. A typist could come in on Fridays to type the week's letters and perhaps operate the PAYE. Arthur was certain he could do those jobs too, but was unwilling to allocate the time.

Throughout the autumn, Edith busied herself in making her preparations for the wedding. As the number of guests would be large and the village hall unable to accommodate so many, she arranged for the reception to be at the Midland Hotel in Derby. The bridal pair would catch the three-thirty London train from the adjacent station and carry on to Southampton where they would embark on a night-sailing boat for a cruise to Tangier. The wedding was arranged for Saturday, December 2, and they hoped to return to their new home at Stokenchurch on Thursday, December 21.

The event became a topic of conversation which cropped up every evening at Oakleigh. On one such occasion, Arthur magnanimously announced that he proposed to give his sister a new Consul for a wedding present. Edith was thrilled and overwhelmingly grateful until a sudden thought struck her and she added anxiously, 'It won't be out of the farm account will it?'

'Trust you to think of that,' Arthur replied with mock severity. 'Of course not! I'm paying for it myself. I'll have your old car in part exchange though!'

'I thought there was a catch in it,' Edith said in pretended disappointment.

She went on to discuss her choice of bridesmaids.

'Bridesmaids?' queried her brother. 'What on earth does a woman of your age want with bridesmaids?'

'Don't be so bloody rude about my age,' Edith flashed. 'It's my wedding! I shall have exactly what and whom I want. I'm going to ask Linda and Alison.'

'Good God, that's worse than ever,' her brother groaned.

'Alison, yes, because she's not too tall, but Linda's taller than you are. Better have Caroline Salt; she's about the same size as Alison.'

'I'll make my own choice, thank you! I don't know Caroline all that well, but I've known Linda and Alison all my life and I think it's more appropriate to have local girls. Anyway, you're not going to be best man, so what's it to do with you?'

Arthur shrugged and fell silent. In that household Edith always achieved the last word. However, a few days before the wedding Arthur received an urgent request from Desmond – practically an SOS – to officiate as groomsman at the wedding, as Robin would be abroad on important business. Edith was doubly displeased; she thought her marriage was more important than a business conference, wherever it might be held, and she was not keen on having her brother participating in the ceremony.

Saturday, December 2, produced a morning with a sharp frost and clear air, promising sunshine later – a promise which it wholeheartedly redeemed. Desmond came up to Oakleigh on the Friday afternoon but, to conform with tradition, left before midnight to stay at the Midland Hotel where Arthur would join him in the forenoon and present him at Hartnall church just before one o'clock. Edwin and Betty Salt, with their daughter Caroline, also spent Friday night at Oakleigh. To the older Salts, their presence here recalled tender memories of their own wedding from this house in 1922. Robert had given his sister away – very willingly as he now jokingly reminded them. Tomorrow he would give away his daughter who in his eyes was as like her mother as one peach was like another from the same branch.

At eleven o'clock Arthur departed in his Jaguar to fulfil his duties and at five minutes before one o'clock Robert Felton shepherded his daughter into the bridal car for the short run to Hartnall church. As they threaded through the crowding villagers to pass under the lychgate he thought tenderly of how he had similarly escorted Betty on her great day, and then further back in time to his own wedding just before Christmas in 1914. For a second, he felt Meg was beside him once again, then the rich voice of the new organ recalled him to the present. He and Edith paced down the aisle with Linda and Alison dutifully following, to join Bob's nephew and son standing patiently at the altar steps.

Robert had always had a great affection for this village church which had been the scene of all the key moments of his life. Standing there with its imposing Norman spire for eight hundred years, it seemed remote and changeless, yet at the same time close to the heart and comforting to the spirit. The beautiful coloured windows, rich in their portrayal of Christ's ministry, had looked down on his son and daughter through all their childhood Sunday-school days, and indeed on their mother's before them. Over to the right was the Ratcliffe aisle, sombre with effigies and plaques of Linda's forebears. He wondered idly if Linda's thoughts were in the same channel. His reverie was so deep and distant that his eyes misted and he felt his head swimming. As he pulled himself together to perform his own small function, it seemed as if Meg were there beside him. She was speaking, 'I, Edith Mary take thee, Desmond Edwin . . .'

Robert pulled himself up again. His wandering mind was missing the beauty of the current ceremony. He should be happy in the present for his daughter and her husband, not wallowing in sentimental nostalgia for the past. He was proud of Edith, for she looked so regal in her charming yet simple outfit. Her cream calf-length dress which had a faint slimming effect on her strong figure; the small hat with tiny floral trimmings and a veil over the eyes only; the little bunch of button chrysanthemums of variegated colours; all combined to present a picture of supreme elegance. Linda and Alison also carried similar posies and looked most attractive in their pretty golden-brown – Robert thought he had heard the colour referred to as russet – dresses. Linda was tall and queenly with the faintest tinge of aristocratic disdain in her bearing, and Alison, dark, but with a simple beauty that was heart-warming. Robert could not help thinking that if Arthur got either of them he would be a lucky man.

Arthur was thinking how thrilling it would be when as best man he could kiss Alison legitimately. He intended to make the most of his opportunities and the first occurred as the party emerged from the church. A pale sun shone feebly from a cloudless sky, pleasing the bride and the photographers, both professional and amateur. Arthur seized Alison and kissed her voraciously, hugging her tightly, refusing to relinquish his hold even when she thumped him hard between the shoulder-blades. Alison was dutiful enough but this was too much of a good thing, although she felt she could hardly make a scene in a merry wedding group. Arthur was wearing the lightest of shoes so she trod hard on his toe and he painfully took the hint.

He casually limped over to kiss Linda, who however did not

intend to be kissed casually. She flung her arms round his neck and hung on like a reaching bramble, much to his embarrassment. He did not so much object to Linda, but since he had been much closer than kissing, and since he knew he could take her more or less any time he desired, the public embrace had no novelty. He could hardly tread on her toe as Alison had done to him, so he lowered his hand and slapped her hard on the bottom, not caring who noticed the action. Linda did not care either, although she flinched and coloured, for she hoped that to bystanders it implied a secret intimacy.

The church had been filled to capacity, for Edith was a native, a member of a well-known family and had personally been popular all her life. Not every member of the huge crowd had been invited and among these was Linda's father, the former squire, Major Mortimer Ratcliffe, who, in addition to knowing the bride all her life, had also known her mother since early childhood. Ordinary villagers moved respectfully aside as he approached her and said courteously, 'Edith, allow me to offer my very best wishes for your total happiness. My dear, you look radiant, quite the loveliest woman of my time.'

Edith blushed deeply, her father looked very straight while Linda whispered sharply, 'Don't overdo it, Daddy!'

The George Clark family were there too. Clark himself, massive, bland but pugnacious; Mrs Clark, slight, pale, insignificant and patient; the eleven-year-old daughter Patricia, taking everything in with wide eyes, and Colin looking happy and involved at the thought that the bride had been his friend, tinged perhaps with melancholy that he would probably see her no more. Mostly his eyes were on Alison who looked so sweet in her pretty bridesmaid's dress, and he looked positively angry when Arthur kissed her with such obtrusive ardour.

The Oakleigh farm staff were present in force, led by Dick Marshall, upright in spite of his bulk, and smart in his new grey suit. Mavis was with him, big and homely, and their four sons and daughters. Edith looked across and caught his eye, which glistened for he was recalling that as a teenage youth he had often guided her toddling steps. Impulsively Edith walked over, put her arms on his shoulders and kissed him full on the lips. 'That's for thirty years' loyalty, Dick,' she said with a tremulous laugh and handed him her tiny bouquet. 'You know what to do with this,' she murmured and nodded towards the churchyard stile.

'Ah do that, Edith,' he muttered and Edith was further moved when Linda and Alison handed him their own flowers. Followed impulsively by Betty Salt, Dick carried them down the churchyard path to Meg Felton's grave.

The bride and bridegroom entered their beribboned car and headed the long motorcade to the Midland Hotel where, after the luncheon, the cake-cutting, the toasts and the speeches, Edith and Desmond left by the afternoon express for London, on their way to Southampton where they spent their wedding night aboard the vessel which was to convey them to Tangier.

Arthur and his father, together with Betty and Edwin Salt, remained to entertain the guests with music and dancing which extended into the late hours. Arthur, who loved dancing and considered himself an expert, had no shortage of partners. As well as Linda and Alison whom he favoured most, he found he was expected to dance, and indeed enjoyed doing so, with Aunt Betty and Cousin Caroline, Mavis Marshall and the other farm wives as well as numerous friends from the village and other relatives who had gathered together for this major event in the Felton/Ratcliffe family. He danced with Linda as if by right and thoroughly enjoyed himself, for having been well coached in childhood she approached perfection. He partnered Alison many times too, and was pleased that she did not resent his continual invitations. Although mainly self-taught, Alison danced well, too, with a natural grace and did not lack other partners. As the evening wore on and her shyness evaporated, Alison began to feel that the party had been a personal success. She felt she now had the measure of Arthur and was convinced that he would go no further than she allowed, so she enjoyed herself thoroughly.

Linda was in great demand by all the males and could be reasonably described as the belle of the evening. She was not quite so happy when at about eleven o'clock she saw Arthur and Alison leave the hotel together. Alison had no car of her own and no regular escort, and when Arthur enquired considerately if he could drive her to Hilltop Farm she saw no reason to refuse.

Chapter 13

The night was bright and clear as they set off. Arthur swung easily into Midland Road, across the London Road into Regent Street and turned left into Osmaston Road. To get home he must cross the Trent in one of two places, Swarkestone or Willington, and decided on the former as being not only nearer, but offering one or two riverside pull-offs if such were needed. So he headed south-east down the long straight highway. There was no need to hurry for they had the whole night before them.

Alison complained that the car was stuffy and wound down her window to its fullest extent. In fact, the keen air cut in sharply and Arthur looked across in surprise. He thought the atmosphere was much more intimate with the windows closed, which was exactly what Alison thought. Seeking entertainment, she explored the dash, fingering a knob or two.

> Put another nickel in,
> In the nickelodeon,
> All I want is loving you,
> And music, music, music,

sang the rich brave voice of Teresa Brewer.

The song pleased Arthur. He looked across at his passenger.

'That's a lovely tune, Alison. Quite my favourite among the current hits.'

'We certainly hear a lot of it,' she agreed. 'That's about the sixth time to-day.'

> Closer, my dear, come closer . . .

the chorus came round the second time. Arthur leaned his body across so that their shoulders touched.

'Alison,' he said softly, 'that's exactly what I'd like you to do!'

'Oh Arthur! I thought we'd done with that! Look out . . !'

A roaring, low vehicle with blazing headlights swung madly out of Osmaston Park Road, tried to straighten up, wavered, then skidded obliquely towards them across the main thoroughfare. Instantly reacting to the pressing danger, Arthur pushed hard on the brake and snatched his steering wheel to the left. He had overdone it and before he could correct his violent manoeuvre, the Jaguar checked, its nearside front wing struck a lamp standard. As the metal crunched and the glass tinkled, Alison, with a gracefulness which was terrifying, sailed head first out of her window, to land on her head and shoulder with a flat, sickening thud, on the flagged pavement.

Arthur's firm grip on the steering wheel, one foot braced against the brake pedal and the other on the clutch, wedged him firmly in his seat and prevented his crashing through the windscreen. Apart from a slight bruising of his lower chest he seemed unhurt. He conquered his nausea and his feeling of shock and scrambled out of the car on to the pavement. Alison was lying in a crumpled heap, shivering slightly and either moaning softly or breathing noisily – he could not be sure. He was sure she was alive, however, but for how long? He had seen plenty of dying and dead in his six years of war and knew the dangers of moving a person indiscriminately. The temptation was strong, but he refrained from touching her.

There was no other traffic about and all the houses in this part of the road were dark and silent. It might take minutes to rouse somebody and demand the use of a telephone. Then he recalled there was a sub post office not too far up the road; he could run there quicker than he could waken a sleeping household. He took one step, then vaguely remembering from his first aid courses the urgency of keeping the patient warm, he darted back to the car and snatched a heavy rug from the rear seat. Hastily adjusting the pretty bridesmaid's dress, of which Alison had been so proud, he tenderly covered her up to the neck. Then he was off with long, loping strides, his light evening shoes scarcely touching the pavement. His memory had not been at fault for the red-framed glass box stood beside the kerb less than two hundred yards back. Breathlessly he dialled for the ambulance and the police, giving the exact location, then sprinted back to his crumpled car.

Sickeningly, his radio was still emitting its programme of popular music.

> I've got a luverly bunch of coconuts,
> There they are, a-standin' in a row
> Big ones, small ones, some as big as your 'ead . . .

With an expression of revulsion he reached through the open window and switched off the hideously inappropriate Cockney song.

Under the rug Alison was now very still, apart from the slight flutter of her quieter breathing but, true to his training, he declined to touch her although he knelt on one knee close to her pallid face. The ambulance arrived ahead of the police car and the attendants efficiently prepared to move the injured girl. Glancing at her position and her bruises the senior man muttered, 'Looks like a back injury, Jack. We'll treat it like that, anyway.'

They laid her, fully extended and padded securely, on the stretcher. 'Watch the tongue, Jim,' said the man and they lifted the stretcher, keeping it perfectly level, and slid it into the vehicle. Arthur went to climb in after her, but paused when the police sergeant spoke to him. 'About a statement, sir, – and the removal of your car!'

'Good God, man, I must go with the girl! The statement can wait awhile, surely! The car? – Yes, I leave it to you to get it moved to the nearest breakdown garage and let me know in due course.'

'Very well, sir. We'll follow you to the hospital and take particulars there.'

The journey in the ambulance was short, since Alison was to be taken to the Derby Royal Infirmary at the upper end of Osmaston Road. The attendant told Arthur this, and tried to make other conversation but got no reply. The young man's only concern was for the injured girl – his mind refused to function on any other topic.

The ambulance changed direction, turned round gently to the faint splattering of gravel, invisible hands opened the doors and Alison was carefully transferred to a wheeled stretcher and pushed through an entrance marked 'Casualty'. A burly, handsome staff-nurse and her assistant fluttered round in anxious attendance.

'Oh, what a lovely dress,' the junior girl said as the blankets were removed. 'Was it for something special?'

'She was a bridesmaid less than twelve hours ago,' Arthur answered, hardly able to keep his voice from breaking. He moved in to the trolley as close as he was allowed. The staff-nurse scrutinised him with formal but genuine sympathy.

'You were the driver?' and when Arthur nodded wordlessly she went on, 'You've had a severe shock. Do you feel OK? Sit down in the corridor. You are going to wait?' Arthur inclined his head again. She became business-like. 'How long has she been unconscious?'

'Twenty-eight minutes,' Arthur said with military efficiency, after glancing at his watch.

'As near as you can, tell me exactly what happened.' Arthur complied and she continued, speculatively, 'It's possibly a fracture, and there'll be some concussion, of course. Is she a relative? Your wife, or fiancée, perhaps?'

'No, but she was about to be. I'm a very close friend!'

'The doctor will be here in a few seconds, and after an examination and an X-ray we will be able to tell you the extent of her injuries.'

The two nurses pushed Alison into the examination room and the senior made preliminary tests to gauge the depth of the unconsciousness. She found the pulse rapid and weak, raised the eyelids and examined the pupils with her pencil torch. Alison's breathing was shallow and quick.

'We'd better get her things off. Watch carefully; we must keep her airway clear.'

The young house-surgeon arrived on the scene, walking briskly as he buttoned up his impeccable white coat. He was fresh and alert, for although it was past midnight, this was the first casualty since he had come on duty.

'What have we here, nurse?' he asked cheerfully. 'Road casualty or domestic squabble?' He looked down at the patient, visualising her appearance in full health. 'My God, what a lovely girl! It's always the prettiest who get carried in here!'

'That's true, doctor. The prettiest and the unluckiest. This one's straight from a wedding reception – one of the bridesmaids.'

'How long has she been out?'

'The man who was driving her said the crash occurred at 11.35. She's deeply unconscious, doctor – here's her chart.'

'You're right. She appears to be badly hurt at the top end, but there are no complicated fractures of the limbs. Get her on oxygen and give X-ray a ring. We must know the extent of her injuries as soon as possible. She can have her test dose of ATS on return. Better prepare an intravenous drip. Clean her up while you're waiting.'

'Yes, Doctor. Nurse Bailey can get on with that.'

She went out into the corridor where Arthur was still conversing with the policeman.

'Sorry to interrupt, you two, but I must have some personal details for the file.'

She took down Arthur's replies to her questions and when it

140

came to the enquiry for the next of kin, Arthur said hastily, 'I will notify her parents myself.'

'Sorry Mr Felton,' the policeman interjected. 'that's our job, and one we must not pass on to anybody else. I'll phone the station, and they'll deal with it.'

The nurse continued, 'We are taking Miss King up for X-ray in a few minutes and so we shall be able to tell you the extent of her injuries in, say, half-an-hour. Would you like another cup of tea? It would do you good.'

Arthur assented, for the mug of the strong sweet beverage supplied earlier had nearly restored him to normalcy and had enabled him to face the police questions without trepidation or impatience.

'A little later on, we'll have a look at you, Mr Felton,' the nurse said, becoming authoritative. 'Your involuntary movements indicate there might be some frontal bruising. It won't take long to give you the once over.'

'I'm all right, I tell you! Young woman, I fought in Burma for three years, and other places before that, and I've seen plenty of wounded men! I know what injuries are!'

'No doubt! But when you were in the army, Mr Felton, I'm sure you followed the orders of the Medical Officer. We'd like the same compliance here!'

'Oh, all right!' Arthur glowered at her so she added, 'I'll run over you myself.'

When she had disappeared, the police sergeant took over again.

'Did you see the other fellow's number, sir?'

'No, of course not! His headlights were blazing so I obviously couldn't read the front plate and equally obviously I didn't scramble out of a crashed car quickly enough to read his rear plates!'

'Quite so, sir. Did he really drive wide enough to force you into the lamp standard?'

'I don't know for sure. Possibly I misjudged. One can't always gauge the margin of evasion necessary in a split-second judgment. My reaction hasn't done any good, apparently. If I'd let him crash into me the result could hardly have been worse – certainly for Miss King.'

'Where were you coming from, sir?'

'From a reception at the Midland. My sister's wedding. Alison was one of the bridesmaids.'

'You'd been drinking then, sir?'

'Of course! One does at a wedding.'

'Well sir, you're bound to be in some state of shock after this dreadful occurrence, so it's not much use applying the usual sobriety tests. Are you sure you were fit to drive?'

'Of course I was,' Arthur said, showing irritation for the first time. 'Do you imagine I would have attempted to drive home in a drunken state with a girl I was very fond of?'

'It has been known, sir.' He put his book away. 'You'll be hearing from us in due course. Certainly your statement will be needed if there is an inquest.'

'Inquest?'

'Yes, sir. Not all road casualties recover, as you must be aware, and this young lady's very badly injured. Now, can we take you home?'

'No, thank you. I must wait to see how Alison is. I suppose there are all-night taxis? I'll get one home in due course.'

The police car roared away. Arthur waited impatiently in the corridor, sitting on one of the highly-polished forms occasionally, but mainly pacing up and down the mosaic floor with all the pointlessness of a caged animal. He shivered from time to time and assumed this was due to the freezing conditions outside instead of his own emotional state, for the building was well-heated. One interruption, surprisingly not unwelcome, came when the buxom staff-nurse called him into another examination room where he resignedly stripped to the waist. The girl pushed and prodded until she was quite satisfied.

'My word, you're in splendid condition, Mr Felton,' she said admiringly, 'and there's nothing wrong at all except that nasty little bruise on your lower chest. I think it is only superficial, but if you're in any more pain tomorrow, call in and see your doctor. Thank you for being so co-operative.'

Arthur dressed and resumed his pacing in the corridor but at one o'clock the pleasant nurse came out again, called him and waved him silently to the open door of the duty office. Behind the flat-topped desk sat a young doctor, fair-headed, fresh-faced and confident.

'Mr Felton, I understand? I suppose I ought to say "Good morning", although it seems a little odd at this very small hour. You were driving Miss King, I think? Were you engaged to her?'

'Well, not yet. Why do you ask?'

'We cannot disclose intimate details of a patient's condition to someone who is a mere friend. However, as you were driving the car you are entitled to know the broad outline. Miss King is still suffering from concussion and until she recovers consciousness we shall not know for sure if there is any brain damage. I can only say at present that there appears to be none.

'However, there is a fracture of the upper spine, caused by the violent impact. Various nerves could be affected, some badly, some slightly. This part of the spinal nervous system controls the movement of the limbs. It seems possible that she will be unable to move them for some time. In short, Mr Felton, your girl-friend has broken her neck and will be in hospital for a very long time.'

'May I see her now?' In his misery, Arthur could think of nothing else to say.

'I'm afraid not. Her parents have been notified and are on their way, but no one else can see her to-night. I suggest you ring tomorrow and enquire if any visitors other than her next of kin can be accepted. I offer you my sympathies, Mr Felton, but it was inevitable that the injuries would be severe. The human body cannot land headfirst on a stone surface and remain unaffected.'

He held out his hand which Arthur took mechanically, accepting this as his dismissal. Sick and shivering, he telephoned for a taxi. The driver, being unfamiliar with country roads, had to be supplied with running directions and this alone prevented Arthur from sinking into a stupor of melancholy. When they arrived at Oakleigh, he was surprised to see the lights still on in the kitchen and was further astonished when, on entering, he found his father, comfortably drinking coffee but wide awake and very bad tempered. Feeling totally exhausted, Arthur sat down heavily and reached for the coffee pot.

Robert's resentment had been shaping itself for a couple of hours; his reprimands, criticisms and complaints were already formed into words and the words into sentences, ready to be launched at their target. They were too pressing and too pithy to be delayed. He delivered his broadside without even noticing his son's shocked and despondent bearing, and Arthur was too weary to interrupt.

'Where the hell have *you* been? Shooting off like that with Alison and leaving Linda to take care of herself. I left it to you as best man to look after both the bridesmaids. Disgraceful, leaving Linda to practically hitch-hike a lift home!'

'Charles was there with the cricket team; why didn't he take her home?'

'He'd already gone with some of his pals before I knew Linda was stranded.'

'Couldn't she have got a taxi?'

This casual solution inflamed Robert still further. He considered he was justly angry and intended to express it.

'She'd no money with her! A girl doesn't go to a wedding with a fistful of pound notes! You acted damned selfishly and upset everybody else's plans. I had to see Dick and rearrange the farm chaps and their families. I reclaimed my car from him – which was a bit much – put him and Mavis in the back and wedged their two girls in with 'em, so that Linda and I could sit in front. All the rest of the farm people had to cram into the Land-Rover and Edith's Consul, except for two who couldn't squeeze in and they piled into Edwin's car. He wasn't very pleased either! Made a hell of a squash, I can tell you. Worse than that – when I'd dropped off the Marshalls, I drove Linda home, naturally. She invited me in and I'm damned if her father wasn't still up. It was a whole bloody hour before I could get away. Of course, he was very gushing, but I don't want to spend time in Mortimer Ratcliffe's company. I've disliked and despised him for forty years and I'm not going to change my opinion now! Only got home a few minutes ago. Betty and Edwin and Caroline have been in bed an hour or two, I reckon.'

Having freed his mind of these strictures, Robert's temper went quickly off the boil, and he allowed himself the indulgence to look at his erring son with seeing eyes.

'My God, man! What's the matter? You look as if you've seen a ghost and he's knocked you down! What's happened?'

'Crashed the car!'

'How the hell did that happen? You've never even scratched it before – nor any other car!'

'Some bloody fool in a sports car came charging out of Osmaston Park Road and headed straight for us. I swerved and hit a lamp post.'

'Oh hell, no wonder you look bad. But you're not hurt, that's one good thing, and you easily could have been. Alison's all right too, I hope?'

'No Dad. She's broken her spine and will be in hospital for evermore, or something like it.'

'What? What? Broken her spine? For God's sake, Arthur, what are you saying? I can't believe it! Oh no! It can't be! How could this happen to such a delightful girl, and on Edith's wedding day too?'

Robert Felton was so agitated he got up and paced the room, clenching and unclenching his fists, striving to comprehend the tragedy which had enveloped them.

'Nothing we can do about it, Dad. God, how I wish I could relive the last three hours!'

'Do her parents know?'

'They were notified by the police and were trying to get to the hospital, I think. It'd be difficult from their place at that time o' night – short o' hiring. I didn't stay to see them – couldn't ha' faced them just then. I must call and see them after breakfast, though. God knows how they'll take it.'

'Why the hell didn't you ring me? I'd ha' gone over there and took 'em in. Be glad to!'

'I didn't know if you'd be here, or where you'd be! Could ha' tried I suppose. Too dazed to think of it, I reckon.'

'It's like a blight on the wedding! Every guest will be affected by it. What about Edith? Can we let her know?'

'She's on her way now, Dad! I suppose we could get in touch by radio, but it wouldn't be easy, and what good would it do. The boat was due out at ten o'clock. It can't turn round, and they can't get off it! No! Let her enjoy her honeymoon, I say – she's earned it. But when she gets home she'll kill us for not telling her!'

'As you say, Arthur. But let's try to get some sleep now. The tragedy of it! Hartnall'll be a sad place i' the morning.'

He turned as he reached the door to the hall.

'If there's any mortal thing that Alison needs – attention, appliance or whatever – it'll be on us!'

'Of course, of course. What's a thousand pounds or two compared with the wreck of a girl's life? I'm fully covered, of course, and the insurance company will pay up, but months may elapse before that happens. In the meantime, I'm her banker.'

'The farm is her banker, you mean. Neither I nor Edith will be shut out of this!'

Oakleigh Farm was certainly struck by melancholy when Arthur told them the sad news. Although it was Sunday, most of the men had minor chores to do in connection with cows, sheep or other stock. Every member of the staff, complete with his whole family had been guests at the wedding, and Alison was a general favourite. Arthur would have liked to visit Gene and Kathleen King straight away, but knew that on a dairy farm the interruption of the morning milking would not have been favourably received. He decided to go over just before nine o'clock, when breakfast would be finished. He went into the house for his own meal at eight o'clock, feeling hungry in spite of his ordeal, absorbed Mavis' tearful comments and sat down to breakfast with his father and the Salt family who were also visibly affected. The breakfast hour on a busy farm is a recognised telephoning time for business contacts, but not on Sunday, and halfway through his bacon and eggs, Arthur was astonished to receive a call – from Linda.

'Why are you calling at this time in the morning, Linda?' he said irritably. 'We've enough to deal with here, without spending time in idle chat.'

'It's not idle chat to offer sympathy for poor Alison, is it?'

'Sorry Linda. How on earth did you know?'

'The press has been on the phone already this morning – you know, the *Derby Telegraph*. I knew their girl who covered the wedding. Their night staff heard of the accident and Sarah rang me to confirm it. Arthur! I'm just overwhelmed! How utterly tragic for that poor girl and her parents!'

'It just doesn't bear thinking about, Linda.'

'What about you? Not hurt, I hope?' the voice sounded particularly anxious.

'No, I'm hundred per cent physically but pretty low in spirits, I can tell you. I wish it had been me instead of, or at least, as well as Alison. I feel hellishly guilty.'

'You weren't to blame.'

'I can't say that, positively. I swerved too much, or perhaps not quickly enough – through not paying attention, maybe. I'm carrying a heavy load, Linda.'

'Oh come, Arthur. Don't talk like that! I won't have it! You're the most skilful driver in the county. You must pull yourself together, and we must all look after Alison's interests.'

'It's nice of you to say that, Linda, in view of the – well, competition between you and Alison. Or is it?' he ended coldly.

There was silence for a few seconds. Then Linda spoke again, subdued, yet passionate.

'Arthur, I've always wanted you; still do want you and always shall. But I don't want to win you this way. Not this way! You shouldn't have said that.' She put down the receiver with a broken sob.

Arthur finished his breakfast quickly and drove over to Hilltop Farm, using Edith's former car which he had temporarily retained. Her new car, shining and unblemished was locked in the spare garage until after the honeymoon. He had been proud of his wedding gift to his sister; how unimportant it all seemed now.

Gene King was just leaving the kitchen when Arthur arrived. He paused when the car appeared in the yard, and Mrs King hastily finished clearing the table. The older man was struck by Arthur's haggard look, for the young man's night had been sleepless as well as being short. Arthur was shocked by Mr and Mrs King's expression of total melancholy and utter exhaustion, and did not know how to begin what he felt he ought to say. It was left to Mrs King to break the awkward silence.

'Good of you to come over, Mr Felton. At least you can tell us exactly how it happened.'

'There were no monkeyin' about i' the car, was there?' King asked, half accusingly.

'There was not, Gene. Alison would never have stood for it, as you should know – at least she wouldn't have stood for it from me!'

'I dunno. Parents don't know much about what the youngsters get up to these days.'

'I'm not saying I'm blameless,' Arthur said miserably at the end of his story. 'I either reacted too quickly or not quickly enough, but at the rate the other chap was going, if we'd collided we'd all have gone up in smoke which would ha' been worse.'

'It could hardly 'a been worse for Alison,' her father said mournfully. 'Whatever they may say to cheer us up or to smooth it over, a fractured spine is about as bad as anything could be. It's the nerve-centre of the body!'

'True enough,' Arthur muttered sadly, wondering what else he could say. He knew himself to be pessimistic by nature and must try desperately to conquer it. 'But I haven't seen her yet. How is she this morning? I phoned, but they wouldn't tell me anything. Said they preferred to have telephone calls from near relatives only.'

'Aye, that's how it is. Her come round while we were in there between two and three this morning – she knew us, thank God. We can see her this afternoon, some time between two and four.'

'They said I could see her now. Will it be all right if I go? Can I run you in?'

'Well, my old car is off the road at the moment, so we were going by bus from Repton. Can't stand many taxi runs like this morning!'

'I'll drive you in, then. Call for you at one-thirty, so that we're there early. Alison mustn't think she's neglected.'

'That's thoughtful, Arthur. We'll come out in time for you to go in and see her for a few minutes. Only two at a time, you know.' He took the younger man's hand. 'One thing I'm certain of, it warn't intentional. If there were owt you could ha' done to avoid it, I'm sure you'd ha' done it. It's just Alison's bad luck – and ours! Things'll never be the same at Hilltop Farm again – never.'

'Things'll never be the same at Oakleigh again, either,' Arthur said to himself as he drove the car out of the yard. 'Not with this load on my conscience. How can I ever find enjoyment in anything again?'

Chapter 14

Arthur bolted his lunch – much to Mavis Marshall's dismay – and picked up Alison's parents at exactly one-thirty. Dropping them off at the hospital entrance, he parked the Consul in a nearby street, for on Sundays business traffic was negligible. Then he hurried back and waited impatiently in the passage outside the orthopaedic ward. The Kings had already gone in and there were bold notices displayed outside the door, positively limiting visitors to two per patient.

He sat there for more than an hour, tapping his feet with impatience, wishing he had brought a Sunday newspaper. Not that he was interested in that sort of reading, but he would have felt more at ease with something in his hands – something behind which he could hide his head. Other people were waiting too, and some of them nodded and smiled sympathetically. It would have been easy to enter into a conversation, but Arthur had never felt less like chatting in his life.

Alison's father and mother came out of the ward together, Mr King in the act of blowing his nose vigorously, while Mrs King's eyes were unashamedly wet. They sat down on the bench vacated by Arthur who, with a chilling feeling of guilt, strode unsteadily in.

He spotted Alison at once, halfway along the ward and when he was still two or three beds away, he saw her large eyes roll sideways towards him. Only her eyes and lips were moveable, for she lay absolutely flat, with pulleys and weights suspended from her head and feet to keep her in that position. Heavy bandages covered the dressings on her facial injuries. Her pitiful appearance almost choked him, but he forced a smile, placed his hand gently on the uncovered part of her cheek and said, 'Hello, Alison! May I kiss you?'

'Yes, Arthur,' she said weakly. 'It can't do any harm now.'

He bent over and kissed her on the lips. A tear dropped on the bridge of her nose which he hastily wiped away with his own hanky, for her hands hung limp and useless.

'I'm sorry about this, Alison – utterly shattered! My God, I wish it was me lying there instead of you!'

'Don't say that. It wasn't your fault! If that crazy fool hadn't come round the corner . . . I'm so glad you're not hurt. The nurses told me you were all right. It's much better that it had to be me instead of you. You've always been so active, with your soldiering, your cricket, farming, shooting and all that. I'm going to be here a long time, I'm afraid.'

'You mustn't want for anything, Alison. Everything you can possibly need or use will be on me. Any attention, any specialist, any appliance, any convalescence – just say, and it'll be provided.'

Alison made a feeble attempt to smile.

'That's kind, Arthur, but not necessary. My people are not penniless, you know.'

'Are you all right for money now?'

'Yes, and I shall be. The revenue pay my full salary for six months, and half salary for another six months, and I'm sure to be back at work by then!'

Arthur caught his breath. He hoped there would be some miracle to make that possible.

'I'll come in to see you as often as visits are allowed, Alison. I think a hell of a lot of you, as I'm sure you know – more now than I did before.'

She smiled sadly and tried to turn her head away, but it would not move.

'You'll have so many visitors, we may have to work out a roster,' he went on. 'All our chaps will want to come in to see you, then there'll be your office colleagues as well and, of course, your fiancé – he must be out of his mind, poor chap!'

Alison seemed surprised.

'Adrian? Didn't you know? He went to Australia in October and I was to join him as soon as he'd saved up enough to pay a deposit on a house.'

Her eyes filled with tears and Arthur cursed himself for bringing the matter up.

'We'll have to do all the more to make it up to you, Alison.'

To his relief, the bell for departure tinkled at that moment, and he kissed her again, gripping her upper arm through the blankets, hoping she could feel the fond pressure. Halfway to the door he paused and looked back. Her eyes had followed him to the full extent of their movement, and he raised his arm, silently and sadly. Feeling ill at ease, he rejoined Alison's parents and led the way to his car for the journey home. All the talk was of the injured girl and Arthur, in his guilt-ridden mood, could find little to say. Mr King expressed his intention of going to the infirmary every visiting day and looked forward to having the repairs to his own car completed. This put Arthur conversationally on firmer ground.

'If you're ever stuck for a car for the hospital trip, Gene, let me know a bit beforehand and we'll fix you up with something. Either this or the Land-Rover or the old Commer pick-up. It would get you there. In fact, if your car's off the road for any length of time you could keep the pick-up over at Hilltop until you get your own back.'

'That's right kind of you, Arthur. I appreciate it and I understand your feelings.'

'Another thing, Gene. If you get in a flap with the milking because of your hospital visits, I can send someone in to act as relief.'

'Thanks again, Arthur. It's not likely to be necessary. My cowman, Stanley, is a good sort o' chap, steady and reliable and not likely to let us down. But you never know – he might fall ill, and it's comforting to know there'd be somebody in the background to slip in.'

When they arrived at the Kings' home, they were all surprised to see Colin Clark's car in the yard, with the owner sitting patiently behind the wheel. Arthur would have liked to speak to the young man, but realising that Colin was there to offer sympathy to the Kings, which was clearly a private matter, he merely waved an acknowledgement and drove away. He had no doubt that Colin was consulting Alison's parents about his own proposed visits to the girl, which, since the boy's office was in Derby, would present no difficulty. Arthur was relieved to think that Alison would have an unending stream of visitors.

For days Arthur went about his work with a heavy heart. Everyone at Oakleigh was similarly subdued and, appreciating the young gaffer's position, were sympathetic to a man. Robert Felton was sad, too. Essentially a kind man, he could hardly bear the thought of such a pleasant young woman, of whom he was quite fond, being struck down at the crest of her youth. He visited Alison once and she was touched by his obvious concern, just as he was touched by her own observant solicitude.

'You're not walking so well as usual, Mr Felton!'

'No? I was wounded in that leg in the first war, you know – well over thirty years ago now, by gum! It still plays me up sometimes when we get a succession of wet days, and I start limping badly.'

'I wish I could limp,' Alison said in a very small but matter-of-fact voice, almost as if to herself, and Robert choked back his emotion at this unconscious disclosure of the girl's feelings.

As there was a group of other visitors crowding in the corridor he did not stay long and decided he would postpone further attendance until some of the early enthusiasm and imperativeness of her more distant friends had worn off.

Arthur had no such inhibitions. He timed his visits to take place when her parents were not present and cared nothing for mere colleagues waiting outside for he thought he had both a prior and proprietary right to stay with the girl. He was even more drawn to her in her helpless state than he had been when she was in full vigour, but as their general interests diverged their conversation was restricted.

As he and his father sat by their fire in the evenings, Alison's plight would erupt in every topic, and thoughts of the girl filled his mind as he went about his work on the farm. He began to welcome all distractions from it, necessary, expected and unexpected. Consequently he was not displeased when Jimmy Dunn, who had been trimming the long hedge which separated the Oakleigh land from that of Mrs Foster at Lower Sucklings, appeared at the farm for new instructions, and told him that Mrs Foster would like to see the young gaffer, 'rather urgently'.

'Er said if I towd you, it'd save the cost of a stamp as it warn't urgent enough to warrant that expenditure.'

Arthur could not help smiling to himself in spite of his inner melancholy, for Mrs Foster's parsimony was well known in the district. He decided to drive round there that very day, have a look at Jimmy's work, and call at Lower Sucklings at the same time. He drove into the little yard which was neatly kept in an economical way, and knocked on the kitchen door. The old lady appeared at once. She was tiny and frail-looking, although she moved quickly for her eighty-odd years, and her eyes flashed strong and keen from her lined face beneath the thin grey hair.

'Good morning, Arthur! I'm glad to see you. Don't often come into my yard, do you? I can do with some advice and I know you'll give it me free. Is that Edith's old car? I thought it was. I suppose your fine new one was smashed up in that terrible accident!'

'It was a sad business, Mrs Foster.'

'Indeed it was. That poor girl! I liked Alison. She wasn't always flashing her money about like some of these youngsters. But do you know, Arthur, somebody told me that the government will pay her wages in full for six months! Isn't that a terrible expense for the country? Full wages for no work at all. In that sense, she's a lucky girl!'

Arthur could hardly control his anger as he replied,

'I understand that's the usual procedure in the Civil Service. They're not making an exception especially for Alison! But I'm sure you didn't ask me round here to discuss her financial position!'

'No, indeed! But I was thinking how impossible it would be for a farmer to do that with an injured employee. Thank goodness we don't have to pay our labourers when they fall sick.'

'There's no law to prevent us!' Arthur said coldly.

'Oh dear, you're joking, of course. But I'd like your view on a very important thing which has just occurred to me. It's about my man in the cottage. I don't charge him any rent for it although, as you know, we're allowed to deduct six shillings.'

'No farmer round here deducts the allowable rent!'

'Oh, really? Well, this chap Harrison has his mother living with him as well as his wife and two schoolgirl daughters. Now, this old woman gets the old age pension and I think she should pay me something out of it each week – say ten shillings – for the use of the room. What do you think?'

Arthur was silent for a minute or two, groping with this new angle of labour relations.

'They're not overcrowded in there, are they?' he said at length.

'Oh no, it's a three-bedroom cottage. You've seen it enough times, but I daresay you've never been inside. It's in splendid condition too, now. Harrison had redecorated it all through, and hasn't asked me to pay for any of the materials, which is a great relief.'

'He seems to be a good workman from what I've seen of him.'

'Oh yes, I'm very pleased with his performance. He's probably the best man I've had here.'

'And did this aged relative live with him at the time you engaged him?'

'Yes, she's lived with him for some years, I believe – at his employer's expense, of course.'

'Then she's a regular member of his family, or at least of his establishment, and he has the right to occupy the house with his family as part of his wages. One does not expect members of a workman's family to pay bits and pieces as their share of the rent! It's unheard of – indeed, unthinkable.'

'Well, when the two girls leave school I shall expect them to pay me a few shillings out of their wages in return for their bedroom. I'm not sure your view is the legal position, Arthur.'

'It may not be the legal position, but I can assure you it's the customary practice, which is what matters in country life, and farming in particular. If you doubt my knowledge, why ask me at all? Why not apply to the secretary of the NFU? It's part of his job to answer queries.'

'I'm not a member.'

'Then you should join, of course. Every farmer should belong to it. The subscription is less than one-and-six an acre per year, I think.'

'Heavens above! That would be more than two pounds a year! I couldn't possibly afford that from this little place!'

Arthur, unwilling to trust himself to say any more, turned to get into his car. Mrs Foster called out, 'One moment!' and scurried into the kitchen with surprising agility. She returned almost immediately with two large wrinkled eating apples.

'Perhaps you'll take these in to Alison next time you go. Tell her they're from me. I'm not sure that I can get in myself; the bus fares are so high.'

For the rest of the afternoon Arthur's mind was so occupied by this extraordinary encounter that, for the first time since the accident, he quite forgot Alison except when the two apples in his jacket pocket bumped against his hip.

'The old leopardess can't change her spots,' Robert Felton chuckled when the incident was recounted to him.

Unless he was actually conversing with some one, Arthur's mind seldom strayed from the subject of Alison King. The first shock of the accident and her subsequent perilous condition wore off, but his application to the matter did not flag, nor did his sense of duty fail. After breakfast one morning his father found him carefully pacing out the ground behind the rear of the scullery, where the newer wall of the office, which had been erected in 1937, joined the older brickwork of the original house.

'What's on?' the older man said briefly.

'I'm just looking into the possibility of building on another room – a large bed-sitter or perhaps a two-room flat suitable for a wheelchair. Alison might need some such provision.'

His father looked surprised and said nothing while Arthur completed his measuring and noted the figures in his diary. Finally he said, 'Whatever you want to do, lad, I'm with you all the way. But I would suggest that you don't do anything in a hurry.'

'You can rely on that, Dad.'

'If you want some authentic information about building an invalid flat, why don't you go along to the Hall. The lad there has

154

just had one fitted up, I understand.'

'Yes, he has, but if I went to see Colin I might meet his father and we're not exactly friends. I'll ask Edith; she's been in there.'

'Edith? Oh lord, she's due home soon isn't she?'

'The boat's due in this evening.'

'So soon? Oh dear! She's bound to telephone! Will you tell her or shall I?'

'I'll tell her, Dad. It's my pigeon!'

'I'm surprised Linda hasn't been round. She was so happy and so intimate – with me, that is – at the wedding. Have you seen her?'

'No,' Arthur said, so shortly that his father raised his eyebrows. 'She phoned. I know she's seen Alison several times. She works in Derby and pops in to the infirmary on visiting evenings straight from her office. Have any more sugar-beet permits arrived?'

'Er – they may well have. There was a letter from the Sugar Corporation but I didn't open it – left it with the others on Edith's desk.'

'It isn't Edith's desk now, Dad, and we'll have to open the letters ourselves. We've about ten more trucks of beet to send off and I'd like to load two of 'em before Christmas. The Co-op are shouting for more potatoes, too. We're going to have a busy time this pre-Christmas week. I think we'd both better go and give a hand with the sorting and weighing today to release Dick and Frank for loading the beet.'

Unused to such sustained physical effort as bagging and loading potatoes, both father and son were sufficiently tired to enjoy the relaxation of fireside chairs in the evening. Their conversation petered out and they both nodded off, but at eight o'clock the phone rang.

'That's Edith,' Robert said, as Arthur got reluctantly to his feet.

It was Edith, bubbling over with enthusiasm, pleasure and excitement.

'Oh, that's you, Arthur. We've just got back. Had such a marvellous time and a comfortable, restful journey home.'

'Where are you speaking from?'

'From our new home – Westmead Farm. Aunt Betty's been so good, everything laid on for our arrival – fires, meal and all that, so we're going to spend a quiet evening together by our own fireside for the first time.'

'Is Desmond satisfied with his new acquisition? Is he pleased with you?'

'He'd better be! What a nerve you've got! How's Dad?'

155

'Dad's all right.'

'You don't sound very cheerful! Is everybody else OK?'

'Well – not exactly, Ede. Alison's had a bad accident.'

'Alison has? Oh, poor girl! I am sorry! How did it happen and how bad is it?'

'It's bad enough! And I caused it I'm afraid. Taking her home after the wedding, I ran into a lamp post.'

'*You* ran into a lamp post? I don't believe it!'

'It happened, Sis. Alison fractured her spine and I came out scot free.'

'Her *spine*? Good God, how awful! Why wasn't I told? I've been enjoying myself in the sun of Tangier, having the most gorgeous time of my whole life while my bridesmaid was lying with broken bones on a hospital bed! Arthur, it's not bearable! You could have radioed the boat!'

'There was no point, Edith! You couldn't have done anything. Nobody could. I thought it wicked to spoil your honeymoon with news of a tragedy. It wouldn't have helped Alison if you'd spent your time in misery and self-recrimination!'

'But I feel such a selfish pig, Arthur, and I've sent Alison such a pretty card saying how gloriously happy I was. I'll never forgive myself.'

'She got your card. Her parents took it to her. She's in the Derby Royal, by the way. Alison said how glad she was that you couldn't be told until you came home. She's got everything, that girl – a sweet nature, courage, endurance and optimism, and she'll need them all, believe me!'

'I'm coming up tomorrow, Arthur.'

'So soon? What will Desmond say?'

'To hell with what Desmond says! We intended to drive up Friday afternoon and spend Christmas Eve and Christmas Day with you and return home Boxing Day morning. Desmond won't want to come away yet – he's got things to do on the farm, but I'll come by train tomorrow. Don't send anybody to meet me. I don't know what time I shall arrive and I shall walk across to the Infirmary – it's only a few steps – as soon as I get off the train. I'm sure they'll let me in if I explain the connection. Then I'll get a taxi home. Oh Arthur! What a wretched homecoming it will be!'

Much to her husband's dismay Edith kept to her plan and travelled to Derby on the midday train from Aylesbury. It was after five o'clock and quite dark when her taxi drove in to Oakleigh yard. Robert and Arthur had postponed their evening meal, which they normally ate earlier in the winter months, until

156

her arrival. Robert jumped up at once and met his daughter as she entered the kitchen. After a long embrace he stepped back and surveyed this daughter whom he loved so much.

'Why, Edith! You've been crying!'

'Well, who wouldn't?' The young woman said, choking back more tears. 'To see that poor girl lying there in pain! She was so keen and happy at the wedding it was a pleasure to see her. Now – oh – it's such a shame – so unfair!'

'Sit down and have a meal, love,' her father said. 'We can talk about it all while we're eating.'

Edith took off her coat and scanned the table.

'Why, what's this? You haven't got everything out! No side-plates, no slop basin, no butter knife, a great crumby loaf stuck in the middle of the table and precious little else. Where's this meal you're talking about?'

'We generally get the tea ourselves,' Arthur muttered, 'and don't bother too much.'

'Then it's about time you did!' and Edith stalked into the larder, carrying with her the offending loaf, and returning a few minutes later with the missing utensils, a cold pie which the men had been saving for another day, tinned vegetables, and fruit which had been transferred to the appropriate dishes, a jug of cream and a plate of bread and butter, grumbling to the men as she did so.

'You two will really have to do better than this,' she admonished them. 'Disgraceful! I shall really have to square you up again before I go back. I wonder what sort of state the office is in.' Arthur pulled a wry face behind his hand. 'Yes, I'm looking at you, Arthur!'

Notwithstanding Edith's scolding, the men ate their improved meal with much enjoyment, and Edith, after her tiring afternoon, also ate heartily. She recounted the highlights of her Tangier honeymoon, but the conversation soon veered round to the plight of Alison King.

'She lies there so patiently,' Edith said mournfully, 'and seems so resigned to things. Oh God, if it were me, I think I'd go mad! I'd bought her and Linda a swim-suit from Tangier – very French and very chic. I just daren't offer it to Alison now – nor to Linda in case Alison hears about it. Oh dear! What a tragedy to come back to. She was so pitifully glad to see me, I just couldn't keep back the tears. I overstayed my time considerably, but the nurses were very kind and discreet. They told me one important item of news – after Christmas Alison is to be moved to Stoke Mandeville, where they

157

specialise in spinal injuries. It's the best place there is, apparently. I'm glad she's going there. It's only fifteen or twenty miles from Westmead Farm and I shall go and see her every visiting day.'

'That'll be very helpful,' her father remarked. 'It's probably a hundred miles from here and Gene King might not be able to make the journey too often. By the way,' Robert continued, feeling that his son might not broach the subject, 'you called to see Colin Clark in his new flat, I remember. Did you take note of any special contrivances – other than the obvious ones, I mean – that are needed by a person spending much time in a wheelchair?'

'I suppose so – yes I must have done. Why? Alison's parents can get professional advice on these things.'

'It's not Alison's parents I'm enquiring for, it's Arthur. He's proposing to build a flat for her adjoining the office.'

'Oh.' Edith opened her mouth to speak then closed it with a snap. Silence ensued for a minute or two and she tried again.

'Are you sure you should do that, Arthur? No – as you were that question. I feel it's not a matter I can comment on!'

'I'm going to marry Alison,' Arthur said bluntly, 'when she has learnt to cope with her disabilities, which may take some months. And I'll fix a place up ready for her.'

'No immediate hurry, though, surely,' Edith murmured, then added hastily, 'Of course whatever you spend will be shared jointly. I insist on paying half.'

'There are three of us, so I'm afraid you can't pay more than a third, Edith,' her father said quietly.

'Let's put this sombre subject aside for a while,' Arthur exclaimed irritably, 'and talk about something else. Your honeymoon, for instance. You look absolutely terrific, Sis, better than a new coat of paint. I'm really glad to see you looking so well, 'cos I didn't expect it. You told me that Desmond's pleased with his new wife. Are you pleased with your new husband?'

Edith blushed deeply as she giggled, 'Of course,' and there was no mistaking the sincerity in her voice.

'How are you going to take home my splendid wedding present – that smart car which is languishing in the garage?'

'I've been thinking about that coming up in the train, and I've decided that you must give Dick a couple of days off and he can drive it down to me.'

'Can't you drive it yourself when you go back on Boxing Day?'

'No, certainly not! I shall ride with my husband! It will be a nice weekend for Dick and he can bring Mavis with him. After all, they've both worked for us for the whole of my life and have earned

158

a reward or two. They'll stay with us, of course. He can drive down on the Friday, spend Saturday and Sunday looking over the farm and I'll put them on the train on Monday morning.'

'Don't you think Dick might feel out o' place, staying in your stylish house? He doesn't know Desmond – well, hardly at all, other than when he spent a few holidays here as a child.'

'He knows Edwin though, Arthur,' interposed his father. 'They worked here together for nigh on three years. Dick taught him quite a few wrinkles, I think.'

'Of course,' Edith remarked, 'and he's known Aunt Betty longer. And there's another thing. If he waits until Alison has been transferred to Stoke Mandeville, he and Mavis can visit her on the Sunday. She'll be thrilled to have visitors from the village. It might mean waiting a few more days for my new car, but I'm sure I can bear it.'

Chapter 15

Edith applied herself vigorously to preparing for what she assumed would be her last Christmas at Oakleigh – her last Christmas in charge, that is. She did her own Christmas shopping in Derby, using her new car. On her return she pleased Bob by declaring herself entirely satisfied with it, and with her shopping expedition generally. After seeing the parcels, large and small, which his sister unloaded, Arthur remarked that he should have bought her a van.

Desmond Salt arrived on Saturday afternoon, also with a car-load of parcels. Edith had decorated the house throughout with holly and streamers – and mistletoe, although she commented that she didn't know who was going to make use of it. In the sitting-room a towering Christmas tree sparkled its seasonal message while beneath its branches sheltered heaps of gaily-wrapped parcels. For some years it had been the custom at Oakleigh to give a party on Christmas Eve for the farm workers' children and the distribution of presents from the tree was not the least exciting part of the evening.

'This blessed party seems to get bigger every year,' Arthur remarked to his father.

'When you get a few children of your own,' Robert said affably, 'it'll be bigger still.'

'That'll be the day,' Arthur muttered, wishing he had not raised the matter. He certainly did not begrudge the youngsters their annual event, for he liked to keep the staff happy. Farmwise, he had no reason to be discontented. All orders for potatoes, swedes and cabbages had been filled; all the allocation of sugar-beet tonnage had been taken up. The milk yield was steady at a high level; the ewes were content to be halfway through their pregnancy, and the beef cattle equally so, replete with their appetising rations and supremely comfortable on their deep bed of straw.

'It's Christmas for both man and beast,' Robert said more than once, voicing an opinion his father-in-law had expressed for many years.

Edith declined to take any of the part-time domestic helpers away from their homes on Christmas Day and set herself the task of cooking the enormous lunch single-handed. She demanded the not-very-competent help of Arthur and Desmond, and was not backward in pointing out their shortcomings, which criticism they took in fairly good part. 'After all, it is Christmas,' Arthur said, a trifle grimly.

After a heavy meal, the men were inclined to be soporific, but Edith quickly had them on their feet for the washing-up. With her penchant for organisation, Edith had made arrangements with Alison's parents and a few special friends to operate a carefully regulated timetable of visits to the injured girl, and the Oakleigh group had been allocated the first half-hour. Arthur was not consulted, but fell in with his sister's arrangements gladly enough. He and his father went in first, carrying fruit, flowers and chocolates as well as presents in gift wrapping. Alison's bed seemed like a village Christmas treat in miniature. Her locker was so crowded that Arthur wondered where later visitors would deposit their offerings. To Robert, the whole of the ward seemed a dazzling, exotic world of colour – balloons, streamers, tinsel and floating lights everywhere.

Alison, touched by so much attention, tried hard to be cheerful and succeeded so well that Arthur felt his heart lighter than it had been since the accident. With military precision he hustled his father from the bedside after exactly fifteen minutes and was surprised to see Edith approaching, not with her husband, but with Linda Ratcliffe.

'Aren't you going in, Desmond?' he asked his brother-in-law.

Desmond shrugged his shoulders.

'Apparently not. Edith's doing the arranging. She said I would have plenty of opportunities to see Alison at Stoke Mandeville – which is true, of course.'

It was Arthur's turn to shrug his shoulders when, as the party left the hospital to walk to Desmond's car, Edith said, 'Linda's coming back with us, Arthur. You'd better ride in her car.'

'What is this in aid of?' he asked rather coldly as he squeezed into the little Morris.

'Edith's invited me to Oakleigh for tea,' Linda replied brightly.

'The devil she has!' Arthur exclaimed in astonishment, then almost at once, 'I'm sorry! I shouldn't have said that, especially at Christmas. Delighted to have you! I'd have invited you myself if I'd thought of it!'

He was somewhat nettled to notice that Linda was smiling with high amusement as she always did when he was discomfited.

The tea to which Linda had been invited was not the dainty afternoon function so common in well-to-do houses. At Oakleigh, the Feltons still followed the old-fashioned custom of a meal at the table, and on Christmas Day, a large meal at that. Seemingly unlimited quantities of cold turkey, pork pie, ham, salad, tinned fruit and jugs of cream, trifle, tarts, bread and butter, home-made jam, home-made small cakes of different kinds and, lastly, a huge Christmas cake, heavily sheeted down with almond paste and icing, so beloved by Robert Felton and his son. Edith, too, threw caution to the winds at Christmas and, in spite of her oft-declared intention of dieting to restrict her weight, ate largely of every sweet thing in sight.

Robert sat at the head of the long deal table with his daughter on his left and the visitor on his right. He was glad to see the young people so happy and, apparently, so hungry. Even Linda was tucking in enterprisingly, which somehow he had not expected. Arthur seemed relaxed too, much more so than usual when Linda was present. Robert looked at his son with pride, but not uncritically. The lad had been through a tough time since Alison's accident, but he had surmounted the initial shock and was taking practical measures to minimise the effects of the tragedy. Pity he was so big-headed, Robert thought, but no doubt he would grow out of that as he got older and experienced a few more failures.

Robert turned his head and looked at his daughter, in his eyes the image of her mother. The same bold features, full lips; the same set of her head, the same silky hair, but fractionally darker, the same robust and comely physique, and sweetest of all, the same mannerisms.

The table was crowded with far more food than they could possibly eat at one sitting, even if their numbers were doubled. But it was always so at Oakleigh – especially at Christmas. With a shock Bob realised that it was his fortieth Christmas in that room and at that very table. His mind drifted back, unbidden, to his first Christmas there – in 1911 – and to the family who had absorbed him. Arnold Ratcliffe, the old patriarch, and his understanding, lovable wife; Sam, the huge elder son who lived for nothing but the farm; the twelve-year-old younger son Arthur, gentle, cheerful, clever and competent, but always wanting to run before he had properly learned to walk and, lastly, the blue-eyed, golden-haired Meg who had instantly captivated him with her fresh beauty and her winning but imperious ways.

162

Were their shades in the room, looking down on the modern scene? Yes they were, for he could see them quite clearly, superimposed on the figures of this present gathering, and he could even hear their mealtime badinage. He hadn't lost them altogether, then . . . and he broke out of his reverie with a start, for Linda's small hand was gripping his right wrist. He fancied he could feel the affection pulsing through.

He smiled at her as she said gently, 'The present is still with us, Mr Felton!'

After the meal the conversation veered round to Alison, and Arthur bluntly stated his intention of building a flat for her, which would join the office, and described his plans in detail. Linda paled a little and, although listening with apparent interest, took no part in the conversation.

Later in the evening the farm men and their wives arrived in a body and took up all the available seats in both the kitchen and the sitting-room. It was a convivial party and, greatly to Arthur's surprise, Linda was in her element, moving from group to group, chatting to everyone with complete sang-froid. Both Edith and her father were pleased at this, while the farm people were delighted to be fussed over by this charming and modern representative of the old squirearchy.

Edith engaged in detailed conversation with Dick and Mavis concerning their proposed trip to Westmead Farm soon after Christmas. She described the route in such detail that Dick began to feel hurt and irritable at her lack of faith in his ability.

'Ah'll find the road, never fear Ed – er Mrs Salt,' he said at last, rather shortly, and Mavis nudged him. Edith, quick to sense the atmosphere, tried to recover her lost ground.

'Mrs Salt? You usen't to call me that, Dick, when I went out in the float with you on fencing jobs and foddering.'

'Them days are long past,' Dick replied heavily.

'But our friendship isn't, Dick! That goes on for ever, I hope.'

For the rest of the evening Dick and Mavis felt on top of the world. Nevertheless, it was he who kept his eye on the clock and dropped a hint or two to the others when he thought it nearly time to leave. So much drink of such great variety had been consumed that it was not surprising when some of them walked out unsteadily. Foreseeing this, Robert had insisted that they must all attend the party on foot, notwithstanding that all had bicycles and one or two of the younger men boasted a van.

When the family sat round the fire for the next hour or so, Robert could not help noticing how easily Linda fitted into their

163

circle. The thought made him faintly uneasy with himself when he dwelt on how much he disliked her father. Of course he was aware that her upbringing had made her adept at merging into any social group.

At eleven o'clock Linda rose to go. She moved across to say goodbye to Robert and he said solicitously, 'Linda, you've had several drinks over the evening. I don't think you should drive home!'

She was touched by his concern.

'I'm quite all right, Mr Felton, really I am, and it's only a mile or two.'

'It would please me if you didn't drive home!'

'In that case, of course I won't, Mr Felton. Perhaps Arthur will drive me.'

'I don't think any of us are fit to drive,' persisted Robert. Arthur, remembering with a sense of guilt the tragic occurrence the last time he had driven a girl home after a festive evening, picked up his queue and said unenthusiastically, 'I'll walk you home Linda, if I may.'

'My dear Arthur, how could I possibly refuse?' Linda replied with such obvious delight that it caused smiles all round, but in fact Linda was despondent. She knew she had lost a round. Arthur, fully committed to his high-minded project to provide for Alison, would bitterly resent any attempt to coerce him from it. So they walked through the village to Home Farm like ordinary friends, Linda carefully restraining her real feelings and Arthur pleased and surprised that he had not to fend off this lovely but unusually importunate young lady. He even unbent sufficiently to give her a friendly peck on the cheek, which she returned, rather more warmly, on the lips. Arthur was more touched by her responsible attitude than he was prepared to admit to himself, but as he walked home in the frosty moonlight he decided there could be no deviating from the course he had mapped out. He would marry Alison and alter or add to the farmhouse to make it easy for her to live there. He would not mention it to Alison until she was about to leave hospital and wished he had not spoken of it at the tea-table.

On Boxing Day Edith set off with Desmond to return to her bridal home. Dick, who with his two sons intended to spend the day ferreting, turned up to wave a friendly but respectful goodbye, and to assure Edith that he would definitely deliver her car as soon as he received word. Edith felt a tightening of the heart as she left Oakleigh, for the certainty that she would never again enter her well-loved home as its mistress affected her deeply. When she visited the place again she might well have a baby in her arms – an event which her husband anticipated with composure and certainty.

Robert and Arthur, too, were sorry to see her leave, for they now realised they would have to make firm arrangements both for the housekeeping and the office work, or at least the typing. Now that Christmas was over these changes would have to be incorporated in the farming programme to which the new year demanded urgent attention.

Alison spent another fortnight in the Royal Infirmary and on January 8 was taken by ambulance to the hospital at Stoke Mandeville. Visiting there was restricted to Saturday and Sunday only and as her parents would obviously visit her the first weekend and in addition Dick and Mavis, staying at Westmead Farm, would call and see her on both days, Arthur decided to postpone his own first trip for another week.

Collecting the Marshalls from Derby Midland Station on the Monday afternoon, he was surprised to be told that Colin Clark had presented himself at Alison's bedside on Sunday afternoon.

'Good God! Did he manage to drive all that way himself, Dick?'

'Don't know. We didn't see him to ask, but Alison towd us he'd been in, and she was quite chuffed about it.'

'I should think she would be. I'd better call and see Colin and find out if I can give him a lift down there. It can't be easy for him even if his car is specially fitted. I'll have the Jaguar back before next weekend and it'll be a much faster journey.'

Arthur drove down to Hartnall Hall the following evening after supper. Not wishing to run into George Clark or any other member of the family, he made straight for Colin's private entrance as described by Edith. When he rang the bell he was surprised that the door opened by itself, presumably by remote control, and Colin Clark's voice from the interior called, 'Do come in and straight up the passage!'

Arthur complied and found Colin working at his desk which was covered with neat stacks of invoices and other papers.

'Oh! Glad to see you, Mr Felton. Do sit down. You're here about the cricket club I take it? I'm getting on with the fixture list and my typist has done the letters for all our opponents' secretaries and I hope to get them all away this week. I hope to get the list confirmed by the end of the month and everything should be plain sailing from then on – perhaps a few whist drives and dances in February and March. There are still a few subscriptions outstanding – I haven't had yours yet, by the way.'

Arthur grinned and selected a fiver from his wallet.

'I can see you're going to be the best secretary we've had. Nobody else ever had the nerve to ask for my sub.' He chuckled with real amusement as he handed it over. 'But I didn't come in about cricket at all. I came to talk about Alison.'

'Ah! That's a sad affair, Mr Felton.'

'Call me Arthur. I asked you to once before, you know!'

'Sorry – Arthur, then. What is it you wish to say?'

'I understand you've been in the habit of visiting her and I'm sure she's been very appreciative. Our man Dick Marshall and his wife, who called to see her at Stoke Mandeville on Sunday evening, told me that you had been there in the afternoon. I don't know how you got there, but if you drove yourself, I think it's a tremendous achievement. What I would like to suggest is that you should travel with me. I shall be going practically every week, and while you may not wish to go as often as that, you're quite welcome to come as frequently as you like, and I would enjoy your company. It's nearly a three-hour drive, even with a Jag.'

The emotions shown on Colin's face varied from annoyance to gratitude. He struggled to find the right words.

'I'm really very grateful, Arthur, so grateful I don't quite know what to say, except that it really wouldn't be convenient to do that, as we might not want to be in there together. Another thing – Alison's mum or dad might like to come with me sometimes. Yes, I know you're concerned about my stamina, and it's very thoughtful of you, but in fact I'm quite capable of driving two hundred miles in a day. I've done it once and as I get more experienced I shall manage it with less effort. I'm young and strong, you know' – Arthur winced – 'so there's really no problem.'

'All right! If that's how it is –' Arthur began slowly, but Colin interrupted him.

'There's also the problem of filling in time, since it's not to be supposed that we should drive straight to the hospital and straight out again. We each might have different things to do!'

'My sister lives down that way now, Colin, and naturally I shall call in and see her some time – most times, in fact. Edith would be delighted to see you, or any one else from Hartnall.'

'I'm sure she would, and I'm really most gratified to hear you say it, but I think it would be better all round if we go independently. And I think it would be an advantage if we long-distance visitors called on Alison at the same known time every week. Say, if you took early Saturday afternoon as your stint, I might keep to early Sunday afternoon.'

'I see.'

Arthur was quite taken aback by Colin's positive manner. It was clear he had given the matter much thought, for he had been so pat with his objections and proposals. Groping for words Arthur managed to say, 'Very well, Colin. I was only trying to help, but if you're so sure you don't need it – well, I'm delighted for your sake. So if we're not going to meet at Stoke Mandeville, I look forward to seeing you at the cricket ground in due course.'

He took his leave, feeling puzzled and somewhat deflated. Later he called at Hilltop Farm on the same errand.

'We're grateful to you, Arthur,' Gene King said, 'and I daresay there'll be a time or two when we might take advantage of your offer. We can't go just every weekend – not all that distance – but we'd like to be sure that Alison has at least one visitor. I understand your sister is going to call in there regular, and we appreciate that more than I can say. But if you're going sometimes and Colin Clark goes as well, Alison won't be short of visitors. Mostly, we shall try to drive down in our old car, but if we do want a lift from either you or Colin, we shan't be backward in asking.'

'Very well, Gene, I understand, and I want to make it clear that I've no intention of deserting Alison. I shall see her through, no matter what happens.'

'You're a true Felton,' Mrs King said. 'We've no cause to worry on that score.'

Robert and Arthur Felton tried hard to settle down to the new life they must now endure at Oakleigh. Edith had looked after them well since 1946 and she was badly missed, but since her departure was permanent, they were forced to consider other housekeeping arrangements. However, when the subject was broached to Mavis Marshall she was indignant at the implied suggestion of belittlement. She told them that she considered herself quite capable of running Oakleigh house, and if necessary would put in more time there, and persuade the other two dailies to do likewise. Not wishing to offend Mavis, who had come to the house originally as Edith's nursemaid, Robert quietly dropped the idea of installing a resident housekeeper.

The office work was also in disarray. It was very much a part-time job and since it was not feasible to engage someone for an hour or two each day, Arthur compromised by arranging for a young woman, who had been a typist before her marriage, to attend every Friday to make up the wages and type the week's letters. The result was far from ideal, for she was not very efficient with the PAYE system and letters had to wait up to a week for a reply, unless Arthur undertook some typing, which he detested.

The new year raced on its way as the Feltons tried to keep up with their farming commitments. Many tons of potatoes had still to be graded and despatched, swedes and cabbages to be marketed, and there was still much ploughing to be done. There were dairy cattle to attend to, numerous calves to rear, several groups of beef cattle to finish off in covered yards before being sent to the abbatoir or grading centre. The lambing started early in March and, as in previous years, Robert and Arthur assisted Bert Rawlins in this exhausting and extended task.

In addition to all this, because of the continuing national meat shortage, Arthur persuaded his father to agree to keep pigs again, a practice which had been discontinued at the end of the war. It was finally decided to instal a number of breeding sows at Clayfields and in the preliminary absence of a pigman, the two young tractor drivers had to attend the pigs between them, much to their disgust and discontent.

Throughout these weeks of application to the farming programme, Arthur drove down to Stoke Mandeville nearly every weekend. He invariably called in at Westmead Farm for a meal with Edith and Desmond, and less frequently made a courtesy call on the elder Salts at Stoneleigh. Robert accompanied his son once a month. He enjoyed the ride, the visit to the gentle girl in hospital, and the subsequent calls on his daughter and sister. Alison was always glad to see her visitors but had very little to say, which Arthur found strange and irksome. He had not yet told the girl of his plans for her, preferring to wait for a suitable opening which did not materialise.

Careful planning ensured there was no overlapping by visitors and Linda went down twice during the winter, unbeknown to Arthur. Not that it would have made any difference to his own plans had he been informed. Thoughts of Alison filled his mind when he was not mentally occupied with farming, and it was Alison who brought Linda to his attention.

'I had Linda down to see me last Sunday,' Alison said to him early in March. 'It's a long way for a girl to drive on her own,

168

especially if you're coming down the same weekend. I think it's a little unkind of you, Arthur, not to offer her a lift. Why don't you find out when she's coming and bring her with you?'

'If that's what you want, Alison, of course I will. But I don't go straight home from the hospital, as you know. Sometimes I stay quite a few hours with Edith.'

'I'm sure Linda wouldn't mind that, and neither would Edith. In fact, I mentioned it to her and she said she'd be delighted. It would please me, Arthur.'

'Oh all right, then.' He was not very gracious, but when he said goodbye, it seemed that Alison kissed him with more affection than usual.

Reluctantly he telephoned Linda and was relieved when she told him she could not accompany him on his next visit.

'I'd like to go the next weekend though, Arthur, and would be glad of the chance to go with you. Driving my little car such a long way is rather tiring.'

'I shan't be going myself that weekend. I have business here at Oakleigh and in Derby.'

'The following weekend would suit me just as well. I know you're not likely to miss two consecutive Saturdays.'

'All right, Linda. I'll pick you up on Saturday morning the twenty-fourth. I'll probably be on my own.'

He was not anxious for her company, for he had never felt at ease with her since the incident on Egginton Common but he could not restrain his admiration when, on calling for her at Home Farm, she appeared immediately, wearing a most becoming two-piece suit of pale blue.

'By gum, she certainly knows how to dress,' he muttered and ran round hastily to open the door for her. Linda was agreeably surprised at this mark of politeness, for Arthur normally reached over from his driving-seat and opened the door from inside in a casual, brotherly fashion. Throughout the journey, much to his surprise, Linda was pleasant, decorous and demure. She was no longer sure of her position with Arthur, nor was she quite sure of his total commitment to Alison, so she decided, for the time being at any rate, to play the role of an unassuming acquaintance. Arthur was delighted at the change in her and felt that he did not mind her company at all so long as she kept in that mood.

However, he was not so pleased with her when she insisted on accompanying him to Alison's bedside, but the disabled girl seemed so glad to see them together that Arthur forgave his companion's importunity. Later on, at Westmead Farm, Linda shed her inhibitions for she saw no reason to put an act on for

169

Edith's benefit. She played her usual extrovert self, charming Desmond, somewhat to Edith's displeasure, and giving Arthur an unwarrantable feeling of jealousy.

They left Edith's very late, and Arthur drove home at great speed in the early morning hours. Nothing improper occurred or was even mentioned. What little conversation they had was confined to matters concerning Alison and Edith. After a while Linda fell silent and Arthur, looking across with approval, saw that she had dropped off to sleep. How pretty she looked, curled up in the corner as naturally as if she were in a settee at home. He was so touched by the impression that, when they arrived at Home Farm between three and four o'clock, he had no hesitation in asking her to accompany him on the journey down on April 14.

By this time Arthur felt that very soon he must do something positive about his future with Alison, and decided he would present his proposal to her before the end of the month. He had received the plans for the mooted extension to the farmhouse and as a preliminary had set Jimmy Dunn the task of clearing away the shrubbery behind the office, marking out the footings and preparing to excavate them.

The man had made a start on this a day or two before Linda was to accompany Arthur on his next trip to Stoke Mandeville, and as a variation of the usual routine she decided to cycle to Oakleigh and meet Arthur there, possibly still at his breakfast.

The door was opened by Robert Felton, overflowing with delight and courtesy.

'Do come in, Miss Ratcliffe! I'm so glad to see you! My word, how charming you look. But then you always do, my dear. Arthur's getting ready. He'll be down in a few minutes.'

They stood in the kitchen, pleasurably facing each other. From behind the rear walls came the sounds of heavy labour as Jimmy vigorously plied his axe or spade.

'Whatever's going on, Mr Felton?'

'Oh that? Arthur's got a chap there preparing the ground for the extension. You knew about it, I suppose? Arthur's going to build a flat there for Alison.' He sighed, raised his eyebrows and shook his head gently. 'It was a sad business for that poor girl.'

Linda felt the questions building up in her brain – questions she desperately wanted to ask but could not get out, while her heart seemed to die inside her. She took a deep breath to recover her composure, then said simply, 'It's all settled then, Mr Felton?'

Her relief was inexpressible when Robert Felton replied casually, 'Oh, I don't think so! He hasn't said. Nothing's settled until it happens, Linda.'

Chapter 16

Nevertheless Linda was worried and throughout the journey to Alison's hospital she was utterly subdued. Arthur wondered at her unresponsiveness but did not comment on it. He told himself that he liked Linda as a passenger rather better when she was not so talkative. He glanced across at her now and then, thinking that, talkative or speechless, she still looked as lovely, as charming and as well-dressed as ever. He knew well enough she was fond of him. Nothing wrong in that – it was quite natural – but he knew that he must discourage it, for his duty and his inclinations were centred on Alison – tragically injured, possibly by his own lack of attention. So he talked to Linda considerately, but his thoughts were on the girl in the hospital bed, thinking that he must soon declare his plans to her and wondering when he could make the opportunity. Next weekend, possibly? He really ought not to wait longer – there were busy times ahead on the farm. He looked across at his passenger.

'Oh, Linda, I've decided to go down to the hospital again next Saturday?'

'So soon? I suppose I may come with you, though?'

'Well, I don't know. My father is coming along . . .'

'I'm sure Mr Felton won't mind my coming too. I think he'll be pleased to have me as a travelling companion, and I him, of course.'

'No doubt,' Arthur said, becoming ruffled by the girl's persistence. 'But in fact it won't be very convenient for you to be around. I need to have some vital private talk with Alison, and I think next Saturday will be opportune.'

'I see! Well, I certainly don't want to embarrass you with my presence. It's kind of you to have driven me so often as you have. I'm very grateful, but of course I knew it could not go on for ever.'

Linda felt utterly miserable and for the first time realised she might not win Arthur after all. They shared a very quiet lunch in Aylesbury and arrived early at Stoke Mandeville where they were delighted to find Alison dressed and in her wheelchair for the first time. Her face lit up with pleasure to see them together, which Arthur thought strange although he was pleased with the improvement in her condition. Alison seemed quite merry and

Linda, thinking her good humour was caused by Arthur's own jolly mood, although in fact it was the other way round, swallowed her misery and forced herself to be equally lively.

There was a congestion of visitors that afternoon, for Edith arrived to dispossess Arthur and Linda. They waited for her in the corridor so they could travel to Westmead together and while they chatted, somewhat absently, Mr and Mrs King arrived to replace Edith, who, although not having met them personally for several years, immediately invited them over to Westmead for a meal before returning to Hartnall.

A long time was spent in explaining the route to Gene King and Arthur furnished several diagrams, but in due course the three young people set off for the Salts' home. On arrival, the enthusiastic Desmond insisted on taking Arthur round the farm immediately. The sowing of spring corn and grass seed was now completed, the planting of the potatoes well advanced and the remainder of the ground fully prepared for the other root crops, so the arable fields were naturally at their tidiest. Many of the beef cattle had been turned out to graze only a few days previously and the ewes, having finished lambing, had also been moved with their offspring to fresh grazing, so the farm as a whole was in a shop-window condition.

Arthur accompanied Desmond willingly while Linda, equally willingly, remained behind to pour out her heart to Edith who for once could find little room for optimism.

'I'm terribly sorry the way things have turned out, Linda. I was so sure you'd win in the end. Poor Alison's accident has spoiled things for everybody. Arthur is so stubborn and, according to Dad, he's become very secretive lately – won't discuss his plans with anybody. He used to be so predictable, but not now! I think he feels terribly guilty about Alison and is determined to make amends.'

'Quite noble of him, really,' Linda said in a small voice, 'but then, there's never been anything wrong with Arthur's character, basically. Just a little self-centred, perhaps.'

'You were meant for him, Linda, for you're fond enough of him to tolerate his little faults and, by God, there are plenty of them! But I'm bound to say there's nothing you can do now – nothing that you should do, or could do, without causing distress to others. But there are many imponderables. Just keep your fingers crossed and pray – if you haven't forgotten how!'

Linda smiled.

'Oh Edith! Somehow you always manage to imply there's a

silver lining. I can't see one here, I'm afraid. But I suppose I may still come and see you irrespective of Arthur?'

'I shall be very cross if you don't. Hartnall was my home for thirty years and Hartnall people have been, and still are, my friends. I'm still retaining a share in the family farm, you know!'

'I'm so glad! I shall think of you every time I pass by Oakleigh!'

'Pass by? You must call and see my father. I insist on it! He doesn't have many highlights in his life now, and your visits would provide some!'

Linda looked wistful.

'I don't know, Edith. Suppose Alison is there? It might be awkward for all of us, you know!'

'I'm not going to think of it! I won't advise Arthur, I can't advise Alison, I don't have to advise my father, but I can advise you, and my advice is simply, don't panic! Say nothing, do nothing! Just wait in the wings! And now I think I must get a meal ready for our other guests. They'll probably be here before our men are back from their totally absorbing farm appraisal.'

Linda helped Edith prepare a high tea to which Mr and Mrs King, as well as the two young men, applied themselves with relish. The Kings, not very able conversationalists in a strange environment, said little, and Alison's affairs were not discussed. Gene King did mention, with some pride, that Colin Clark was coming to see her on the following day, and added that he had never missed his Sunday visit. Arthur commented that it seemed rather wasteful of petrol for three parties to journey so far in one weekend, all in separate cars, and thought there was scope for some co-operation. He was mildly chagrined when no one bothered to agree.

Mr and Mrs King left about eight o'clock, but Arthur, who was beginning to enjoy his visits to his sister's new home, stayed on through the whole evening without consulting Linda, who however was equally pleased. They spent a homely evening with television and music, which lasted until nearly midnight. Arthur then prepared to leave and became impatient at the extended farewell embrace of the two girls.

Linda's resolution to keep silent about Alison was severely tested on the journey home. She managed to confine her remarks to farming topics and asked pertinent questions about the differences between the policies and practices of Oakleigh and Westmead and, much to Arthur's surprise, made knowledgeable comments on his replies. In spite of the deadness of the hour, their conversation was lively and informed, lasting the whole of the trip and Arthur was sorry when the time came for him to deliver his passenger to Home Farm.

'Goodbye, Linda,' he called cheerily. 'See you again at the start of the cricket season, no doubt. It won't be many weeks now!' And he drove away leaving a forlorn young woman standing with half-raised arm in the porch of her home.

During the next week Arthur's thoughts were centred entirely on Alison, except when he was actually dealing with farming matters. He urged Jimmy Dunn to greater speed preparing the site for the extension and ordered two loads of hardcore for him to wheelbarrow and spread on to the cleared ground. On Saturday morning he harried his father to greater haste in order to leave early.

'I may have quite a lot to talk to Alison about, so I'm going to drive you straight to Westmead, have a quick lunch with Edith and then drive to the hospital on my own. If you want to see Alison, you can go in later with Edith.'

'Of course I want to see Alison,' his father observed tartly. 'That's why I'm making the trip! You don't have to regard yourself as her only visitor!'

Arthur arrived at the hospital early in the afternoon. To his surprise and disappointment he found Alison confined to her bed 'because of some infection,' she explained. 'Nothing very important.'

Her visitor placed his usual offering of flowers and fruit on her locker.

'You were getting on so well,' he said and the disappointment was evident in his tone. 'Quite mobile, in fact. I certainly hope this little setback is not important, because I've got something important to say to you, and I want to get it over before anyone else turns up. Dad and Edith will be here in an hour; you're not expecting anyone else before that, I hope?'

'Nobody that I know of. This is all very mysterious, Arthur. Why is it so essential to-day? And why haven't you brought Linda? She's always so lively and cheers everybody up.'

'The reason I haven't brought Linda will soon be obvious,' Arthur said seriously. 'You know how fond I am of you, Alison – in love with you in fact, more so now that you're disabled, for which I must accept the blame.'

'I don't think that at all,' Alison said quickly.

'At least, you were riding in my car when it happened and the result's just as disastrous. I've looked on it as my responsibility, and I want to make you my continuing responsibility for the rest of our lives. I'm asking you to marry me, Alison!'

'Marry you, Arthur? Marry *you*? You can't mean it!'

'I do mean it, my dear. I've made all the plans to build an extension on to our house for you. It will be fitted with every device known to medical science. No expense will be spared. I can assure you.'

'You don't have to stress that, Arthur. I know perfectly well that you don't do things by halves! But consider – you're a busy farmer! What use would I be as a farmer's wife?'

'I've gone into all that, Alison. I'm sure that with your new mobility and your increasing skill with all the appliances, you will be able to manage my household admirably. There'll be plenty of help in the house, of course – you'll only have to direct them and do the organising. You have a flair for that, as I well know.'

The girl looked extremely worried.

'It's all so sudden, Arthur. I'm very grateful, of course. I'm overwhelmed and just don't know how to explain . . .'

'I'm sure your parents won't mind. They've known all along what I've been thinking, and appeared to be much in favour.'

Alison tried to be gentle although she was displeased at Arthur's calm assumption of her acceptance of his proposal.

'Arthur, you're an active man with your farming, your cricket and sometimes your hunting. You'd find life irksome married to a woman who couldn't join you in all those things. You think you love me – perhaps you do, now – but how long would it last?'

'How long?' Arthur pictured the hundred miles or so of rich farming country through which he driven that morning – fresh green pasture, bursting with growth, the paler shade of the leys and the twisting barley; the bluegreen of the young oats and the hard, steely green of the wheat. 'How long, Alison?' he said again. 'As long as fields are green, my dear, that's how long!'

Alison looked even more worried.

'That sounds very pretty and well thought-out, Arthur, but it won't do, you know. Life isn't all green fields, and fields aren't always green anyway. Oh yes, they're green enough in the spring, I grant you – like now. But in the winter some of the greenness gets trampled into mud. The land floods sometimes and gets left looking washed-out, lifeless and tide-marked. Sometimes the fields get buried in snow – whited sepulchres, if you like! Married life's like that, I reckon. Everything's smart, fresh and beautiful to begin with, but it doesn't stay like that. I can't marry you, Arthur! I won't marry you!'

The young man was utterly shaken by her attitude and groped

for words to express his astonishment.

'What – why – what are you talking about, girl? I'm offering you all that you need – all that I've got. You're foolish to reject it all like this. Give yourself time to think it over.'

Alison sighed miserably. She had hoped to avoid a direct confrontation.

'As a matter of fact, Arthur, there's someone else.'

'Someone else? How can there be?'

Alison ignored the unflattering implication.

'Last Sunday Colin Clark asked me to marry him.'

'The devil he did! I'm just a week late, then? Why the hell didn't I bring it up last Saturday? And you've decided, just like that?'

'Arthur! Colin understands my position and my needs far better than you possibly could, no matter how you tried. I haven't said "yes" yet, but I may do tomorrow.'

'Well, I don't know!' Arthur still seemed bemused. 'Alison, you've taken something from me which I've lived with for a year and which has taken possession of me this last six months! You've cut the ground from under my feet. What am I going to do now?'

'Marry Linda, I hope! She's just right for you, Arthur, and you're the only one who can't see it!'

'I'll never marry anybody after this,' he said bitterly.

'Oh, rubbish!' Alison was rapidly regaining her spirits. 'You'll have to readjust! Farmers have to replan for a change of weather, why not for a change of direction or of mind?'

Arthur sat fidgeting for a few minutes.

'You won't mention this to anyone, will you?'

'Why ever not? You're not ashamed are you? I'm not! I'm proud. There's not another man in the county in your condition and state of life who would have offered me what you have. No! I'm deeply touched and shall remember it all my life. I could boast about it and so could you, but it might be better all round if we didn't.'

Arthur bent down and kissed her.

'I'm sure you'll be very happy with Colin. He's a grand chap. We'll still be seeing each other.' He turned and walked quickly out of the ward. When he returned to Westmead he found that his father and sister were on their way to the hospital and although he must have met them, he was so preoccupied he had not noticed their car. He was glad of their absence since it left him free for a farming discussion with Desmond.

At the evening meal Robert and Edith spoke at length about Alison, both of them sharing the opinion that she seemed much more relaxed than formerly.

'It seemed as if a heavy load had been removed from her shoulders, or more accurately, a weight from her mind,' Edith commented, giving Arthur a searching look which he totally ignored.

Throughout the drive home, and all the following day, he remained silent and thoughtful. His father diplomatically refrained from pressing him for information and, wisely, did not comment on Monday morning when Jimmy Dunn, having finished wheeling in the hardcore, was despatched to other work at the far end of the farm. By then Arthur, with characteristic resilience of mind had switched his attention entirely to farming matters, throwing himself into it with as much vigour as if he had been playing truant from his work. Metaphorically he had, and although he would not admit this to anybody, and certainly not to his father, he was determined to make up for lost time. He certainly gave no thought to Linda, having already decided that Alison's reference to her was girlish impertinence.

During the next few days of his contrition, he spent much time in the office trying to restore the meticulous order of Edith's long reign. All he managed to achieve was the transfer of documents from one place to another which later he was unable to locate. On the Friday when Mrs Tunnicliffe, the one-day-a-week secretary appeared, she could not find anything either, and made caustic remarks in a not too respectful tone. She became further flustered when later in the morning Arthur stood over her telling her exactly how to operate the PAYE system which she knew rather better than he. Finally she protested.

'Mr Felton, do you mind going away and leaving me to continue on my own? I need neither your help nor your instructions!'

Arthur was furious and strode away in a cold temper, neglecting even to reprimand the woman as she deserved, in case she resigned on the spot. Muttering imprecations on all women, he went off to Derby market and did not return in time to distribute the wages. His normal practice was to visit each man at his job and hand over the pay packet.

Very crossly, all the men lumbered up to the farmhouse at five o'clock, and Robert Felton, equally annoyed at this unexpected disruption, had to search for the envelopes in the drawer where Mrs Tunnicliffe had safely hidden them, and then half-apologised to his staff for the delay in payment. This caused some heated exchanges between father and son when Arthur returned home for a late tea.

At Oakleigh, ill-temper had never been allowed to persist and harmony was fully restored by midday on Saturday, for the work programme for the week had been over-achieved. Arthur offered no explanation as to why he was not making the usual trip to Stoke Mandeville, and Robert tactfully did not enquire. He did say, gratuitously, 'This grand spring weather is too good to spend on driving halfway across the country! It's better sometimes to stay home on the farm and relax!'

On the next day, which was the last Sunday in April, the weather was still bright and sunny with a warm drying breeze. A group of steers had been turned out in the River Fields more than a week previously, which was early for Derbyshire. However, the spring had been dry and the Feltons considered it was better to turn the cattle out before the grass was long and lush. An early start would enable them to keep on top of the growth and if the grass could be kept short they would put on weight more quickly. Arthur decided he would stroll quietly through them to see how they had settled down.

He selected a stick from the hall stand, reached for his hat, then glancing at himself in the mirror and appraising his curly light brown hair, decided he would look smarter without it. After all, it was the first warm weekend of the year. He retraced his steps through the kitchen, pausing there for a moment, thinking of the flat he had proposed to build Alison. Shrugging his shoulders he passed out into the yard, leaving the farmhouse empty, for his father was already making a Sunday afternoon survey of a distant corner of their farming empire.

Arthur strode down the drive, fittingly content, for the fields on each side looked splendid to him, the resurgence of spring showing on every twig, every square yard of ground. The last flock of ewes to have lambed had just been moved on to fresh grass in one of the driveside fields and the speckle-faced lambs looked happy and thriving as they bounded about to explore their new pasture. It seemed as if they were glad that it was Sunday afternoon and thrilled to be away from the shabby, jaded untidiness of the lambing paddock adjacent to the steading which they had occupied for so long.

As he emerged from the drive on to the road, intending to cross over to the gateway of the pastures, Arthur glanced to his left and saw a car parked, half on the road and half on the grass verge which was wide enough to provide almost a lay-by. The registration number, the make, shape and age of the car all seemed vaguely familiar as did the rear view of the head of the driver, apparently reading at the wheel.

Out of mere curiosity Arthur turned left up the road and strolled casually towards the car, but before he was halfway towards it he realised that the car belonged to Linda and the studious driver was none other than the girl herself. He quickened his pace and when he stood beside the driver's door, Linda looked up from her book, but waited for him to speak first.

'Good afternoon, Linda,' he went to raise his hat but found he was not wearing one so casually dropped his left hand to the roof of the little car. 'Reading is a strange way of spending this very pleasant Sunday afternoon!'

'Indeed? What do you suggest I should be doing?'

'I suggest you walk with me down to the Trent to have a look at our young cattle – we can talk about the cricket season, too.'

Linda was out of the car before he had finished speaking, but then blushed as she realised her haste was unseemly. Arthur stood back and appraised her. She was wearing a roll-neck sweater of pale blue which looked well with her glossy fair hair, a light-coloured heather mixture pleated tweed skirt, lisle stockings and strong brogue shoes. Arthur whistled in bold admiration.

'My word, Linda, you look absolutely lovely this afternoon.'

The girl coloured with pleasure.

'You're looking fairly smart yourself.'

Arthur thought so too, for he was wearing his fully-cut riding breeches, knitted socks with decorative tops, polished brown market boots and his favourite hacking jacket which was a reddish pattern. His pale green shirt and college tie provided a look of casual dignity which pleased him.

'Aren't you going to lock your car?' he asked as they turned to walk away.

'No! Who'd dare to touch it when it's parked on Felton property?'

Arthur coughed and smiled. Sarcastic baggage, he thought, but if that was to be her tone, he thought he could match it. He opened the gate and as she passed through it in front of him she felt she had never been so happy in her life. Looking down at the deep fresh grass which almost covered her shoes, she said knowledgeably, 'Are the cattle in here, among this deep growth? Surely not?'

'Not yet. They're in the bottom field by the river. If that will keep them, and I hope it will, I'll make hay of this. Let's go on across.'

They walked over and through the next gate, then down to the drinking-place where the Trent widened to very shallow water on the Oakleigh side. There was a shingled approach and the current rippled fast and noisily over the shining pebbles.

'What a delightful picture,' Linda murmured, 'As rich as a Constable painting.'

The cattle were drinking deeply, a few at a time, while the lesser animals stood back on the grass and waited their turn. The arrival of the two humans caused the foremost beasts to gaze with brief curiosity then splash out of the water with excitement. But they did not disperse and Arthur was able to walk through them slowly and appraise each one carefully. When he had finished his examination, Linda said casually, 'They've settled down quickly, haven't they? They're looking well, and I'm sure most of them will be fat before the end of the summer.'

Arthur looked at her with surprise for he had never credited her with any farming knowledge.

'Time enough, but I didn't know you were on judging terms with beef cattle.'

'There are still *some* things you don't know about me, Arthur,' and she blushed at her own thoughts, but her eyes twinkled. 'It's lovely down here by the Trent,' she went on. 'The river's so beautiful in spring – so fresh and lively and inviting. Let's walk along the bank as far as your land goes.'

'It's got to be a lot warmer than this before I accept its invitation,' Arthur commented, 'but we needn't go right along. There's a pleasant willow copse just round the bend.'

As he spoke, his memory went back, unbidden to that spring day before the war when his mother very embarrassingly revealed that she and his father had discovered themselves in that clump and had made ardent love there, of which he, Arthur, was the result. What a peculiar thought! Barely imaginable.

Other thoughts entered his head as he looked at Linda again, thoughtfully and with relish and anticipation. He was thirty-five, had been almost a celibate for some months but now the spring sun was warming up the blood in his veins and he felt other stirrings. He moved close to the girl and put his left arm round her waist. With a contented sigh she allowed her head and shoulder to rest on his upper arm. He faced her, pulled her closer, putting out his right hand to fondle her curves. She pushed it away and shook her head. He released her and they wandered on again, following the river, admiring its still silent pools, its shallows and gurgles, enjoying the insect and bird life, where overhanging bushes gave an element of solitude and mystery. They reached the clump of willows. It was strongly fenced to keep out the cattle and the grass within was clean and fresh but damp-looking. Not too damp though, Arthur thought and seized Linda again, crushing her to his body.

Linda said simply, 'You're unlucky, Arthur. It's the wrong day, I'm afraid.'

He released her at once, losing interest, but she stood close up and guided his arm round her waist again. Reluctantly, as it seemed, he tightened his grip. She waited for him to speak, but he did not, so she looked straight up into his face, pouted and said sulkily, 'You ought to marry me, Arthur, you really ought! We've been through many things together – in the car, and all that . . .'

'Marry you?' Arthur sounded startled, 'Why? And about the car at Egginton – you're not going through all that again? Good Lord, Linda, I didn't ask you down here to propose to you!'

She could have knifed him but, restraining her anger, she looked up into his handsome face as tenderly as she knew how.

'Oh come, Arthur! You know you ought. I'm so fond of you, and I know you love me really, although you pretend not to.' She paused and then, with the flash of a new idea, she continued, 'It would be better for everybody! I know what sort of state you're getting into, with your household management and with your paperwork too. I'm a trained secretary remember, and could do your office work just as competently as Edith!'

Arthur made a theatrical gesture as if a blindfold had been torn from his eyes.

'Of course! Why didn't I think of that before? Oh dear, what a blind fool I've been!' His eyes glinted mischievously. 'You'll be a splendid hostess, you're a very nice girl to take around, I'm sure you can be a competent housekeeper. You're one of the prettiest girls in the district, and I'm certain you'll be an efficient secretary – yes, and you could be exciting as a wife if you chose – especially in bed! Yes, I will most certainly marry you Linda, and the sooner the better!'

Linda put her hands on his shoulders. Her eyes showed she was enjoying her triumph but she was a little piqued as well for she could not be sure just how much his attitude was simulated.

'Arthur! If I thought you were marrying me for those reasons only, I . . . I . . . I'd push you into the Trent!'

Quick as a flash he stooped down, put his left arm behind her knees, his right arm under her shoulders, snatched her off the ground and advanced the few feet to the river bank. Linda thought it was delicious to be held so, but immediately below her the water ran deep and dark and cool and she was uncertain of Arthur's mood. For a moment she thought he might be reckless enough for anything. She snuggled closer and flung her arms round his neck, determined to hang on should he be tempted to drop her. To balance her fears, she was conscious of a deeper thrill from such close contact.

'Arthur! How dare you? Put me down at once!'

Actually she was content to be in his arms. All that she wanted was for him to move back from the river's edge.

'Put me down at once, Arthur!' And she hammered his shoulder-blades with her fist.

'Say "Please".'

'All right. Please put me down!'

'Say you're sorry, then!'

'I'm sorry, damn you!'

Arthur seemed to be enjoying himself for he grinned broadly, set her down precariously on the brink, then snatched her a foot or two away.

She straightened her clothes and tried to look serious.

'If I'm to marry you Arthur, I shall demand more out of the deal than simply being a house-keeper/office-girl.'

'Linda, you'll get a lot more. I promise you.'

She kissed him and he continued, 'You'll get everything you deserve, perhaps more.'

'Damn you, Arthur! You conceited wretch! When we're married I'll cut you right down to size!'

The twinkle in his eyes vanished and was replaced by a frosty sternness. Impertinent minx, he thought and was strongly inclined to swing her round and slap her. But no, he mustn't upset her and cause a hitch. That sort of thing could wait until they were married. It would be a pity to spoil things by being too clever or too Victorian. God, how lovely she was! Perhaps he ought to say something that would please or amuse her. His eyes twinkled charmingly again as he replied, 'Cut me down to size, will you? Ah well, it's about time somebody did!'

Their eyes met and this time there was no mistaking the message. Shaking with laughter Linda fell into his arms, proud that at last she had got her man. Arthur was exultant, too. All his problems were to be solved in a most delightful way.